ASYLUM

ASYLUM

JEANNETTE DE BEAUVOIR

MINOTAUR BOOKS

NEW YORK

ASYLUM. Copyright © 2015 by Jeannette de Beauvoir. All rights reserved. Printed in the United States of America. For information, address St. Martin's Press, 175 Fifth Avenue, New York, N.Y. 10010.

www.minotaurbooks.com

Designed by Molly Rose Murphy

Library of Congress Cataloging-in-Publication Data

de Beauvoir, Jeannette.
    Asylum : a mystery / Jeannette de Beauvoir.
        pages   cm
    ISBN 978-1-250-04539-3 (hardcover)
    ISBN 978-1-4668-4403-2 (e-book)
    1. Women detectives—Fiction.   I. Title.
    PS3604.E1125A98 2015
    813'.6—dc23   2014040208

Minotaur books may be purchased for educational, business, or promotional use. For information on bulk purchases, please contact the Macmillan Corporate and Premium Sales Department at 1-800-221-7945, extension 5442, or write to specialmarkets@macmillan.com.

First Edition: March 2015

10 9 8 7 6 5 4 3 2 1

For the orphans

ACKNOWLEDGMENTS

For giving me a wonderful creative home to live in when I'm in Montréal, my thanks to the Leblanc family, owners of the original Théo d'Or.

Much gratitude and love to Lukas Ortiz of the Philip G. Spitzer Literary Agency: your name, *mi amor,* is synonymous with perseverance! And many thanks to my fabulous editors at St. Martin's/ Minotaur, Kate Ottaviano and Daniela Rapp, as well as copyeditor Rebecca Maines, who improved this novel by light-years.

As always, thanks to my first readers, Carem Bennett, Marion Hughes, and Dianne Kopser. Carem has been my first reader for more years than I care to remember, and is a steadfast source of support and love. You're all the best, and give me far more than I deserve.

Finally, thanks to Rod Vienneau, spokesperson and advocate for the remaining Duplessis Orphans and author of *Collusion: The Dark History of the Duplessis Orphans.*

ASYLUM

PROLOGUE

The woman sitting in the backseat shivered and drew the child closer to her side. But it was a warm morning, promising summer.

"Just over there," said the man sitting next to the driver, the man wearing the clerical collar. "Pull over here; the gate's just ahead."

The car shuddered to a stop and for a moment no one inside moved. The sun was just about to come up, the eastern sky behind them streaked with bits of pink cotton candy; but inside the taxi the dark of night lingered.

The woman spoke to the child. "You have your bag?"

"Yes, maman." Large eyes looked up at her, round with fear. The little girl had been awakened and made to dress in the dead of night. "I don't understand. Why do I have to, maman? I don't want to go!"

The woman blinked back the tears suddenly flooding her eyes. "You have to," she said, her voice unsteady. She took a deep breath. "*You have to go. This is your new home,* mon chou. *I can't come with you.*"

"*But I don't want a new home! I want to stay with you! No!*"

The priest in the front seat turned and looked back at them. "It's time," he said unnecessarily.

"*No," the little girl said again, but this time she said it without hope.*

The woman opened the door and got out, extending her hand to the child, who followed obediently. A tall wooden green-painted door loomed ahead of them. "You have to go," the woman said again, looking not at the child but at the door.

The girl cried out, something incomprehensible, and the woman turned and sank to her knees so that their eyes were level. She dashed at the tears and forced herself to smile. "My dearest love. You must. It is for the best, it truly is." She put her arms around the child and pulled her close. "Don't forget me. Don't forget that your maman *loves you.*"

"*I love you, too,* maman." *Her voice was trembling, heavy already with loss.*

The woman didn't relinquish her hold. "Gabrielle, je t'aime . . .*" Her words were muffled against the child's brown hair.*

There was the sound of the car door opening and the priest's footsteps crunched across the gravel toward them. "You must let her go now," he said to the woman, not ungently. He put his hands on her arms and pulled her back from the child; she stumbled against him as she stood up. "It's for her sake," the priest said. "They'll take good care of her. We've been over this, Lucienne. It's the best thing you can do for her."

"Yes," the woman said again, but there was nothing in her voice but pain.

The priest took the child's hand and pulled the chain beside the door; from somewhere inside came the sound of a bell pealing. A few moments later the door opened and a nun stood framed in it. "Good morning, Sister," said the priest.

Her eyes took in the woman, standing shivering by the car; the priest; and finally the little girl. "Yes?"

"This is Gabrielle Roy, Sister," the priest said. "I've written Mother Superior about her."

The nun nodded and opened the door wider as the priest transferred the child's grip from his own hand to hers. "Come along, then, little one," she said.

The girl looked back. "Maman?"

The woman stood still, sobbing, her hands to her face. The priest turned and put his arm around her shoulders, pulling her away, steering her back to the waiting taxi.

Behind them, the green door closed with a click.

"She's safe now," the priest said. "You did the right thing, Lucienne. She couldn't have lived in the village. The children there would have tormented her. She's safe now."

"Yes," the woman said again, but her heart was as empty as the clear bright sky.

CHAPTER ONE

It was Ivan who started it all.

My husband is an avid consumer of the morning news, but does not ascribe to the time-honored spousal mealtime practice of hiding behind a newspaper; he has his electronic tablet at the breakfast table, where he scans news in two languages: the Montréal *Gazette*, the *Globe and Mail*, and, on occasion, CNN, while scarfing down rolls and orange juice. Me, I'm not ready to face any of these options—morning is not exactly my finest hour—and so I generally sip coffee and just listen to his running commentary.

"They've found another body," Ivan said that Friday morning, his voice somber.

I looked up from my café au lait. "Another woman?"

He nodded. "On another park bench, over on the Plateau," he said.

I didn't have to ask what he was referring to. Montréal had been experiencing a spate of apparently random killings that summer—three, to be exact—that were now spilling into fall with number four. The police, the news outlets assured us, were following leads. In the meantime, women all over the city were advised to take precautions: not to take the bus or Métro alone, to purchase extra locks for apartments and lofts, to ask service people for identification.

I leaned so I could read over Ivan's shoulder. One Danielle Leroux, thirty-four, apparently hadn't taken enough of those advertised precautions.

I shuddered and put down my coffee. "I should get ready for work," I said. But I didn't move, fixed in the moment, fixed to the spot. It was as though Danielle Leroux's tragedy had, for a passing shivering instant, become my own.

And then the moment was over and I met Ivan's quizzical dark eyes. I shrugged. "It just sucks," I said, using one of the many English-language colloquialisms at which I have become so proficient since marrying Ivan, an Anglophone living in a predominantly Francophone city.

He nodded. "You're being careful, right, Martine?" No husband likes to hear about other women being murdered, especially this close to home.

I stood up from the table and carried my bowl to the sink. The ghost of Danielle's presence paused, lingered, and then disappeared, a bright shimmer in the air. "I'm being careful."

Ivan got up and stood behind me, slipping his arms easily around my waist. "It's just," he said, "that I've gotten used to you. I'd hate to have you disappear, too."

I twisted around so I was facing him, our bodies still touching. "Used to me? That's the best you can do?"

Ivan smiled, pulling me closer to him. "We Russians," he said softly, his lips millimeters from mine, "are the masters of understatement." And then he kissed me.

Ivan, it has to be noted, consistently makes something of a show of his Russian heritage; but the truth is that it was his great-grandparents, aristocrats, who fled St. Petersburg for Paris a week before the October Revolution, not Ivan himself. To the best of my knowledge, no one in his family has ever gone back. His father was raised in France and spoke some Russian at home; but my father-in-law left Paris for the United States right after earning a degree at the Sorbonne, to take a post teaching at MIT, and Ivan's own accent reflects the academic corridors of Boston far more than it does the tea rooms of Moscow.

Which doesn't keep him, of course, from appropriating any Russian attribute that he cares to claim when the occasion arises.

I held him for a moment, tightly, then released the pressure in my arms. Ivan immediately let go and turned back to the table, folding his tall body back into the chair. "So what's on your plate for today?" he asked, his voice casual, an undercurrent of the kiss we'd just shared still running through it.

I cleared my throat and turned back to the sink. "Meeting with the mayor *et compagnie* at ten," I said, briefly, glancing at the clock. "The usual check-in to make sure that the world still thinks well of our fair city." My job is to make sure that it does; my title is *directrice de publicité*—publicity director—for the city of Montréal, so I'm responsible, in an odd way, for everything from street performers to press releases. Anything that

can make Montréal look good—or bad—passes across my desk
at one time or another.

I alternately adore and detest what I do; but one thing I can
say for sure: it's never dull.

"Sounds like a summons to me," Ivan remarked, taking the
last swallow of his espresso. The beep of his e-mail sounded and
he frowned down at the tablet display.

"I hope not." But he was probably correct. The mayor only
noticed my existence when something was going wrong. And
another murder certainly qualified as being very wrong indeed.
Calling in the troops in order to spread the blame among them
was pretty much his style.

Ivan was scanning e-mails. He was already moving away
from me, his mind skimming across the river to the casino and
its own set of myriad unique problems. Ivan is the director of
poker operations for the Montréal Casino and, in some ways,
his job is not unlike mine. Making sure that people are happy,
that operations are running smoothly, that those who come to
our fair city to play are playing both well and fair.

Every day is a special day for those of us whose professions
are to provide fun and frolic to others.

I knew better than to interrupt. Instead, I ducked into my
own study and assembled the papers and accoutrements
I'd need for my day, replaced the ballet slippers I wore at home
with the heels I was wearing to the office. In the hallway
I stopped for a last check in the mirror, putting on my lipstick,
smoothing my often-rebellious thick black hair, adjusting the
scarf around my neck. By the time I was ready, Ivan was wearing his raincoat, preparing to leave through the back door to

pick up our Volvo in the mews where we kept it garaged. "Gotta run, love."

"*D'accord.*" I leaned into him for our ritual good-bye kiss. We had agreed, when we first were married, that we'd never part without one, and we were pretty good about keeping the commitment. It was Ivan's idea: his own first marriage had died from lack of—what? Oxygen? Rituals? Passion? Whatever it was, he was going to make sure it didn't happen a second time. "Be good, be happy."

"Be good, be happy," I echoed, and he was gone.

I managed to snag a seat on the Métro and peered over the shoulder of my neighbor, reading the *Gazette*'s French-language version of the news about the new murder. There wasn't much more than what Ivan had shared with me. This victim was young, pretty. Too young, too pretty. I gave myself a mental shake as I got off the train. Starting the day depressed didn't bode very well for the rest of it.

I work out of City Hall, down near the port, in what's called the "old city," *le Vieux-Montréal*, a warren of twisting cobblestone streets and ancient secrets, art galleries and tourist attractions.

Every time I'm down here—which is, of course, every day— I'm convinced that it's the prettiest section of Montréal, but in reality I'm deeply and passionately in love with the whole city. Every *quartier* has its charms: Chinatown, the Plateau, Little Italy, Gay Village, the mountain itself with the city spreading up its slopes to the Oratory at almost eight hundred feet, even the chrome-and-glass and massage parlors of the official downtown area.

I love that we have municipal bicycles to grab and use at regular intervals, that there are bike lanes crisscrossing the city, that we take being green to heart. I love that we're all bilingual, often in the same sentence, shopkeepers' greetings usually consisting of "*bonjour*, hello." I love all the neighborhoods, with their odd and twisting outside staircases and their brightly painted doors and window boxes, the heat of Montréal's summers and the cursed snowbanks of its winters.

But maybe what I do love best of all *is* this small section of my city, this place where I work, the original Iroquois village by the life-giving river, once called Hochelaga and then Ville-Sainte-Marie when the French moved in . . . where now tourists are taken about in *calèches*, the clopping of the horses' hooves echoing off the buildings in the narrow streets, where Roller-bladers skim along the waterfront, and museums guard the past and welcome the future.

I flipped my ID badge to the security guard in the lobby of the (even I have to admit) extremely impressive *hôtel de ville* and took the elevator up to the fourth floor. My administrative assistant, Chantal, looked up from her computer screen as I came in. "Did you see the news?"

"I did," I agreed grimly. "Any messages?"

"You know there are," she said, handing me the stack of pink slips. "And Janine from the mayor's office called twice to remind you about the meeting this morning."

"As if I could forget." I sighed and hooked my foot around the door, closing it behind me, my hands full. Even a moment of solitude would help before facing the politicos for whom I worked.

My office has a decent view of the old city, with the coveted south-facing orientation that enables me to see the river and the beautiful island called the Île des Soeurs, the nuns' island; if I went right up to the window and peered in the right direction, I could make out the casino. Sometimes, when I was feeling lonely or romantic, I'd go and look over there and whisper erotic messages to Ivan. He's never given any indication that he received any of them. Apparently my extrasensory communication skills are a little subpar.

My desk holds the usual paraphernalia—art deco lamp, computer, framed family photographs. Pictures of Ivan and me summering in Nova Scotia, laughing in each other's arms. A serious picture of him, alone, with the Jacques Cartier bridge in the background. And pictures of Lukas and Claudia, Ivan's kids: on the rides at la Ronde, the permanent amusement park on the Île Sainte-Hélène that was now part of the Six Flags franchise; playing with sparklers on our rooftop terrace; eating crêpes down at the Old Port. Family stuff.

The buzzer on the desk sounded. "The mayor is ready," said Chantal's disembodied voice.

And on that happy note, it was time to go.

I suppose that there had been a life sometime before the orphanage, but I could never really remember it—not really, not as a whole. There were only scraps left, understanding a colloquial expression I couldn't remember having heard before, a tune that wouldn't get out of my head, a sense of something almost familiar lurking in my peripheral vision that disappeared as soon as I turned my head to look at it.

They say that you don't remember anything before you're four or five years old, but there are memories, I know there are, they just lack the clarity and specificity of more recent ones.

But there had been a time when I wasn't at the orphanage. There had been a life. It was a small truth, but it was my only one. I had had a life, before.

And I knew that I was lucky in my truth. Some of the others, they'd been left with the sisters, the bonnes soeurs, *as soon as they were born, baskets on the doorstep. No time for memories there.*

I even knew my mother. At least for a while. Until she got married, and didn't come to visit anymore, drawing with her absence a line plainly and firmly beneath who she'd been, so that she could become who she needed to be.

Later, much later, I recognized how brave that was, her coming to visit me, being willing to see me at all. The sisters never tried to hide their disgust at—and contempt for—the moral lapse that had resulted in my conception, and I'm sure they made her continued presence in my life very difficult.

At the time, of course, all I knew was that I wanted her to return—but only so that she could take me away. Every time she came, I begged her to take me with her; I pleaded, crying, and she never did. I think—or maybe it's just wishful thinking on my part, maybe I made this up so I could feel better, feel loved—that her plan was to marry someone who would understand. Someone who could come with her to the orphanage and pluck me out of the long dormitory room under the eaves and take me back to Verchères, the village upriver from Montréal in the Montrégie district where I had apparently been born. He would adopt me; we could be a family together.

But there were few enough men willing to marry a fallen woman, and fewer still eager to raise her illegitimate child; after she married, my mother never came again.

I waited for her, of course; every time I could get to a window, I watched for her, waiting for my name to be called to the front parlor, disbelieving that she would abandon me. There had to be some sort of mistake. She would come again one day.

I don't know that I ever really believed she wouldn't.

I kept going back. For months, I kept going back, lurking by windows, hearing car doors slam and running with wings on my feet to see who had come. One of these days, it would be her; I was sure of it. One of these days she could come for me.

I couldn't believe that I was something she needed to hide.

I should be grateful, I suppose, that she'd kept me away from the nuns for as long as she had. As long as she'd been able. Maybe she knew, in her heart of hearts, the lie behind the cloister door, that the bonnes soeurs—*the "good sisters"—weren't actually all that* bonne.

Maybe she knew the truth behind that lie, that despite what parents and guardians were told in the polished front parlors, the children left with the nuns weren't ever going to be put up for adoption, or educated, or really cared for at all.

It sounds like neglect, doesn't it, when I write it like that? Like their sin (and trust me when I say that sin there was) was a sin of omission, not of commission. But not loving us, not caring for us—that was really only the beginning.

The rest was so very much worse.

CHAPTER TWO

Mayor Jean-Luc Boulanger was prompt. My boss is always prompt; in the next election, he's probably going to run on his ability to be on time.

He certainly has precious little else to run on. He may well have appointed me to my position, but ours was an uneasy relationship: I needed his political connections, he needed my skills and expertise. I didn't vote for Jean-Luc, and working for him hasn't improved my opinion of the man. But we can't always choose the people we work with, can we?

He noted my arrival in the conference room on the first floor with a curt nod. "*Bonjour*, Madame LeDuc."

"*Monsieur le maire*," I murmured politely, sliding into a seat across the table from him, opening my planner and pulling out a pad of blank paper, writing the date and time on the top sheet. September 18. 10:00 a.m. Anything to avoid small talk.

Richard Rousseau, my deputy, came in and sat next to me,

swiveling his chair to move it a little closer. "Do you have any idea what the meeting is about today?"

"*Non*," I answered, under my breath. A lock of hair had escaped and was on my forehead; I tucked it back behind my ear. "But I'll give you three guesses."

He grimaced. "Danielle Leroux?"

"Danielle Leroux, Annie Desmarchais, Caroline Richards, and Isabelle Hubert," I reminded him, appalled that I knew the names by heart. Appalled at the *reason* for knowing their names. "All of the above."

Richard nodded and scowled across the table as the police director, along with the assistant director, two aides, and their public relations officer seated themselves obsequiously around the mayor. They were from the Service de Police de la Ville de Montréal, or SPVM, the city police.

Just to keep our lives interesting, we have three police forces that can potentially all be working in Montréal. They sometimes even actually acknowledge each other's existence.

There was the SPVM (the city police), the Sûreté de Québec—police who cover all of the province—and the national Royal Canadian Mounted Police. Three levels of policing, and they do not always play well together. The city police resent it when the provincial police try to hone in on anything in the city; and they both resent the Mounties, who aren't all that popular anywhere in the province.

Here in the province of Québec we often choose to forget that we are, after all, part of Canada.

Ivan says it's not so different in the States, where there's a general understanding that city cops and state police and the

FBI tend to step on each other's toes. I waved that information away when he was trying to explain it to me: my life was complicated enough as it was; I didn't need to know how they do things in Boston. Police are police are police, right?

I turned to whisper something about the police to my deputy and found Richard staring hard at the director. No surprise there: Richard was constantly at odds with the police. Their public relations representative was as communicative as a brick wall, and my own small department subsequently found itself doing more damage control in more instances of potential public relations nightmares than should have been strictly necessary. One wondered why they'd bothered hiring someone for PR if they didn't plan to do any of it. Most of the consequent problems fell onto my deputy's plate, hence the scowl. I couldn't really blame him.

The mayor nodded to the mousy aide who had just seated herself in the background and she got up to close the door. He cleared his throat importantly. "*Bon.* Time to begin." He looked around the table. "We're rapidly becoming the murder capital of North America," he said, crisply and inaccurately, "and I'd like to know what people are doing to stop it."

We all looked at the police contingent from the SPVM. The director cleared his throat in turn. "We have all available people working on it, *monsieur le maire*," he said uncomfortably. "I'm not at liberty to say exactly—"

"Not at liberty?" barked the mayor. "Not at liberty, you say? The way that you've been running—or should I say not running?—the department over this past year, I'd say that you didn't have a clue what exactly is going on! As for being at liberty, need I remind you for whom you work? It's intolerable, the way that things have been going . . ."

I tuned him out. I'd heard this particular diatribe before, more than once, and it was getting a little more grating every time I heard it. Arguments seldom improve with age. The mayor and the director were famous for hating each other, and for taking any possible opportunity to make each other look bad in public. A dreary exercise at best, but it also engendered a major headache for those of us entrusted with the city's image.

And in the meantime, the body count was up to four. We were in September, still prime tourist season for Montréal, and still with a compelling reason for people to stay away. Which made it my problem.

I sighed out loud. It was everyone's concern. We were all behaving as though these deaths were somehow a great public relations fiasco. Yet to Danielle Leroux, Annie Desmarchais, Caroline Richards, and Isabelle Hubert, they were anything but. For them, it was the end.

I glanced up and caught the mayor's eye, belatedly realizing that everyone had heard the sigh. "So, Madame LeDuc," he was saying, fixing me with a baleful glance, "I want you to be coordinating things between the police director and my office. As from now."

"*Monsieur le maire?*" I'd definitely missed something.

He nodded briskly. "You'll make sure that there's a report on my desk every morning, recounting the previous day's activities and what progress is being made," he said, liking the idea. "And you, *monsieur le directeur,* will give *madame* every facility."

I cleared my throat. There was no way around what was

about to happen. "*Monsieur le maire*, isn't there someone else who is better qualified—who has more experience with police work?"

"Madame LeDuc," he said, a patronizing smile already spreading across his features. "Everyone else is very busy with immediate, important duties."

Say it, I thought. Say that you think my office is window dressing. Say that you think we don't need a publicity department. *Dis-le*.

He managed not to, because he knew it would come back to bite him in the elections. I'd done a lot to bring conventions, tourists, great visiting musicians, new festivals, and important events to the city—as everyone but the mayor acknowledged. "You are the one," he said finally, "who can best work it into your schedule."

I looked across the table at François Desrocher, the police director. He scowled back at me. The mayor hadn't exactly made his day, assigning someone for him to report to. And the fact that it was me—a woman—in particular . . . well, suffice it to say that it wasn't the best news he could have received. Desrocher had a reputation for his treatment of women in the police force—looking the other way when male officers humiliated them, refusing them promotions, assigning them to clerical posts, not sending them for training. Having a woman breathing down his neck now, second-guessing him, was probably last on his list of desirable outcomes to this meeting.

I smiled sunnily back, just to annoy him, and turned to the mayor. "*Monsieur*, have you considered calling in the Sureté?"

"There's no need for that," snapped Desrocher. "We can

handle the situation *entre nous*—among ourselves. There is no reason to think that there is any involvement off the island."

"There have been four deaths," Richard, next to me, pointed out. He wasn't too happy about the director's dressing-down, either. "It doesn't sound like you're handling it."

"Enough!" An aide was whispering into the mayor's ear, and he held up his hand. "We will reconvene tomorrow afternoon. Madame LeDuc, I want a report from you on my desk in the morning. Now for God's sake, *tout le monde,* go and find out what's happening out there!"

Chantal sat at her desk in the outer office and watched Richard and me coming through the door. She summed up the situation with immediate accuracy. "Everyone's blaming everyone else," she said.

"That's about it," agreed Richard, slumping into the chair next to her desk. "Everything short of name-calling."

"There was name-calling," I said, standing in front of the desk and leafing through yet more pink message slips. "They were just trying to be subtle about it. This goes on, it will get more blatant, you wait and see."

"Something to look forward to," said Richard.

I looked at him sharply. "Are you all right?" He looked the same as he always did: very Gallic, elegantly dressed today in an Armani suit that he'd no doubt picked up secondhand—I knew what his city salary was—but managed to make it look perfect anyway. His compelling blue eyes and tousled dark hair made women turn around and look at him, more than once, more often than not. After working together for three years, I'd started to get used to it.

He gave a very French shrug, then delivered the bombshell. "I knew her."

There was a moment of silence. I didn't pretend to misunderstand him. I walked over to my door and opened it. "In my office. Now."

I didn't sit behind my desk; I don't need to assert my authority with Richard. I gestured him to the leather-covered sofa under the diplomas and sat in the matching adjacent armchair. I leaned forward, bridging the distance between us. "Talk to me."

He ran a hand through his hair again distractedly. "Danielle Leroux," he said unnecessarily. "I know her. I knew her." He paused, then said, explosively, "*Merde, alors!*" and buried his head in his hands.

I waited a moment, then reached out a hand and touched his shoulder, keeping it there. "Richard. *Je suis desolée.*" I am so sorry. What an inadequate thing to say, in the circumstances.

He looked up, tears in his eyes. "It's just . . ." He took a long, shuddering breath. "Martine, there may be problems. I'm sorry, but there may be. We—we were seeing each other."

Oh, God. I tried not to let my consternation show; it wouldn't help anything. I kept my hand on his shoulder reassuringly. "I think you should tell me about it, Richard."

He nodded miserably, but didn't speak again for an eternity. "Danielle . . . she was a research librarian. Over at UQAM." That explained how they met; Richard was working part-time on a graduate degree at the Université du Québec à Montréal, my own alma mater. "She . . . at first, we went out for a coffee a couple of times, we liked each other, what can I say? We spent a lot of time together. We took a long weekend, went up into the Laurentians . . ."

I remembered him taking that time off; I'd had to change my own personal plans to accommodate him, and Ivan hadn't been best pleased. That had been at least a month ago. If Richard had met Danielle when classes were still in session, they had been seeing each other throughout the summer.

My stomach clenched with anxiety. Most people are killed by someone they know. Despite the profile pointing to this being a serial killer, there was no way that my deputy wasn't going to be on the list of suspects.

Pretty high up on it, too.

I took a deep breath. "Richard. When did you see her last?"

There was misery in his eyes. "Wednesday night."

Great. And she'd been killed sometime Thursday. It was going to be a very long day indeed.

All of us at the orphanage had one thing, one terribly important thing, in common: we were mistakes. I never really understood what that meant, but Sister said it often enough that I knew it must be true. We came from villages, farms, even the city itself; we were brought with favorite toys or blankets or in harsh cheap unraveling baskets or by some relative who hid us from the light of day.

Those who brought us in were fed the lies. Of course he can keep his favorite blanket. Naturellement, she will have her stuffed rabbit with her in bed at night. Bien sûr there will be a good education. We love them all as though they were our own.

Well, we were theirs, all right; but love didn't have anything to do with it.

It was all about the work. Hard work.

Even the smallest children had something to do. My earliest memories of the orphanage are of floors, of scrubbing floors. Perhaps because we were small and couldn't reach much of anything else, we were made to clean the floors.

I don't know if the sisters even knew our names, or if they ever cared about any of us as individuals. We were their charges, the mistakes that they were tasked to deal with. And that was what united us: the need to be children, real children, with names and pasts and thoughts that were all our own.

Not that they didn't try to hammer the individuality out of us. We looked the same, all of us girls, wearing long scratchy shifts in bed at night and pinafores during the day—we all wore the same clothes, interchangeably; nothing was our own. Nothing showed that one of us was in any way different from any other one.

In the winter we washed in water so cold that we had to break the ice on it, we got dressed and made our beds, lined two-deep the length of the dormitory. Sister inspected all the beds and had a stick ready to rap the knuckles of any child who didn't do it properly.

Needless to say, I got quite good at making my bed.

Then we'd stand in line, single file, down three sets of stairs and out to the chapel for morning mass, which none of us understood on account of it being in Latin, but which we had to stay awake for anyway. I got good at staying awake and attentive there, too.

We had no idea, then, that it could get better—or worse. It was the way our lives were. It was everything we knew. It just was.

CHAPTER THREE

As soon as Richard left, I got on the phone. "I need to come over there now," I told the director's assistant.

"Madame LeDuc, we have you scheduled in for your update at two o'clock," she said smoothly. "I'm afraid *monsieur le directeur* is busy at present."

"Then he will have to be interrupted," I said. "I have information about the most recent homicide, and I need to speak with him at once."

"*Madame*—"

"Never mind," I interrupted. "It doesn't matter. I'm on my way over."

I opened the small office closet and exchanged heels for flats. Never mind whether or not they went with my suit: comfort will always win out in my book. Life is too short.

Chantal tapped on the door and put her head in. "Monsieur Petrinko is on line two," she said cheerfully.

I picked it up. "Ivan, I haven't much time—"

"Hi, babe. I'll be quick."

I relented, told myself to back off, and drew in a deep breath. It wasn't Ivan's fault that everything else in Montréal seemed to be falling apart. "Sorry, sweetheart. What's up?"

"Just a minor domestic emergency," he said. "Margery has to be in the hospital. Well, she's there now, actually. Down in Boston. Gall bladder, or something like that. Something really serious." Ivan gets a little flustered sometimes.

I grimaced. Margery is Ivan's former wife and the mother of his children. Any sentence that begins with her name inevitably ends in something somewhere between inconvenience and disaster. It isn't Margery's fault, it's just the nature of shared parenting. "And?"

"And the kids are already on their way to Montréal," Ivan said. "Some neighbor dropped them off at Logan, and their flight will be in—oh, hell, in about half an hour. And I have this meeting—"

"No," I interrupted. "I can't go pick them up at the airport."

There was a pause. "Martine, I wouldn't ask if this wasn't an important meeting. You know that."

"I know that," I agreed, trying to reach across the room for my briefcase and not disconnect the line in doing so. "And you know that I wouldn't say no unless *this* was really important. I'm on my way to police headquarters. I *seriously* don't have time."

There was a longer pause. "We're going to have to have them for the weekend anyway, babe, and I'm sorry," Ivan said, exploring my mood. "I can't send them back to Boston, not with all this going on with their mom. I don't want to ask Rob to deal with them, with everything else on his plate." Rob was Margery's husband. I didn't know him well enough to pick him out in a crowd, but he seemed to make her happy, and the kids liked him. "He's probably at the hospital with her now, anyway. I think she's at Mass. General."

Wherever she was being treated couldn't figure into my plans. "Ivan, I have to go," I said.

"Okay, okay, I'll manage to get them. Or I'll send somebody from here. Maybe Sylvie." He was thinking out loud. "But—well, I thought you should know that they'll be staying with us for a few days. At least through Sunday night. Sorry, I know it's not our weekend to have them here, but I couldn't say no."

He was repeating himself, which meant he was nervous. It gave me pause. Was I really that awful, that he needed to feel me out that much? But . . . yeah, extra time with the kids wasn't exactly the way I'd planned on spending the weekend.

I shouldn't really say that. It's not so much that I don't like them—in unguarded moments I'll even admit to loving them—it's the fact of giving up our only free time together, of constructing a weekend that centered around Claudia and Lukas. Normally there would have been a conversation here about it. Today, not so much. "Of course you couldn't," I said. "I get it, I really do. But listen, Ivan, I really have to run. I'll see you later. We'll figure out the weekend then." I disconnected the call before he could say anything else.

It was time to concentrate on the easier of my two jobs, that of publicity director. The stepmother thing? Sometimes I felt like I'd never get a handle on it.

Let's face it: everyone's got their own ideas about how children should be raised, but try getting four adults who don't necessarily like each other attempting to co-parent together, each with their own past and thoughts on the subject, and it isn't pretty.

After staring uselessly at the phone sitting in its cradle, I roused myself and headed across town to the Plateau, where the headquarters of the SPVM lives on the Rue St.-Urbain. Twenty minutes via Métro: a new personal best.

I had barely arrived at François Desrocher's office before he started in on me. "Beside Mademoiselle Leroux's telephone is a pad of paper. On that pad of paper is the number of your deputy," he said accusingly, fixing me with a sharp look.

"I know," I said calmly. "He was dating Danielle. However, he did not see her at all yesterday, and so can be of limited help to you."

"You knew this?"

"Not when we met this morning," I said. "He told me of it after the meeting. Monsieur Rousseau is devastated, as you might well imagine, *monsieur le directeur*. We have spoken of it since then, he and I."

"You were *unaware* of their connection before?"

It was my turn to glare. Wasn't that what I'd just said? "I am not in the habit of inquiring into my staff's personal lives, *monsieur*," I said tartly. "Monsieur Rousseau is an excellent deputy director. His job performance has always and consistently been exceptional. Beyond that, what he does in his personal life is none of my affair."

He ignored me. "We need to question your assistant," he

said, his voice brisk, making sure he was showing who was in charge here. "He should be relieved of any further involvement in this case."

"He *has* no involvement in this case," I said with as much patience as I could manage, wondering how many years of prison I'd get for decking the director. A lot, probably. Though mitigated by his attitude and behavior, surely, as anyone who knew him would have to concede. "It is not my office that's doing the investigating, as you know, *monsieur*: that is your task. I am merely to assist you in any way I can, and to report back to *monsieur le maire*. As was made clear at this morning's meeting. My deputy will continue to assist *me* as necessary." I took a deep breath. "You may, of course, speak with him in order to gather information about the victim, as you would with any other witness. He has assured me that he will make himself available to the police."

He frowned, making a show of sitting back in his chair, steepling his fingers, regarding me with disfavor. "Madame LeDuc, I would not wish to interfere." Yeah, right. "But you must understand that I have a police force to run and a series of murders to investigate. Your deputy will no doubt be summoned."

Hadn't I just *said* that he could interview Richard? If he was trying to make a point about being in charge, he could have just said so. It was time to take the offensive here. "In the meantime," I said, as sweetly as I could manage, "perhaps, as I am here already, *monsieur* will give me an update on the current progress of the investigation? Perhaps bring me up to speed on whatever evidence you've gathered, on what leads your detectives are pursuing at the moment?"

He didn't like it, but he already knew this wasn't a battle he was going to win. He made a show of sighing and of unlocking a drawer in his desk before withdrawing a folder and passing it across the expanse of desk to me.

"A summary," he said sourly, "of the investigation to date." He looked at his watch importantly. "As I cannot allow you to leave the premises with these documents, *madame*, and as I myself am very occupied, my assistant will indicate a quiet place where you may go to read these materials."

I stood up. I couldn't have asked for anything better; I hadn't been looking forward to listening to him sigh and tap his watch while I went through the material, and being spared his scowl did a lot to brighten my day. Alone, I could really think about what I was reading, maybe even wrap my brain around exactly what was happening in my city.

Maybe.

I opened the folder in a small airless room procured by a constable who made it clear she had more important things to do than show me around, and flipped through the reports on the latest victim: her autopsy results, crime scene photographs around the park bench where her body was displayed, a notation of drugs found in her body, the first narratives written by the responding officers. My stomach lurched and I swallowed hard, several times, until the bile went back down.

The drugs didn't mean much to me; I've been fortunate in my good health, and perceive medications taken by others as I might a strange custom practiced in a foreign land. Still, it seemed like there were a *lot* of them for someone so young. I scribbled the names down and decided to Google them later.

I steeled myself and looked again at the bench—and felt the

nausea again. How could anyone sit on one of those ever again, after seeing this? The lifeless body was naked, and streaked with some dark brown substance I could only interpret as blood; it was curled up on one side of the bench, the head leaning against the back, as though taking a catnap.

I swallowed again, pulling my eyes away from the photograph, and glanced through the rest of the autopsy report. She'd been in good health when she was killed. I struggled to read the minutiae of the descriptions written up by the doctor who'd performed the autopsy, by the crime scene techs. Rape, it said. Mutilation, it said. I swallowed hard.

And then, without really being aware of what I was doing, I pulled out another photograph and came face-to-face with Danielle Leroux, alive and vibrant and far more real than what had been left on that city bench.

No wonder Richard had been attracted to her. She looked younger than her thirty-four years, with dark hair swept up into a barrette on one side, eyes sparkling with humor, and a smile that invited one in return. No one's idea of a librarian, I thought.

Someone's idea of a victim.

CHAPTER FOUR

I looked at that photograph for a long time. It seemed inconceivable that this beautiful, vibrant girl had any connection to the chilling autopsy report, inconceivable that those laughing eyes weren't laughing somewhere anymore. It had to be someone else, the rational part of my brain was insisting.

I sighed, finally, and put it aside. There was little else in the folder to see; we were, after all, still in the first day of the investigation. I knew that there were homicide detectives out there now, interviewing neighbors, contacting family members, piecing together a life that somehow met with a killer on a warm night on the Plateau. One of them would be speaking, soon, with Richard, another piece in the puzzle. I should probably give him some time off.

And I should probably have thought of that before, when he'd first told me.

The next folder was a lot thicker, though it had just as few answers. I flipped quickly through what I didn't want to see, didn't want to know: rape. Stabbings. Mutilation of the face in particular. My stomach lurched, and I flipped away from those pages.

And flipped to a photograph of Annie Desmarchais alive and well, and even though I had already seen it on the front page of the *Gazette*, I was still taken aback. What little I knew of serial killers had come from the pages of mystery novels and the occasional movie; and that, along with common sense, dictated that victims look similar, that serial killers are attracted to a certain appearance.

Annie Desmarchais had celebrated her sixty-fourth birthday a mere two weeks before she had been murdered, back in the early summer. She was attractive, slightly plump, with a warm smile and exquisite grooming; but she was still, undoubtedly, a woman of a certain age.

I pulled Danielle's picture out from the first folder, put the two women side by side, and frowned. Aside from the twinkle that managed to penetrate the lens of a camera, there was nothing that I could see that the two had in common. Flipping open the other two folders, I looked at the faces of Isabelle Hubert—one of the most beautiful women I'd seen, and this in a city of extraordinarily beautiful women—and Caroline Richards, who wore glasses and had slightly crooked teeth. Nothing in common, but there had to be something, hadn't there? Didn't serial killers run to a type?

What was it that their killer had seen in them that I wasn't seeing?

"You won't see any similarities," a voice said from behind me, making me jump. "There aren't any." The chair next to me was pulled out and a young man sat down. "Mind if I join you?"

"Not at all," I said, hoping he couldn't hear my heart pounding. Maybe it was just because I was new to this murder stuff, but having someone creep up on you when you're looking at pictures of dead people is enough to make you seriously come apart at the seams.

The young man looking at me was clearly and unabashedly Anglophone, a rarity in a police department run by an ardent card-carrying member of the *Parti Québecois*, the political party advocating endlessly and repetitively for secession from Canada. "I'm Julian," he said, almost apologetically. "Julian Fletcher."

"Martine LeDuc," I said automatically, putting out my hand to shake his. "You're not in public relations, are you?"

He snorted. "Public relations? Not if the chief has anything to do with it. I'm kept strictly under wraps. Not politically correct enough." He grinned vividly. "In fact, he'd probably get rid of me altogether if I wasn't so good at what I do."

"Which is . . . ?"

"Detective," he said. "*Détective-lieutenant*, actually. There are still enclaves in this city where speaking English isn't regarded as heresy, and I know everybody in them."

A light was dawning. "Oh, my God. Fletcher . . ."

He nodded. "Yep. *That* Fletcher. One of the *Westmount Fletchers*." He sketched quotation marks around the name with his fingers. Westmount was the oldest and wealthiest—and most Anglophone—section of Montréal. "I'm the proverbial black sheep in the famous family. Silly boy who chose public service over commerce. Never to be spoken of again in the hallowed halls of the family mansion on the hill." He grinned suddenly, vividly, and I found myself smiling back. "The name comes in useful, though, and no one in this building has ever discarded anything that might be remotely useful." His tone was brisk, suggesting that he didn't altogether mind being a black sheep. "So," he went on, nodding at the papers spread out in front of me, "what is it you want to know?"

I gestured helplessly. "Everything. I'm not seeing a connection, and I'm only on the second folder."

Julian sat back in his chair. "You're taking it in the wrong order," he said, frankly. "You should start at the beginning. That's where *he* started."

"You're sure it's a he?"

He shrugged. "Even if all the odds weren't with it being a he—and almost all serial killers are male, so there are your odds—there was a sexual component to all of them. Didn't you know?" He slanted a look and saw my face. "They were all raped," he said gently. "I'm sorry. I guess no one's been talking about that part."

I swallowed. "I guess not."

He sighed, drummed his fingers on the edge of the table for a moment. I had the impression of a great deal of energy pulsing behind all his movements. "Okay. Do you really want to sit and read all about it, or shall I show you?"

"Show me?"

He nodded, standing up, already helping me out of my chair. "The director assigned me to you, but he doesn't have to know that we didn't spend the day poring over records. Let's take a ride, Martine LeDuc," he said easily. "Put the ladies in context."

"Okay," I said, bemused, trailing after him. "It's kind of you to take the time. You know I shouldn't be doing this at all." I grimaced. "I appear to be the only department head who doesn't have what the mayor considers important things to do, hence my availability to be the messenger girl between him and the director."

"Never mind," Julian said encouragingly. "All the better. You may see things we don't. And I get to boss you around. I don't get that very often in my job. It's win-win, you ask me."

We went out to where his car, an Audi TT that he certainly had not bought on a policeman's salary, was illegally parked in a resident-only space. Julian kept talking even as he slid behind the wheel and eased us out into Montréal's moderately terrifying traffic. "So, Isabelle Hubert," he said, maneuvering in front of a truck with millimeters to spare. I checked my seatbelt to make sure it wasn't going to give out on me. "Victim number one. Pretty. Young—twenty-three. Blonde, but that wasn't what nature had intended." He glanced at me. "Prostitute, but not one of the girls working the corners down on Sainte-Catherine. She worked for an escort service. Higher class clients, lower risk environment."

"Not low enough," I commented. I remembered what the papers had said when Isabelle Hubert's body was found, also on a park bench; in her case, stretched out across it, lying down as though asleep. Everyone seemed to think that violence was an acceptable risk and a foregone conclusion for prostitutes, call girls and streetwalkers alike. There was almost an air of, well, what did she expect? What did she expect, indeed? To be allowed to live?

Even Ivan had said so. Not one of our better moments together.

"Yep, so you might think," Julian replied now, noncommittal.

We were driving north, into the Little Italy section of town. Julian pulled off Rue St.-Denis onto a side street and pointed to the third building, solidly built of gray stone, the trademark curving outdoor staircase—in this case painted a gay and charming purple—going up to the second floor where Isabelle Hubert had lived. "Nice place," he said, ignoring the horns of motorists who were trying to squeeze by us on the narrow street. "A piano, though it's hard to figure out how she got it in there. Copper cooking pots hanging from the ceiling. Lots of plants, lots of books, a cat."

"What happened to the cat?" I swear it felt like a logical question.

Julian didn't know. "Point is, she had a life. She worked evenings, and during the day she wrote poetry, she went for walks, she hung out at a little café back on St.-Denis. She was taking an art class, doing some genealogical research."

Julian was still looking at the shuttered windows, as if they might yet tell him something about their former occupant. "She saw a client at eight," he said. "That's what these girls call them, clients. We talked to the guy, he was one of her regulars, saw her every week. We looked at him hard as a suspect, at first, but it wasn't him. He was more broken up than if it had been his wife. He left the apartment where they'd met at the same time Isabelle did, went and played racquetball with a regular partner, was still having an after-workout glass of red wine with the guy when they found her body. Hey, did you hear about that? They're saying that's good for you now, red wine after a workout."

I ignored him. I found my eyes drifting to the windows just as his had. She had written poetry. She had played the piano. She had loved her cat.

I was still wondering what happened to that cat.

Julian put the car in gear and drove off without, as far as I could tell, either signaling his intention or looking in any of his rearview mirrors. "She didn't have anyone else scheduled that night," he said. "We checked with her madam. She was supposed to be on call—she had a cell phone, and if a client asked for her, the madam would call her and tell her where to go."

We were driving south, down the rue Guy, toward the center of the city. "She didn't keep an appointment book or have a smartphone or anything helpful like that," Julian said. "There was a calendar on her wall at home but nothing was scheduled for that night after the client. So we don't know what her plans were."

I closed my eyes. Maybe if I didn't *see* how aggressively he was driving, my stomach would stop twitching. "It was beautiful weather," I said, my eyes still shut, remembering what I'd heard when the city had learned of Isabelle's murder back in May. The kids had spent the weekend with us, one of our scheduled times with them, and it had been fantastic. We'd taken them to la Ronde, the amusement park, all of us getting delightfully sick on twirling rides and junk food. Spring is greeted with open arms in a city entombed in snow and ice throughout the winter, forced to go underground.

"She may have just wanted to walk," I said. I could imagine her, blonde and pretty, her jacket open to the soft air, the lights of restaurants and shops spilling out around her, highlighting the glitter of her jewelry as she passed.

"The client," Julian said, "lived on the Plateau, too. Or at least that's where he keeps the apartment he saw Isabelle in; his wife and kids live somewhere else, somewhere off Sherbrooke.

Isabelle walked down to the Latin Quarter. We think she had some sort of purpose, somewhere specific to go, someone to see. If she were just enjoying the night, why not go to a café, a bar, sit outside with a drink?"

It was a good question. "That's close to UQAM," I said suddenly, sitting up straighter, opening my eyes despite my better instincts. "Danielle Leroux worked at the University of Québec."

"Good girl," Julian said, approving. "We'll make a detective out of you yet. Unfortunately, while that thought did occur to us, too, we couldn't find the connection." He pulled over at Berri-UQAM and indicated the Métro stop, the bushes, the one lone bench. "Isabelle was left on that bench sometime after midnight. She wasn't killed here, she'd just been dumped for someone to find. Just lying stretched out on the bench. No clothes on her, and not a lot of trace evidence, either."

"Trace evidence?"

He nodded, again not looking at me, but rather at the bench. Today, a young couple was sitting on it, talking intensely together, her arm linked through his, oblivious of its former occupant. "Edmond Locard—a Frenchman—made the observation sometime around the turn of last century that when two objects—people, in this case—touch each other, each of them leaves some trace behind on the other. Got to be called Locard's Exchange Principle. Hairs, skin oil, dirt, stuff like that. The forensics people love it, and I'll be honest, it's nailed quite a few people. In this case, we were looking for skin cells under her fingernails, which would indicate that she had struggled, tried to defend herself, but which might also have given us a sample of the killer's DNA. We also looked for pubic hair transfer, and semen." His voice changed a note, a shadow flitting across. "There was some thought in the department that her profession made that point moot."

"What?" I hadn't heard that. "Why, because prostitutes are just asking to be raped? To be killed?"

"Take it easy," said Julian. "I'm on your side, okay? Turns out, it *was* moot. Mademoiselle Hubert practiced safe sex with her client that night; and her killer, unfortunately for us, did the same. *Rien.*"

"But you know she was raped?" It was difficult to get the words out.

Julian nodded. "Unless the client was violent with her, which he says he wasn't, and I believe him: they saw each other regularly." He put the car into gear as he spoke.

Again the dramatic entrance into the stream of traffic. I was starting to get used to it. "But the blood," I said. "Am I remembering right?" I was thinking back to the newspaper accounts that I'd read with such consternation, the first dramatic murder in the city since I'd become publicity director. "There was a lot of blood, wasn't there? She was stabbed, I know I read that . . . wouldn't her blood have been all over him?"

"Undoubtedly." Julian checked his rearview mirrors before pulling a sudden exciting U-turn. "But he could have been prepared, he could have worn some sort of covering, or nothing at all. Forensic countermeasures. Then he could have changed back into street clothes after he left her on the bench. Her heart had stopped pumping by then." We passed a taxi with inches to spare. "If that's the way it happened, then that would put him in the organized and not-too-crazy section of the bus, by the way. There were a lot of people out that night, even that late, and you can be sure that if anyone had been staggering around covered in blood, we'd have heard about it."

We were heading west and north, into the English-speaking part of town. Street names were gradually sounding more and more Anglophone as we went up the hill, and houses were getting grander and grander, and then we were, suddenly it seemed, in the heart of McGill University on Sherbrooke Street. And Julian was continuing his tour. "Moving along to Caroline Richards. You'll recognize the name, of course."

I did, as I had when her mutilated body had been discovered, back in the beginning of July. Caroline Richards had been an investigative reporter, writing for the English-language *Globe and Mail* newspaper. She had failed to show up for a staff meeting on a Monday morning; her body was discovered that evening by a family strolling along the St. Lawrence River, over in the working-class section called Verdun. She, too, had been displayed on a park bench. Unlike Isabelle, who had been lying on the bench, Caroline had been sitting up straight, as though relaxing and watching the water flow by in front of her.

I'd wondered at the time how long that family would have to stay in therapy. Collateral damage.

"She lived up here," Julian was saying. "Got divorced sometime last year, he got the house, she moved into an apartment near campus, wanted something closer to the action. You know the drill."

"I'm happily married," I pointed out, a little tartly. "So I wouldn't know."

He shrugged. "Good for you," he said. "Thing is, she was grabbed the night before, on the Sunday; the medical examiner says she died then, sometime during that night. But he had to hang on to her body for a while, all day in fact, 'cause that path where she was found? It's real popular, even on a Monday. Joggers, cyclists, elderly people out walking, half of Verdun is all over those paths when it's good weather. She had to have been dumped just minutes before she was found. Raises a lot of interesting questions." He slanted a look at me.

"Why didn't he dump her during the night, like Isabelle Hubert?" I asked obediently. "Why hold on to her, and where? What's the significance of park benches?"

He nodded approvingly, his eye wandering over a group of young women passing by the car, books and notebooks clutched to them as they chattered together. "Good questions. And three months on, the answers are, we don't know, we don't know, and we don't know."

"I begin to see why the director is having a coronary," I said.

He put the car in gear and eased off the clutch. "Next one. Annie Desmarchais was killed in August," he said. "Both Isabelle and Caroline were in their twenties. Annie, as you saw, was in her sixties. She was a widow, lived with her sister—also a widow—over in Westmount."

"Was the sister helpful?" I asked.

He shook his head. "Wanted to be. The sister's sixty-eight, and all I can say is, I hope I'm that energetic when I hit that age." For him, I thought sourly, that was probably a matter of light-years away. Ever since I'd turned thirty-five, I was very conscious of time—and youth. "She and Annie spent a lot of time apart, it's probably why they got along so well. The sister—her name is Violette Sobel—teaches yoga at the community center on Maisonneuve, plays bingo, takes an art class, and has a boyfriend, himself being almost seventy and not a suspect by any stretch of the imagination. Annie was pretty much up there with Violette in terms of activities, but hers were more cerebral. She worked as administrator for this foundation, a place called the Providence Foundation, some kind of local philanthropy that the Demarchais family started and funds. She read books, and was working on her first novel."

"Did she have a boyfriend, too?"

"Nope. Claimed she wasn't interested, though I gathered that Violette did her part to try and change Annie's mind. She says she hadn't set her up with anybody recently. Annie said she was too busy. Said she'd been married once, that was enough for her, thank you very much."

Some days, I knew how she felt. Some days, once was more than enough.

"Anglophone?" I asked, assuming I knew the answer. Living in Westmount was a dead giveaway.

"Interestingly, no. Desmarchais is the ladies' maiden name. Apparently Papa made it big as a medical doctor and bought a place where all the rich folks were living, but the family's Francophone."

We'd turned south again, and Julian was pulling over. "There's the house. It's in both their names."

"She lived the farthest from downtown," I observed, wondering if it meant anything. Cars passed by. The house, large and elegant and aloof, stood silent.

"True, but she spent a lot of time down there, our Annie, and over on Sherbrooke, too: that's where she worked, at the

Providence Foundation. It was kind of *her* foundation; actually, she and her sister started it, though Violette was strictly hands-off." He paused. "Annie was last seen there on a Thursday night, fairly late. There was a meeting that apparently ended acrimoniously. Someone offered her a ride home, but she called a taxi and left to meet it outside."

"What happened then?"

It was, I thought, a very Gallic shrug coming from someone as determinedly Anglophone as Julian Fletcher. "Who knows? A city worker heading out for the night shift found her up in the Plateau, in the Parc Saint-Louis."

I felt a headache building. "I think I can guess."

"You got it. The interesting thing is, by now he's either getting sloppy, or less creative, or else he's just feeling at home in the Plateau, because that was where we found Danielle Leroux, too."

Oh, great. Ivan and I took the kids there. A small park flanked by brightly painted houses. Picture-postcard pretty. Maybe we'd have to find another place to feed the pigeons—at least until I could look at the Parc Saint-Louis without flashing on the image of women's mutilated bodies propped up on benches.

It was after the winter that it happened. It had been a bad one, that winter, even by our usual standards, with the orphanage and convent cut off from the rest of the city by snow and electrical failure. We generated our own electricity, so that mattered little; but we were unable to bring any of the work we did to market, or the meat or eggs that we sold, and so everyone looked a little pinched.

And the cold—Jesus wept, the cold. There was snow coating the inside of the dormitory windows, and when the lights were put out at night, all you could hear was the chattering of hundreds of sets of teeth. No one slept much, not when it was that bitter, and several of the youngest children died, and we couldn't even bury them because the ground in the small graveyard beyond the chapel was frozen under six feet of snow.

So as you can well imagine, when spring came, it was cause for celebration.

Something was going on, though, and we all knew it; we just didn't know what "it" was. There was an undercurrent of something among the sisters, and more than once voices were raised behind closed doors—something expressly forbidden. I suppose that should be some comfort to me, shouldn't it? The fact of there being a rebellion? The knowledge that some of them, at least, tried to protect us?

I suppose I should be grateful. But it's hard to see beyond what happened, and feel anything at all.

That day . . . Every detail is etched in my mind as clearly as if it happened yesterday. I am the small child standing in line, looking lost. What I didn't know was that I was standing at the edge of a cliff, about to topple over.

They never told us what was happening. Perhaps I blame them the most for that. There was no announcement. There were no reasons given. There was only Sister waking us up before dawn, urging us to dress in the dark.

When the buses were full, they pulled away from the convent, and as I looked back, all I saw was Sister Mary Martha sobbing into her hands.

On the bus, we just kept going and going, from the outskirts of the city through Montréal itself, then, slowly, the scenery changed,

and what I was looking at was more desolation and more isolation as we bumped along what turned into a country lane.

When we finally stopped, it was after going up a long driveway.
In front of us stood a tremendous gray building that wasn't altogether different from the one we'd left; large and imposing, its stone
walls sweeping up several stories with rows and rows of windows,
all of them in a line, wings flung out from a central staircase and
entrance. There were words carved into the stone above the doorway, but I didn't know how to decipher them. "Where are we?" I
whispered to Marie-Rose, the girl sitting beside me.

She shook her head. "I don't know."

I raised my voice. "Can anyone read?"

One of the boys—Bobby it was—spoke from the back of the
bus. "Cité de Saint-Jean-de-Dieu," he said. "That's what it says."

Which told us exactly nothing.

The bus's engine had stopped and it was getting a little warm
inside. The sun had come up and was shining directly in our faces
over a field across the road. Finally a sister—not one we knew,
and wearing a different habit from "our" sisters—got onto the
bus and stood there facing us. "Your attention, children!"

Most of the chatter subsided.

"My name is Sister Catherine," the nun said. "And this is your
new home. You'll need to learn the rules and do what the sisters
and their helpers tell you. If you do that, you will have a good life
here."

A wave of whispers as we all consulted each other, feeling
grounded not in this woman's words but in the familiarity of the
other children, of knowing each other in this strange new place.

And that was the beginning.

CHAPTER FIVE

There was trouble at home.

I could hear it as soon as I turned my key in the front-door lock. Claudia's wailing voice, then Lukas, sharp and angry. And Ivan, trying to be soothing.

Welcome home, I thought grimly, then raised my voice cheerfully. "Hello! Anybody here?"

Lukas arrived almost immediately from the back hallway. With his tousled dark hair and his brilliant blue eyes, my eleven-year-old stepson looked a lot like the posters his sister put up in her room of baby pop stars, though she never seemed to notice the similarities. "*Belle-Maman!* Dad said you'd be late!" Lukas seemed, on the whole, rather glad that I wasn't. He threw his arms around my waist.

I gave him a hug and a kiss, then slid out of my shoes and jacket, dumping them both in the foyer along with my briefcase, and started toward the back of the house. "Your dad making dinner?" I asked hopefully.

"More like being an umpire," said Ivan, emerging from the kitchen. He hugged me, whispering, "I think they're scared about Margery, but they're taking it out on each other."

Lovely. I forced a smile and went past him into the kitchen, the biggest and brightest of the rooms in our apartment, where the family seemed somehow to spend most of its time. Claudia was perched on one of the high stools at the island, doing her nails. What business a nine-year-old has in growing and maintaining long fingernails is a battle I'd long ago given up fighting, since it was clear that Claudia was going to do whatever Claudia chose to do. There were more important things in life to fight over.

Lukas had disappeared into his room.

I ignored her as I went across to a glass-fronted cupboard, took down a wineglass, and filled it with Merlot. The sun was most definitely over the yardarm after the day I'd had, and besides, I had a feeling I was going to need the sustenance. "Claudia," I said conversationally, sipping, "nice to see you, too."

An exaggerated sigh, which was apparently the current preadolescent response to anything or anyone. "Hello, *Belle-Maman*," she said, her accent slightly worse than her brother's had been. When Ivan and I married, I resisted having his children call me by my first name. "I just don't see it as respectful," I'd told him. After a night of argument, we settled on *belle-maman*, which literally means "beautiful mommy" and can be used (because French sometimes is a very odd language) to refer either to one's stepmother or to one's mother-in-law. As it had no connotations to either the kids or their mother, the name stuck.

Claudia had more to say. "Daddy says I have to set the table, and I'm not going to do it. It's not just that I don't want to, either. It's illegal. There *are* child labor laws, you know."

I looked over her head at Ivan, now back in the kitchen and with a dish towel slung over his shoulder. That meant that he was, at least, preparing to cook. He was trying to hide a smile, though.

"Not in Canada there aren't," I told Claudia cheerfully. Well, no labor laws that prohibited the setting of the table, anyway. "Have you heard anything about your mom yet?" That was the real issue here; might as well get right down to it.

"No!" she wailed, and with a sweeping gesture, spilled the nail polish all over the countertop, jumped down from the stool, and ran from the room. Ivan and I stared at each other in dismay.

"Well," he said, opening the refrigerator, "that went well."

"Yep," I said, taking a hefty swallow of the Merlot. The smell of the nail polish was bringing on a headache, and the chances of getting Claudia in any state to clean it were nil. I got nail polish remover and pulled out some paper towels and started mopping the noxious stuff up. "What time did you guys get here?"

He was laying chicken breasts in a pan, assembling olive oil and rosemary. Did I mention that my husband is a brilliant cook? Nights like this, it's what keeps him alive. "Late. Sylvie picked them up at the airport this morning, and she said traffic at of the airport was horrible, both ways. You'd think on a

Friday people would be trying to get *out* of the city, not into it. And then tonight, traffic from the casino was worse."

I shook my head, disposing of the last of the nail polish as I did so. At least she wouldn't be wearing any of it this weekend. "Montréal's a tourist destination," I reminded Ivan. "That's why I'm gainfully employed, remember?"

"Speaking of which," he said, putting the pan into the oven and turning to face me, "what happened today? Are you all right?"

I took a deep breath. "No," I said, and even I could hear the tremor in my voice. I took another swallow of the wine. "Boulanger's assigned me to monitor the police department until they solve these murders, and—"

I broke off as Lukas entered the kitchen. The kid had enough on his plate with his mother in the hospital; he didn't need to think his stepmother was falling apart, too. "So what horrible task has your father assigned *you* that's in violation of child labor laws?" I asked.

He made a face. "Claudia's just mad 'cause she's scared about Mom, and it's easier to be mad than scared," he said perceptively. He got a soda from the refrigerator and hopped up on the stool his sister had vacated. "Mom's in the hospital," he told me.

"I know," I said. "I'm sorry, Lukas. Has your stepdad called yet? Do you know how she's doing?"

"We're supposed to call after nine," Ivan said. "We'll know pretty soon." He paused, put an arm lightly around Lukas's shoulders. "She's going to be fine," he said.

"I know." Lukas's voice sounded casual, but the fear in his eyes betrayed him.

I drew in a deep breath. "Let's go out," I suggested, meeting Ivan's eyes. He hated giving the kids junk food in about the same proportion that they loved eating it. "Instead of just waiting around here to make the call."

Lukas brightened immediately. "McDonald's?" he suggested. "St. Hubert?"

"*Not* McDonald's," Ivan intervened, but he was already turning off the oven. "That's a good idea," he said to me across the room, relief in his eyes. Even Claudia couldn't sulk, we had found, when eating greasy French fries out of a greasy paper wrapper.

And so we went to St. Hubert, and it was only as we were waiting in line under its bright neon lights that I remembered the fast food place shared a last name with the first of that summer's victims. And found that I suddenly wasn't hungry at all anymore.

Margery *was* fine.

The kids went to bed, exhausted and relieved, and Ivan and I sat together in the living room, our fingers entwined, my head on his shoulder. "So," he said softly, "are you okay?"

"I guess so," I said. I was thinking that I didn't have much to complain about in the grand scheme of things. I wasn't in a hospital, recovering from an unexpected operation. I wasn't dead.

"You need to work this weekend?" His tone was neutral; both Ivan and I have jobs that often demand irregular hours, and we were used to it, used to coordinating fluctuating schedules.

"No," I said, and then amended it. "Probably not, unless

something comes up. I'll find out on Monday what's going on with the investigation, and talk to the mayor."

"So he's using you as a sort of glorified go-between?"

I sighed. "Something like that," I said. "I make fun of him, I know, but I think maybe he's hoping that someone outside the establishment might see something that everybody else is too close to the investigation to see. And it's possible."

Ivan thought about it. "Do you think you can?"

I shrugged and nestled in more comfortably to his shoulder. "I don't know. I've gotten closer than I thought I would, and it's . . . well, it's not easy. I'm working with one of the detectives on the case—an Anglo, Ivan, you'd like him—and so far all I've done is see an overview. I don't know what on earth I can come up with that the professionals aren't seeing, but I'll keep at it as long as *monsieur le maire* wants me to."

"Just stay safe."

"Of course I will. I'm not in any danger," I said, before remembering Julian's driving. Well, not in any danger from the criminal element, anyway.

The telephone rang on Sunday afternoon, the most comfortable time of the weekend for us all: the kids had settled in, we'd done something reasonably fun together on Saturday, I'd been to Sunday mass while Ivan made pancakes at home, and by now we were all relaxed; the preflight jitters prior to leaving again for Boston hadn't started yet.

It was Julian. "Martine? Sorry to bother you at home."

"It's fine," I said automatically. "Has anything—?"

"No, no," he said quickly. "Nothing's happened, nothing like that. Just wanted to see if you'd like to grab a coffee together."

I glanced into the living room, where Ivan, Lukas, and Claudia were all bent over the game of Trivial Pursuit that I'd just left. "Julian—"

"Hey, I know you're probably busy, but this isn't just a social thing." His voice got lower. "I just wanted to run something by you, outside of—well, you know." He cleared his throat.

I looked back at the group huddled around the board: my family. "It's okay, Julian," I said. "I'll meet you in an hour and a half, does that work?" Compromise: the story of my life.

"Sure," he said, sounding relieved. "I'll be at Café Zanetti. See you then, Martine."

"See you then," I echoed, and hung up the telephone, my eyes on my family in the living room. Someone was going to have to win this game, and quickly.

"Okay, here's the thing," Julian was saying, two hours later. Ivan had left to take the kids to the airport; I was still in my weekend uniform of jeans and a comfortable cotton shirt. Julian had a five o'clock shadow and was wearing a leather jacket. My very own *voyou*. "You know, everyone thinks this is a sex crime. I mean, everything points to that, right? Rape and murder, sex crimes, right?"

"Right," I said cautiously. As if I knew that much about sex crimes. Or any crimes, come to think of it.

Julian leaned forward, his espresso forgotten. If his energy level was anything to go by, he could do with one fewer. "So, here's the thing: what if that's what he wants us to think? You know, the park benches, the way the bodies are displayed on them: Isabelle and Danielle lying down, Annie and Caroline sitting up—something doesn't feel right to me. It's way too in-your-face."

I took a sip of my own cappuccino before answering. "Isn't that what some killers do? Taunt the police?" I thought I'd read that somewhere.

He nodded impatiently. "Yeah, yeah, yeah. I know. That's what the profile says. That's what everybody at SPVM thinks, too. But I'm not so sure." He glanced around, lowered his voice again. "I'm thinking, everyone's out there looking for a sex killer. The whole damned police force. We've got a profiler, we've got a shrink, everyone's going down that path. And what if—just *what if* it isn't? What if the killer wants us to *think* that it's all about sex? What if we're not seeing anything else because we're not looking for anything else?"

"What else could it be?" I countered. "Julian, you said yourself, on Friday, that there isn't much connecting the women who were killed. They all had different professions, and all they had in common was that they were single and female. That's not much of a connection."

"I know, I know." He took another quick sip of coffee, grimaced, and reached for an additional sugar cube. "And some shrinks would argue that that's enough, that men have been doing that kind of thing to women since the beginning of time." He shook his head. "But hear me out, maybe that's exactly it: there's nothing about the way they *look* that connects these women—and all the literature says that a sex killer would want his women to look the same." He stirred the coffee, his movements jerky, then took another quick sip. This time it passed muster. "I think that you and I," Julian said, his head bent low as he gestured between us, "we should try another tack."

"Me?" I exclaimed. "Julian, I'm not an investigator. I'm here strictly in the capacity of nanny, because your boss pisses the hell out of my boss."

"I know." There was a gleam in his eyes. "And I'm supposed to be babysitting the nanny, which is calculated to keep us both out of the way of any serious investigation. So who better to go off on a tangent?"

"You're not getting the point," I said. "I don't do this for a living. I don't even *watch* crime shows on TV, Julian. I don't know what I'm doing here. I wouldn't know where to begin."

"Ah, but that's where you're lucky, because I do. You can be Watson to my Holmes." He glanced at me from under fair eyelashes. "You *do* know about—"

I cut him off. "Yes, thanks very much," I said sarcastically. "Okay, so you want us to go off on our own because you're starting to develop an unpopular theory and for me to keep my mouth shut about what we're doing."

"In a nutshell," he confirmed.

It seemed as good a plan as any.

Ivan, of course, was of a different opinion. "You're doing *what*?"

"Just following up on some ideas," I said soothingly. "Probably nothing, *chéri*. All the people who know about these things think it's a serial sex killer, so chances are good that they're probably right. But it beats me hanging out with the director and making him even more defensive than he is . . ."

He glared at me. "And there's no way you're getting hurt, right? This guy Julian, he knows what he's doing?"

I was in no way confident of that one, but why not? "Of course he does," I said, making my voice sound as reassuring as I could.

"Just be careful, babe," Ivan said finally, pulling me close, tipping my chin up so he could kiss me. And that was all that we said for a very long time.

There were some very scary people in our new home. It wasn't just a different orphanage, as it turned out: it was something they called an asylum, a place where people went if they heard voices that weren't there, or screamed all day at nothing at all, or sat in the corners of rooms, talking to themselves.

What I couldn't figure out was what we were doing there.

We weren't mad. We weren't dangerous. We were just children. But very quickly we began to learn that being a child was no protection.

The inevitable happened—sometime during that first week, I think. Dinner was a particularly noisy time I'd very quickly come to dread, when some inmates threw food on the walls and floors and each other, others howled, clanged the tin plates against each other, danced and sang and screamed. How anyone was expected to eat with that going on was beyond me.

And I said so.

"Enough of your impertinence," snapped the sister to whom I'd voiced my complaint.

"I'm not being impertinent," I said. "I'm just asking if I can eat somewhere else."

"Oh, well, yes, then, you can eat somewhere else," she said, her voice cold. *She grabbed me by my collar and propelled me out of the room, down a staircase, and through a locked door onto a long corridor with doors every few feet. One of these was open. "Emil!" she called, and one of the orderlies appeared, dressed in a dirty white uniform. "Help me here."*

I struggled; of course I struggled. But I wasn't nearly as strong as they were, and even though I bit them and kicked them and screamed at the top of my lungs, they lifted me onto a bed of sorts and strapped me down with metal restraints at my wrists and ankles, and another one across my chest.

"That should hold you for a while," the sister said, scarcely out of breath.

"Let me out!" I screamed. *"You can't put me here, I'm not crazy!"*

"You may not be now," said the orderly, leering at me as he closed the door behind himself, leaving the corollary to his sentence hanging in the air: *yet.*

CHAPTER SIX

Monday morning I was in and out of my department in record time. Chantal waved messages at me; I grabbed them and made the calls that absolutely couldn't be postponed. Then I called Richard into my office.

He was looking haggard. "You're not sleeping," I said as soon as I saw him.

He shrugged. "I'm trying."

"Do you need time off? I should have offered before, I'm sorry."

He leaned forward in his chair, his elbows on his knees. "No. No, I'm all right. *Ne vous inquiétez pas.*" He glanced up and I saw the pain in his eyes. "It's better if I'm working."

I wondered if I should say anything else personal, and didn't know what that should be. "Okay, then, if that's the way it is, I've got a lot of work for you." I handed him the telephone messages from Chantal. "I need you to take over for me for a while."

His eyes widened in panic. "You're not going away?"

"No," I said quickly. "No, nothing like that. I'm just going to be assisting the police in their investigation, and I'll probably be out of the office a lot. You can pull Catherine from public affairs if you need help, I'll authorize it."

Richard was staring at me. "The mayor wants you to be working on it full-time?"

"The mayor wants this man caught. None of us will have anything to do, full-time or not, unless he is. So I'm going to be doing what I can to help."

He nodded. "*Bien, alors.*"

"I'll be checking in with you," I said, standing up, reaching for my jacket and purse. His look of misery was getting to me. "Richard." I paused. "I know I already said this on Friday, but I'm truly so sorry about Danielle."

He nodded again. "*Merci.*" His tone answered my question: clearly no trespassers allowed there, so I didn't trespass. I could feel his sadness following me down the corridor like an unhappy wraith, and breathed the air outside with relief.

It was time to check in with my boss.

His assistant was out of the office, so I tapped on his door and let myself in. I'm more of a get-to-the-point type. "Ah, Madame LeDuc," my boss said, for once not upset with my lack of protocol. "You have something to report already?" He sounded hopeful. Maybe his choice of pencil-pusher had come up aces after all.

There was another man with him in the room, a distinguished-looking gentleman in his mid-sixties dressed in an expensive suit, and—it seemed to me—extremely fit. All right, so I notice. As Ivan says, there's nothing wrong with window-shopping. He stood up politely as I entered, a nicety I appreciated, one that my boss never bothered with. "I don't believe you've met. Madame Martine LeDuc, Monsieur Robert Carrigan."

I offered my hand. "*Monsieur*," I said politely.

His eyes were amused. "Madame LeDuc. I hear such good things about you."

Well, that would be a change, anyway. "I'm honored to hear it," I murmured.

"So difficult, I would think," he said, "being the publicity director for such a large city. I trust that my friend Jean-Luc is giving you as much support as you require?" There was an undertone of amusement in his voice and I found myself warming to him.

"As much as he believes I require," I answered with a smile of my own.

The mayor snorted. "I *am* in the room, you know."

We both ignored him. "You have been friends with the mayor for a long time, *monsieur*?"

He inclined his head, an almost royal gesture; he was very stylish. "We have known each other for some years," he admitted. "I am the lead attorney representing a local pharmaceutical company." A quicksilver smile. "But no need to bore you with the details. And now I should leave you to your work together. There is much to be done to keep Montréal's publicity positive, I am sure."

I wasn't sure what that meant, but I was willing to give him the benefit of the doubt. Anyone who could insult my boss that elegantly was okay in my book.

The mayor clearly wasn't sure how to take that. "We were just finishing up here. We still haven't decided—"

The attorney's eyes were twinkling. "My company is honored

to support the mayor in his political endeavors," he told me by way of explanation.

Ah: I had him now. Attorney and—no doubt—lobbyist. Pharmaceutical companies often have deep pockets, and in my boss's worldview, the deeper the better. "I'm sure that he's grateful," I said. The joys of politics.

"We hope he is," said Robert Carrigan smoothly, and I could swear he winked at me. He turned to the mayor. "I'll leave you, then, Jean-Luc. And don't forget about Friday night. Just a short speech will be fine."

"Of course, of course," my boss said, waving him out of the room. "Madame LeDuc, you have something to report?"

The door closed behind the lobbyist and I turned to face the mayor. "I have been doing liaison work with the SPVM," I said smoothly. "A *détective-lieutenant* named Julian Fletcher." I waited a moment for the name to sink in.

It did. "A police officer?" He sounded shocked. The Westmount Fletchers went in for public service, but at a rather higher level than the Communauté Métropolitaine de Montréal.

"A very competent detective," I corrected him.

"Well," said the mayor, "then he will want this wrapped up quickly." As if just wanting it could make it so.

"Of course he does," I said. "As we all do, *monsieur le maire.*"

"*Alors,*" he said, picking up a random piece of paper and scowling at it, "you should shut the door on your way out."

For once, I was happy to do exactly what my boss wanted.

Julian was in high spirits. "We've all been thinking chronologically," he said over the phone. "Even me. 'Cause the theory, you know, the theory goes that someone like this progresses from one victim to the next, establishes a pattern, does what feels logical to them, sometimes decompensates . . ." His voice trailed off and I could almost feel his shrug. "So everybody looks at the timeline. But what if the timeline is for shit? What if it's not about a pattern?" The questions were clearly rhetorical. "Let's start where he left off. Let's start with Danielle."

"My deputy," I said in a neutral voice, "was dating her."

That was news to Julian. "I haven't seen his statement," he said. "They had people in all weekend, didn't see him there."

"I expect that he'll go in to see them today," I said tiredly. "He has a place he rents in the Laurentians, probably went there over the weekend." Richard, Richard, I thought: why did you run? It didn't look good. It didn't look good at all.

Julian was thinking about this one. "Seriously? I mean, were they serious about each other?"

"I don't know. Probably not, or I would've heard her name. But Richard is a very private person." His office, unlike mine, was not filled with pictures of family, keepsakes, or memories. He had art, good art, original art; that was all.

"Okay. Well, anyway, getting back to what I was saying, we won't walk all over anybody's toes. Let's start at work. Where she worked, I mean. You went to UQAM, didn't you?" It was pretty clear that he hadn't; the Fletchers were Anglophones all the way. Stretching back untold generations. "So, anyway, you know the place. Can you go check out her office?"

Pourquoi pas?

The UQAM library was less than bustling, but all the staff seemed preoccupied and busy. I waited until the worried-looking, middle-aged head of the library had time to deal with me. "We have already been talking with the police," she said cautiously, looking at my card. "Forgive me, *madame*, but what is your interest in this situation?"

"I'm working with the police," I said confidently, trying the expression on for size. "Trying to gather more background information."

She handed me back the card, solemnly. "*Bien*. What can I tell you?"

"Danielle Leroux worked for you here?" I asked. Julian had given me a notebook. I opened it to the first page, virginal, waiting for whatever information might come my way. "Don't trust yourself to remember anything," he'd told me before we disconnected our phone conversation. "Everyone forgets. Write down everything."

Holmes to Watson, over and out.

The head librarian cleared her throat. "Mademoiselle Leroux was our research librarian," she corrected me. "As such, I did not supervise her directly, and our work did not often intersect. But she worked here, yes."

I had no idea what information would be helpful, nor what the police would have already asked her over the weekend. "*Madame*, do you know anything about what she was working on? What kinds of projects?"

She shrugged. "It is not my area, you understand, *madame*. But I can show you her office if you like."

"Very much," I said quickly. "For whom did she do this research? For students? Professors?"

"Yes, for both," she responded, leading me down a corridor

and unlocking a door at the end of it. "*Voilà*. The office of Mademoiselle Leroux." She gestured with a flourish. "I will leave you, *madame*. You can find me if you have any more questions." It is Monday morning, her tone implied, and I have better things to do than talk with the *directrice de publicité*.

I was relieved to be alone. Better to snoop in private when one is unaccustomed to snooping, I thought, moving over to the desk, sitting down automatically behind it. It was a small, narrow office, with a grimy window that overlooked nothing much at all, and the kind of bookcases on the walls that are put up using strips of metal into which one fits the supports for shelves. They were filled with reference books, these shelves, most of them in French, in keeping with UQAM's status as part of Québec's primary French-speaking university system.

I sat behind the desk and tried to imagine Danielle here.

The laughing eyes must have turned serious while she worked, I thought; and there was more than enough work obviously taking place here to keep her feeling the weight of her job responsibilities. Piles of papers, folders, and books were scattered around the surface of the desk. I moved a pile and it slid noisily to the floor; behind it I saw what I hadn't seen in my deputy's office, a small framed picture of Richard and Danielle together, both of them laughing; it seemed to have been taken in the countryside, on a hot brilliant summer day.

That did it. I put my face in my hands and cried.

If Danielle Leroux's office held any secrets when I arrived, it still held them when I left.

I'd dutifully taken notes, of course, copying names scrawled on folders, glancing through the contents. She had been doing historical research lately, it seemed, on behalf of two different professors; one was looking into the fur trade, the other into the history of the province's separatist movement. The latter held my attention for a while; there was enough passion on both sides of the separatist issue to provoke violence; but this was an old argument, one that had taken place long ago over issues that were no longer even contested.

Her computer might have held more, but it was password-protected, and no one appeared to know what that password might be. "If it's a university computer," I asked diffidently, "surely there's some way to override the password?"

Ah, yes, the young student at the front desk agreed. The IT department would be able to, surely. But they would not.

"Excuse me?"

"*Non, non, madame,*" she said. "It is not because of you. They are most difficult to work with, even for the smallest of problems. You would need authority before they would consent to come and do such a thing." She shrugged. "They showed the police the password, they had the authority, I suppose."

"Authority?" But even as I spoke the word, I knew that she was right. My own experience working within the political bureaucracy told me that the university would be no different. Better to find another way in. "Thank you," I said to the student, and left.

"We should try and see what's there before they decide to wipe it," I told Julian, my only bright idea of the morning, when we met for lunch. It was unclear whether or not I'd be able to expense it, I thought ruefully as I ordered my favorite *crêpe aux champignons* at the Breton crêperie on Saint-Denis; but I'd fight that battle when I came to it.

Julian had spent the morning with Danielle's landlady, who didn't actually live in the same building as the apartments she rented, but had a small place near Chinatown. Communication had been difficult. "She's ninety if she's a day, and hard of hearing," he pronounced, "so it would have been difficult even if she *did* want to speak English, which she made clear that she did not. Seemed disappointed that I knew how to speak French. Thought she could one-up me."

I could just imagine his accent. "I could talk to her, if you'd like," I offered.

"No problem. We got along well once we started talking about Danielle. Danielle was the nicest tenant you could ever hope for, and why she wasn't married was a mystery, pretty as she was and smart, too," he said, and I could hear the woman's voice coming through in his. "Never forgot her landlady's birthday, if you can believe it, and never any complaints in the building about loud music at night, not like some she could mention."

"So Danielle was a saint," I said, watching the server approach with our *crêpes*. I waited until she had set them down and we'd thanked her. "Who kills a saint?"

"One of those motorcycle maniacs, you want the landlady's opinion," said Julian, forking ham and béchamel sauce into his mouth. "She's not that far off, though, honestly. I think some of my colleagues have been looking hard at the Angels." He shook his head. "But they look hard at the Angels for everything, and they're usually right."

"And the motorcycle gang has a new affinity for middle-aged

women?" I asked, thinking of Annie Desmarchais. As far as I'd been able to see, the women on the backs of the cycles were barely of legal age.

"Well, that's where we're ahead of them, anyway," said Julian. "Hey, you think UQAM is going to wipe her laptop?" he asked suddenly. I hadn't thought he'd been listening before.

"Eventually," I said, sipping cider and thinking about it. "Just like how eventually they'll hire someone and clear out all her stuff. Your people didn't seem to want anything from there; they left her apartment pretty fast. And no one seems to think she's anything other than a statistic. What? Why are you looking at me like that?"

"I'm still stuck on *your people*."

"You know. Your people. The police," I said, gesturing vaguely. "SPVM. Anyway. Does she have family? I mean, someone who's taking care of her effects?"

He pulled his own small notebook from his pocket and flipped back through the pages. "Parents deceased," he read. "There's a brother up in Québec City, came down to identify her, probably still around somewhere."

"He might know the password."

Julian looked at me sharply. "Where are you going with this? You know the police already looked at it."

"What did they find?"

He grimaced. "Nothing. Nothing anyone said was connected to her death, though we may be looking for different things. Why, what do you think is there?"

I shrugged and finished chewing before I answered. "Who knows, Julian, but if you're right and this isn't about sex, then it has to be something more dangerous, more cerebral. And most people keep their cerebral stuff on their computers these days. And no one found a computer in Danielle's apartment, did they? There's just the office one?" I considered. "I mean, okay, at the very least it will give us more information about *her*. I mean, if you wanted to find out about me, that's where you'd look. I have online calendaring, my address book, my personal finances, reports, employee evaluations, e-mail . . . it's all there." I frowned. "Did they find her address book, or her daily planner anywhere? I didn't see any in the office."

He didn't have to consult his notes this time. "*Nada*. So she's probably like you, keeps everything on the computer."

I nodded, thinking of the messy desk, the papers everywhere. "We both use Macs," I said slowly. "We probably have a lot of the same software for keeping track of life, for managing everyday stuff. There might be something there your colleagues didn't see, or think was important."

"Did you try any passwords?"

I shrugged again. "Her name, her street name, that was all. I didn't know her birth date, but honestly, it could be anything. Her mother's maiden name, a nickname, even something completely random. University accounts have really hard-to-guess passwords, and they get changed all the time, so who knows?" Ivan did that, generated a new password every week. But then again, Ivan worked with people whose minds were pretty good at trying to outsmart stuff like that. It was less likely that Danielle would have felt a need to be that safety-conscious. "Listen, I'll write something official for the dean, see if that gives us entrée with the university IT guys. They can probably override her password in two seconds flat, maybe even over the net-work."

He was frustrated. "That'll take time. We need to move on this, because the other computers were wiped. Maybe even re-motely. Let me get it done through the department. Maybe a phone call will be enough." He grinned, suddenly and vividly. "I'm close with one of our IT people. Maybe she can do it, or talk to her counterpart at UQAM. Get us access."

"She?" I smiled back at him.

"Yeah," he said. "*Definitely* a she. You about ready to go?"

I finished my cider. "Where to now? What's the plan?"

He signaled for the bill. "You want to take turns paying? I'll take this one."

"Fine." I nodded. "What's the plan?"

He counted out money. "I'll call Monique and see if I can get the computer stuff started. If you're right, then that's critical." He smiled at the waitress and she giggled. I mean, really, *giggled*. He had the strangest effect on young women.

Julian stood up. "Then we'll go see Danielle's place together. I want you along, you might see something I haven't. And then we'll see about talking to *frère* Jacques."

"That's not really his name?"

"Cross my heart," Julian said cheerfully, and held the door for me. "*Après toi.*"

We were able to do both errands at once, as it turned out, because Jacques Leroux was sitting in his sister's apartment when we arrived. Just sitting. Not reading, not watching televi-sion, not looking through her possessions. Just sitting.

Julian presented his credentials and glossed over mine, then took another look at the man sitting dejectedly in the tapestry chair by the window and turned to me. "Madame LeDuc . . . ?"

Obviously dealing with the grieving was to be my role in this partnership. I said, as gently as I could, "Monsieur Leroux, please accept our condolences. Losing your sister in such a way is beyond terrible."

He looked at me as though seeing me for the first time, a big, burly man, without the laughter that sparkled around his sister's face, even in her pictures. "Yes?"

I sat down hesitantly on the edge of the sofa nearest him and said, as gently as I could, "Though it is no doubt painful for you, *monsieur*, it would help us if you could answer some questions."

"They've already been," he said heavily. "The police." He looked around as though expecting to see more of them. "They just left. An hour ago, perhaps. They have asked me many questions." My, this was fun, following Julian's colleagues around and pestering people in pain for a second time.

"*Je sais, monsieur*," I said. I know. "But just a few more questions . . ."

He made a gesture of resignation. "Ask, then, *madame*."

I opened my notebook. "Were you and your sister close, *monsieur*?"

He shook his head; I had already sensed what the answer would be. In a room filled with books, art, and photographs, this man was simply sitting. They had had, I thought, little in common. "We would see each other for holidays," he said heavily. "She came to Québec for Christmas and New Year's, stayed with us a few days. She sent us cards—for birthdays: that of my wife and my sons as well as my own." That was what Julian had said: she remembered birthdays, Danielle—her landlady's as well as those of her family. The more I knew about her, the more I realized that she was someone I would have liked.

Jacques Leroux was still talking, and I reminded myself to take notes. "Danielle went to university," he said. "I never was interested. I do construction. I like working outdoors." He looked around him again, as though startled anew to be finding himself in this room. "I've sent for my wife," he said helplessly. "She'll know what to do with—all this."

Julian cleared his throat. "When was the last time you heard from Danielle?" I was right: his accent when he spoke French was atrocious.

Jacques seemed not to mind, though I wondered if Julian was having trouble following him. Even for me, the upriver accent was thick and difficult to understand. "It was in the summer," he said. "In July. She called on the telephone," and then, as though such an extraordinary occurrence rated an explanation, he added, "it was my son Luc's birthday. She always called to speak to the children."

Too long ago to be useful, I thought. "*Monsieur*, did you know of your sister's life? Anyone who might have wished her harm?"

He shook his head mutely, then raised his eyes to mine. "Who would?" he asked. "Everyone liked Danielle. Even when we were children, everyone liked her."

"Did she tell you if she was—seeing someone? Something romantic?" I hated myself for asking it.

He nodded slowly. "Back in the spring, yes, there was a letter. She was happy, I think, about him. But she did not say a name."

Julian looked at me sharply; he had probably sensed my sigh

of relief. All I needed was to hear that she and Richard had been fighting, or something of the sort. I wondered fleetingly if he was being questioned at that very moment. "*Monsieur*, if it is not too painful for you, it would be helpful if my colleague and I could look around here. We won't disturb anything."

He nodded again. "Stay if you want, I'll go for a drink," and he rose slowly from the fragile chair.

He looked as though he needed one. We waited until the door closed behind him, then switched back to English. "So?" Julian asked.

"So what? He hasn't got a clue," I said impatiently. "See if you can find any files somewhere around, Julian "

"You're obsessed," he grumbled, but he started looking all the same. I wasn't really sure why: the place was sealed; his colleagues had already been over it and found it so uninteresting that they'd allowed the brother to stay.

Danielle Leroux's apartment was only slightly more orderly than her office, but it, too, practically embraced her personality. Hand-woven fabrics were everywhere: in the wall hanging in her bedroom, in the shawl tossed casually across a chair, in the bright textures of the rugs scattered over polished hardwood floors. Colors were vibrant, from the original oils and acrylics on the walls to the books, hardcover and paperback alike, which filled the bookcases to bursting and spilled out onto chairs, tables, and the counters in the kitchen. She read in both French and English, I noted, and at one time had apparently tried to teach herself Russian; I'd have to remember to tell Ivan about that. There were hand-cast pottery mugs in the kitchen, a used and not yet washed wineglass in the sink, an espresso machine next to a canister of coffee. In the refrigerator, cheese and lettuce and some convenience items; not much there.

She kept a tarot deck in her bedside table along with a couple of novels and a vibrator, which made me smile. Her clothes were more muted than her apartment; like most Montréalers, black was Danielle's main motif, though she also apparently liked blues and greens in their darker varieties. Like me, she preferred flat shoes.

There was absolutely nothing that we saw that gave any indication of why she had been killed.

There was something distasteful about the whole enterprise: like being a voyeur in someone else's life, pawing through dirty clothes and scummed-over glasses. I wondered what people would think of my home, my kitchen, my bed, if they were to go through it as I was doing now. Like undressing an already denuded corpse, finding out what's under the skin as well as under the clothing. It gave me chills.

Julian, happily unaware of my dark thoughts, at length snapped off his gloves. "No secrets," he pronounced. "No laptop, either, so we need to crack the code at school."

I looked around me, feeling suddenly desolate at the apartment's emptiness. Bereft of the young woman who would never open that door again. "Julian," I said quietly.

"Yeah?"

"Let's get him," I said.

That first time, I was in restraints for three days.

Three long days and three longer nights, and if I'd found the howls of the dormitory occupants disturbing, it was nothing to what I was hearing now. These weren't the screams of people haunted by ghostly apparitions; this was pain. I was tied down: I couldn't even cover my ears, shut it out, pretend that it wasn't happening.

I'll never speak out again, I promised myself; if they'll only let me out of here, I'll do whatever they want. Anything. Anything to make this stop.

They gave me water to drink from a long straw and once a day the restraints were loosened enough for me to sit up and eat a slice of bread. That was all. Other than that, I lay there, my muscles cramping, the restraints cutting my wrists and ankles, staring at the ceiling. Twice a day I was brought a bedpan. That was all.

I had nothing to do but think, and hear, and smell, and feel. They were cold and hard, the restraints, and there were no blankets at night. I couldn't stop shivering, even though it was springtime, even though the air should have been warm.

There were people coming and going all the time, and gradually I stopped knowing when it was daytime and when it was night. The clatter of chains, the murmur of voices, doors slamming, children—you couldn't not know that these were children—wailing.

What I heard when I was there—it was the worst. I wanted to pretend that the voices I was listening to weren't human, because I didn't want to believe that a human could make a sound like that.

The metal had rubbed my wrists raw. The orderlies returned me to one of the dayrooms, where I recognized the sister in charge, and she looked at my wrists right away and sent me off with a younger nun to have them cleaned and bandaged. "Sister's always angry they don't take better care," the young one said.

"That's kind of her," I said, my voice tentative, because I didn't yet know what got you in trouble in this place.

"It's not," the young sister said. "Sometimes they get infected, and then the patient can't work, and Sister Véronique hates that."

I looked at her face, hearing the matter-of-fact tone in her voice, trying to stifle my astonishment that someone so young, with hands so gentle, could see nothing wrong with what she'd just said. But there was nothing to be read there, and I went back to the dayroom, tired and aching and feeling despair as I had never felt before.

They put me to work soon after that, and I didn't have time, not really, to contemplate life at the Cité de Saint-Jean-de-Dieu.

If I had, I'd probably have killed myself.

It seemed that the more we protested that we didn't belong in the asylum, the more we were tied up and isolated. Until we learned to stop protesting.

It was easy to feel alone, the only sane person in the midst of so much insanity, so much cruelty. I tried to make friends with the other children, because it was the only connection I had to a world where people weren't tied down, where people weren't made to make the terrible noises I'd heard when I was on the punishment ward.

Those of us who had come from the orphanage naturally gravitated together whenever we could. It was so overwhelmingly big, the Cité de Saint-Jean-de-Dieu, easy to get lost, easy to feel lost. There were other children there, too, from other orphanages—I was surprised to learn that others existed—and then, of course, the masses of people who really did belong in the asylum. Probably hundreds of us in all.

So I looked for familiar faces, and just seeing them, sometimes, felt like a lifeline. Not just a lifeline back to the orphanage, but in some twisted way they connected me to my mother, to my memories of my mother. And now the worst had happened. I had left the only point of connection I had with her. She knew where the orphanage was.

What if she came looking for me, and I wasn't there?

I tried to put it out of my mind as I adjusted to my new life. The work at the asylum was, at first, a lot like the work at the orphanage. Here too was a whole farm, cows and sheep, pigs and chickens, and all of them needing to be serviced in some way or another. I know all of this rather more intimately than I would have liked, because when I was first released from restraints I was placed on farm detail. They did that, I discovered, to all the potential troublemakers. You couldn't get in too much trouble if you were exhausted all the time.

It never mattered how little sleep one had gotten: if one worked the farm detail, one was pulled from bed at four o'clock in the morning, before even the sisters were up for the day, when it seemed that the world itself was asleep . . .

Except, of course, for a barnful of cows, all wanting to be milked at the same time, loud and demanding. Then the straw was to be changed, the chicken feed put out, the eggs gathered in, the pigs fed . . . my days felt as though they should be half finished by the time we trooped in for breakfast.

To tell the truth, I treasured my time with the animals, my mornings and evenings spent tending to their basic needs. The soft breath of the sheep on my hands, the pigs' delighted grunts when you massaged their backs and shoulders, the cows' gentle *eyes. They were kinder and more communicative than the people at the asylum, and I missed them when I was working the fields.*

There were men out on the farm, too, and some of the girls and boys sent there were scared of the men. One of them grabbed me once, but let me go with a laugh. "I'll wait till you're hatched," he said, and I didn't understand, but I ran away.

I quickly found places to hide, and on my third day I came across the graveyard, rows of stones with sisters' names on them. None of the farmworkers ever went there, so I felt safe, even when I was sitting among the dead. I wasn't afraid of ghosts: ghosts couldn't hurt me any more than the living already had. And after that, when I needed to get away, when I needed a moment of peace, I hid among the graves and memorized the names of nuns long dead.

There were always new ones there, too, but they never got stones. I never really thought about why.

And so the first spring moved into the first summer, and by the time the air turned crisp and the wind whirled yellow and crimson leaves around us, I had learned. I had learned to stand up for myself, to snatch back food that was stolen from me, to find a blanket and defend my possession of it. Most especially, though, I had learned to never, ever talk back to the sisters or staff.

I had learned the only lesson that mattered: I had learned how to survive.

CHAPTER SEVEN

Isabelle Hubert, high-end call girl, had no relatives that the police had been able to locate. She had paid her rent through the end of the year, however, so her apartment had been left as it was when the crime scene people had finished, two months ago.

Two months of no one living there, of dust settling, of ghosts sighing. Two months of emptiness, of silence. The floors creaked under our feet. It felt like at any moment we might hear a voice, catch a whiff of perfume, know that someone had been there . . . once.

Julian loosened the shutters, and the afternoon light streamed in. Isabelle, like Danielle, had favored bright colors and an eclectic decorating scheme. In the bathroom was a litter box. "Julian!" I called, thus reminded. "What happened to her cat?"

"I already told you, I don't know," he said, his voice muffled. He was looking under her bed.

In an alcove off the living room was a desk and on it, a laptop.

Since this appeared to be my area of expertise, I booted it. "No password required," I said happily, and waited to see what Isabelle Hubert had committed to her hard drive.

Julian came to stand behind me. "Any luck?"

"Not yet," I said distractedly. "She has a big Mormon genealogy program."

"Mormons? Why? Was she one?"

I shrugged and continued to look through files while I talked. "No, of course not. You don't have to be Mormon to *use* the program, they just make the best ones. It's part of their religion. They believe that you have to convert all your ancestors. You know, sort of retroactively make them Mormons, too. But to convert them, you have to find them. Every member of the church does genealogy, it's required. Go back generations—you're admired if you can go back farther than anyone else." I'd once dated a Mormon.

For about five minutes.

Julian whistled. "Convert your ancestors? What's that about?"

I wasn't in the mood for a theological discussion. "Some other time, when you get me drunk enough, I'll tell you all about it. The point is, they create really great detailed genealogy programs, and Isabelle clearly knew it. Look. She was writing, too. A couple of short stories here . . . Wait, Julian, wasn't someone else writing?"

He checked his notebook. "Annie Desmarchais. She was working on a novel."

"Maybe that's a connection." I kept looking. "Finances. Good God, she was making *serious* money!"

"The expensive ones do," Julian said dryly.

I swiveled around to scowl at him. "The expensive *whats*?"

He had the grace to look uncomfortable. "Um—you know. Hookers."

I looked back at the screen. "Hookers don't make a thousand dollars an hour," I said. "There has to be another name for the profession when that kind of cash is involved. Hey, who *was* that client on the Plateau, the one she saw the night she got killed? You said he was a regular, right? He saw her once a week? How do people *afford* this kind of thing?"

"A matter of priorities, no doubt," said Julian, who probably had never had to budget anything in his life.

"Thanks," I said sourly. "That really does help put things in perspective."

"We aim to please. What else—"

A thought had struck me. "*Merde*, Julian, what time is it? I'm late. I've got to go let your boss tell me how fantastic he is and how close he is to catching the guy. *Merde, alors.*"

"I love a woman who knows how to swear," he said comfortably. "Don't worry, Martine, I'll get you there on time."

I'd been afraid of that. "Alive, too?" I asked as we locked Isabelle's door.

"You want everything, don't you?"

"The profiler," said François Desrocher, a hint of annoyance in his voice, "tells us that these crimes were committed by the same individual."

I waited, but he didn't continue, so I prompted him. "And . . . ?"

"And what, *madame*? We have made some progress."

I sighed. "*Monsieur le directeur*, forgive me, but hadn't that already been concluded? Perhaps it comes as no surprise that this one, too, was killed by the same individual as the others."

He frowned. He was not happy. He rustled some papers and sighed. Finally he decided to surrender something further. "The profiler says that he is white, between thirty and sixty, and probably educated."

He'd just defined about a third of the inhabitants of Montréal. It was time to up the ante, or I was going to be here all night. "*Monsieur le maire* is anxious to find out if you are closer to identifying this individual," I said, trying to sound threatening. "He says that time is running out; there may be another victim before you have made an arrest."

He blew out his breath in exasperation. "These things take time, *madame.*"

"Perhaps this is time that another woman in Montréal does not have," I said sweetly.

He looked as if he were hoping that woman would be me. "All the relatives have been looked at. All the friends. All the coworkers. We are forced to conclude that this individual did not know any of his victims personally." He glowered at me. "What the mayor might not understand is that this is the most difficult killer of all, for the police. He is choosing women randomly to rape and kill. We have no descriptions of him. We have no evidence that he has left behind. All we have is his signature, that is what it is called: that he leaves his victims posed carefully on public benches. This is strange, yes. This is unique. We are working with what we have."

"Well," I said, capping my pen and standing up, "that was all I needed to know. I will tell this to the mayor, *monsieur.* And I look forward to speaking with you again tomorrow."

His glance assured me that he was looking forward to seeing me roast in hell. I smiled and escaped while I still could.

They all wrote, I thought as I drove over to City Hall. Novels, short stories, poetry. Reports on research. Foundation grants. Somehow, they were tied together through paperwork.

"Everyone writes something," Ivan said that night when I shared my hypothesis with him. "There's paperwork involved in every job nowadays."

"Not every job," I said, thinking of Jacques Leroux. "But I concede your point."

He went into the bathroom, started brushing his teeth, came out again and tried to talk around the toothbrush. "But that's the only connection you've found?"

I sighed, slipping under the duvet, considering adding a comforter: nights were already feeling chilly. "Three were Francophones; one wasn't. They were all employed, but at incredibly different jobs and in different parts of the city. Three lived alone; one didn't. Maybe my lord Desrocher is right, maybe it's just completely random. Maybe I'm wasting my time."

Ivan had retreated back into the bathroom and I could hear him rinsing. He turned off the light and joined me in bed. "No," said my husband softly. "You're honoring their lives by trying to find the person who killed them. Not exactly a waste of time."

Ivan always knows the right thing to say.

Mrs. Violette Sobel answered the door on the second ring. "Ah, you will be Madame LeDuc," she said graciously, as if I had been invited to tea. "Please come in."

Julian was right: here was a woman who was managing to

hold her age at bay big-time. Her hair was white, perfectly coiffed; and what one noticed first about her face was its liveliness, not its wrinkles. She was wearing a slim skirt, a soft cashmere sweater, and pearls. I felt as if I ought to check under my fingernails for dirt.

The Desmarchais/Sobel residence was a world away from the other two apartments I had visited the day before. Large rooms with crown molding and high ceilings, ornate mirrors over painted fireplaces, and every room filled with antiques, Oriental rugs, *objets d'art*. Here, too, were original oils; but I was pretty sure that in this case the artists would be recognizable.

Too bad robbery hadn't been the motive.

A Georgian silver coffee service awaited us in the front room, where dour people stared out of dark paintings and a small, incredibly ugly Pekinese immediately launched itself into my lap. *"Voyons!"* Mrs. Sobel remonstrated with it. "Let Madame LeDuc be!"

I was all for that, too. I've never been what one might call a dog person, and the Peke had bad breath. "Just ignore him," she said to me, comfortingly if improbably, and proceeded to pour coffee. "Sugar?"

"Thank you, *madame*," I said as I tried shooing away the beast. It yipped excitedly and attempted to lick my face.

"Well," she said, having handed me my coffee and settled back—as comfortably as one can on a Louis Quinze chair— with her own. "You wish to know about my sister."

I set down my cup so that I could pull my notebook out of my bag, dumping the dog in the process. "Sorry, I need my lap,"

I said to its owner, who looked appalled. "He's very friendly," I offered, trying to make amends. The horrible little thing hid behind its owner's legs. Serves you right, I thought.

I cleared my throat. "What can you tell me, *madame*?"

She lifted the creature into her own lap and stroked it as she talked. "Annie was a warm person, a generous person," she said. "That is my fear, you see; that she was approached by someone needing help, and thus was lured to her death. She could not pass street people without giving them something, some loose change, a dollar or two."

Great, I thought, writing it down. So far, our guy had picked on nobody but saints. People who gave money to panhandlers. People who remembered their landladies' birthdays.

Violette was still stroking the dog. "She was very intelligent, very cultured. More so than I, who came from a better background. I always admired that about her."

I looked up from my notes. "Excuse me? I'm not understanding. How did your background differ from hers?"

"Ah, of course. I always forget to say." She reached around the dog and sipped her coffee. I had already come to the conclusion that it was very possibly the best coffee I had ever tasted. "Annie was adopted, you see. When she was quite old—well, as such things go. She was . . . I think that she was ten at the time. I'd had another sister, a younger one, who contracted tuberculosis and died, may God rest her soul. I think that in some ways my parents were attempting to replace dear Yvonne when they adopted Annie."

I didn't write anything down. I said, "Please tell me how this came about." It could be nothing, I told myself, but it was a piece of information that the police didn't have . . . Somehow, I was starting to see myself in competition with them.

She fluttered a hand. "I really do not know all the details. From the start, from the first day she arrived, Annie was considered part of the family. We were discouraged from speaking of a past that did not include her." She paused, thinking, sorting through old memories, I thought, much as one might do with faded photographs. "It was in the 1960s, and our family was inordinately wealthy, *madame*. Well, as you can see . . ." Her hand fluttered again, encompassing the mansion and its contents as proof. "But we were taught that one must share what one has. We always gave to the Church and had quite a fine relationship with the cardinal, God rest his soul. So when Yvonne died, we turned to the Church. We had an emptiness in our home; but in return, we could give a home to one of God's children who had nothing."

"I see." What I didn't see was how this might relate to why said orphan was murdered fifty-odd years later. "And Annie?"

"Why, she fit in right away, *madame*. She was hungry for knowledge, as I said. Read everything and anything. My father made sure that we both went to university, though I believe Annie got more out of it than I did." There was a slight pause and then she cleared her throat, "I had already met Monsieur Sobel, please understand, and it was—agreed—that we would be married once I graduated. Perhaps I did not pay as much attention to my studies as I might have done." She smiled, a distant smile filled with fondness. She had liked her Monsieur Sobel, I thought.

She caught me watching her, and misread my thoughts. "He was Jewish, my husband; but my father was most farsighted, most broad-minded. It was never a problem."

A guy who in the 1960s sent his daughters to college and encouraged one of them to marry outside his faith. I was beginning to like him quite a lot. "And Annie?" I asked. "Whom did she marry?"

"Ah, we thought for such a long time that she would not!" exclaimed her sister. "After school she traveled, she went abroad. To Paris, to London. She studied there. My father allowed it. He always had a twinkle when it came to Annie." She paused, pondering. "She must have been thirty-two or so when she married. Back then, she was considered to be a bit of an old maid."

Times have changed for the better, I thought. "And her husband?"

"Ah, well, there, perhaps, things didn't work out quite so well," said Violette, with a touch of frost in her voice. "He seemed so suitable, but . . . there was unhappiness. Unlike me, my sister wished to have children. But it seemed impossible. Three, four times she became pregnant, and lost the child each time. Her husband blamed her. He knew she had been adopted, of course, and he went on and on about inferior genes. It was really quite disgraceful."

The Pekinese had abandoned his mistress and was attempting to mate with my leg. I asked for more coffee and while she was refilling my cup, I shook him off and shooed him away yet again. He hid behind her and they both looked at me reproachfully.

"Her husband died, *madame*?" I asked, accepting the coffee

and trying not to be too greedy about drinking it. It really was better than anything I'd ever tasted.

"Yes, he died," she said. "In some ways, his death was a blessing. By then Annie had returned here—to our own home. Our mother had already passed on, and Annie was able to care for our father. There was no thought of divorce, of course; that was not done. But they lived apart for some time before we heard that Louis had died. By then Annie was already using our own family name again, rather than his. She did not go to his funeral."

An interesting story, I thought, but not particularly helpful. "What was your sister's work, *madame*?"

"Ah, Annie's work. It gave her such pleasure. When our father passed on, his money came to us both equally, you see. But my own dear husband had left me rather a lot, as well; so Annie and I established the Providence Foundation. We named it— well, she named it, really—for the order of nuns at the hospital where our father had worked, where she had lived. The Sisters of Providence. Annie was very eager to help those less fortunate than we were, you see. I was never very good at that sort of thing, and I had other interests; but Annie was very involved. She did research to find possible recipients of the foundation's grants."

"She decided who got the money?" *There* was a motive, I thought.

"Oh, my dear, no," Violette laughed. "There is a board to take care of that sort of thing. A process to go through. No, Annie just wanted to find people who needed help." She looked past me, out the window, but I had the impression that she wasn't seeing anything at all. "She loved to help people," Violette said, a catch in her voice.

I stood up. "I've taken enough of your time, *madame*," I said. Useless to ask if Annie Desmarchais had had any enemies. Useless to ask if anyone hated her enough to rape her, stab her, and leave her mutilated body sitting upright on a public bench. Useless to try and figure out any rhyme or reason to what was happening.

The Pekinese was glaring at me through the window as I walked away.

I spent my first two years at the Cité de Saint-Jean-de-Dieu working the farm. I grew taller in those years, and stronger; my skin turned dark in the sun, and there were calluses on my hands where there had once been blisters.

I was tougher in other ways, too.

Alain, one of the boys, had it in for me from the beginning. I was caught off guard once: he waited until I came around a corner and hit me, hard, with a piece of wood he'd gotten from God only knew where, right across my chest.

I fell, struggling to breathe, as he laughed at me. I didn't even think about what I was doing. I saw red and pulled him down by the ankles. I was stronger than most of the boys, because of the farm. I had him against the floor, my forearm across his throat, pressing hard, watching his eyes bulging out. "Leave me alone!"

Alain turned red. I pushed harder against his neck. "Say you'll leave me alone!"

He nodded and spluttered something, and I let him go. He scrambled away to a safe distance.

"You cannot tell anyone that a girl did this to you," I said, seething, and Alain nodded. He already knew that. It would have been the end of him to have the others know.

Only Bobby, the boy who read the Cité de Saint-Jean-de-Dieu sign on that first morning, the one from the same orphanage as me, was a puzzle to me. Sometimes I caught him looking at me with an expression that I couldn't decipher. Something dark, something at odds with the camaraderie that we should have shared. Once he gave me some cake he'd stolen from the kitchens. "We need to stick together," he told me.

"Do you remember it? The orphanage?" I asked him. I was still looking for some touchstone to my past.

He shook his head. "Better to think of the future than the past, you know."

I was cramming the cake into my mouth, fearful of getting caught. "Enough to stay out of trouble," I mumbled.

"Stay out of trouble?" Bobby asked, and laughed. "You just watch me. I'll have 'em all eating out of my hand one of these days, just like you're eating that cake. You wait and see."

I was shocked. "You can't, Bobby. They'll do bad things to us."

"Bad things?" He laughed, but it didn't sound humorous. "You don't even know the beginning of the bad things, Gabrielle."

"What are you talking about?"

He glanced around, a little furtively. "You just got to learn how to make them need you," he said.

I was staring at him. "What do you know?"

"*The doctors, Gabrielle. It's all about the doctors.*"

Perhaps every asylum had them. There was, after all, some pretense at least of caring for the insane. But we seemed to have any number of doctors, all men—of course—all wearing the same white coats that flapped around them like a long cape as they walked.

It might have been comical, if they weren't so dangerous.

How did I know about the danger, at first? Was it intuition? A rumor that I caught in passing without understanding its specifics? Thinking, later, about what Bobby had said, and the cruel smile that curved around his mouth when he said it? I can't really say: all I know is that I feared the doctors even more than the sisters.

Later, of course, I understood perfectly well why.

I only met them in passing; I knew without being told that getting too close to any of them would spell disaster. They didn't even all speak French; English, it seemed, was their preferred language, and I didn't understand any of that, so they were easy to ignore.

But once in a while I glimpsed something there, maybe a trick of the light, but a face would suddenly show compassion, or interest, or kindness, and I realized that under it all these doctors were human. Which, of course, left me with even more questions. If they were human, how could the rumors about them be true?

None of them spent much time anywhere but in the medical rooms on the ground floor and in the basement. When we were ill, we were taken downstairs to see them—but not all that frequently, because it was clear that whatever illness we had was interrupting whatever work they had to do, and no one wanted to go, no matter how sick they felt. Being sick, even horribly sick, was preferable to going downstairs.

It was a long time before I learned what it was they were doing down there. And when I did, I wished I had never known.

CHAPTER EIGHT

By the time I got back to my office, I'd reached the conclusion that Julian had disappeared. For someone who was supposed to be watching the watcher, he was doing a particularly bad job. I left messages on his voice mail both at his desk and on his mobile phone, then thought about the fact that I was apparently on my own.

Fine. I might as well close the circle and find out about Caroline Richards.

I called out to Chantal that I'd be gone for a while. With any luck, I could get out of the building before my boss decided he needed to see me: this case was starting to get serious press, and I didn't want to have to update him on every tiny detail until I had something to report that might actually *change* that press coverage, none of which was currently particularly friendly to the mayor or the city. And for which, *naturellement*, I would be blamed.

I ran into four different people with pressing questions for me on my way out, and dealt with them as quickly as I could. I was turning away when I walked right into someone entering the hall and my purse went flying. Opening en route, of course. "Oh, *pardon*—"

"Madame LeDuc." The voice was amused. "Allow me to help you." He bent down to pick up the sheaf of papers and I recognized the pharmaceutical lawyer I'd met at the police station. "*Merci, monsieur.*"

He straightened up and gave them to me. "*Voilà*. And how are you, *madame*?"

"*Bien, bien, merci.*" I couldn't resist. "And yourself? Making yourself busy working for the mayor?"

He didn't mind the sarcasm. "Ah, yes, as is standard fare in the business of politics. And you? I trust that you are making progress?"

"Making progress, *monsieur*?" I was trying to stuff things back into my purse.

"In making sure that the current crimes do not affect the positive public relations of the city," he said smoothly. "The mayor is anxious that this not hurt his chances of reelection."

Of course he was. And any lobbyist worth his salt wanted him to stay in office, too. My boss, friend to Big Pharma. I paused and met the amused—and, damn it, still attractive—eyes. "Always, *monsieur*."

"Then I will leave you to it." I felt his gaze following me all the way out of City Hall.

The Montréal office of the newspaper was happy to cooperate, the general editor, Francis Russell, assured me. "Such a loss," he proclaimed, making a wide gesture that included the newsroom, the city, perhaps even the world.

"What kind of reporting did Caroline Richards do?" I asked. The name was familiar, but the byline was not; I rarely read English-language newspapers. Ivan or Chantal usually told me anything I needed to know, and I read the *Gazette*—in French— religiously.

Russell was signaling to someone out of my line of sight. "Caroline? Oh, you know, she had a number of interests."

That sounded a little too vague. "What stories has she covered this year?" I tried again.

A harried-looking young man in horn-rimmed glasses appeared in response to the editor's hand signals. "There you are, Mark," Russell said comfortably. "This is Mrs. LeDuc, Mark, from the mayor's office. She needs to see Caroline Richards's archives."

Mark ducked his head, turned, and disappeared, a little *à la* White Rabbit. "Mark will see that you get them," Francis assured me. "In the meantime, you can sit at Caroline's desk while you wait."

"Her position hasn't been filled?" I was surprised. It was a major newspaper, and Caroline had been dead for almost three months.

Francis ushered me ahead of him and pointed to an empty desk, a computer monitor forlornly off to the side. "Oh, her position was filled," he said. "But no one has wanted to—um—"

"Sit where a dead woman sat?" I supplied, amused. Superstition, it seemed, was alive and well in Montréal.

"I'll leave you to it," said Francis without answering my question, and then he was gone.

The room was immense and incredibly loud. Voices talking on telephones, in person, computer keys clacking—I couldn't imagine what it must have sounded like in the old days, when typewriters were used. It was bad enough now. No one was paying any attention to me, so I eased open the top drawer of Caroline's desk. Just to see.

It was a mess: paper clips, staples, pencils, random keys, all the minutiae of paperwork were strewn in the front part of the drawer. In the back, paper, all of it, to my disappointment, blank. I closed the drawer and eased open the next one down.

"Mrs. LeDuc?" Startled, I closed the drawer guiltily as young Mark appeared by the desk. "I have printouts here from the last month that Ms. Richards was with us," he said, as if she had quit or gone on vacation somewhere. A permanent vacation. "But it'll be a lot easier for you to go back further if you use the computer."

I was all for that. "That would be great," I said.

"Excuse me." He reached down below the desk and booted the machine that was neatly out of sight. "I'll get you onto the network; you'll need a password," he explained as we waited for the computer to check itself and make sure everything was in place. I always compared computers starting up to baseball players, touching everything they owned before heading up to bat.

Having decided that it was ready to roll, the computer asked what we wanted of it. Mark mumbled an excuse again and leaned in front of me to access the keyboard, and then I was on the newspaper intranet and Mark was scrolling through lists.

"Here it is," he said. "It's all arranged chronologically, but you can go by subject line, too. Everything Caroline ever wrote."

"Thank you," I said; then, as he seemed about to depart, "Did you know her, Mark?"

To my astonishment, he blushed. "Aye," he managed to say, betraying his own origins as being somewhere in the Maritimes. "Aye, I knew her. She was wonderful." And then he did the White Rabbit thing again. I stood up so I could see over the cubicle, but he had disappeared into the warren. I sighed and applied myself to the computer.

Caroline Richards may well have been wonderful, but it became clear almost at once that not everybody could have shared that sentiment. She did investigative reporting, uncovering things that people did not want uncovered, asking the questions that no one wanted to answer. Of my boss, I noted with wry amusement, on more than one occasion. Odd that her path and mine had never crossed; I made a mental note to ask Richard about her. He did most of the direct work with the press; had he known Caroline?

In the months leading up to her murder, Caroline had reported on financial wrongdoing in the meatpacking industry. She had covered the trial of a reputed mobster and had found that the crown prosecutor wasn't asking the right questions because his wife had not so mysteriously disappeared on the eve of the trial. Caroline had raised so much public outcry when the body of a prostitute was discovered and no one was able to identify the woman that the government relented and offered a free DNA database to sex workers so that if they were killed, they would at least be identified. She did a follow-up on a story that she had originally reported nearly ten years previously about the Duplessis orphans, complaining that there still had been no compensation to survivors. She wrote about . . .

Stop. Back up. The dots were getting closer to being connected. Caroline Richards had done a story that was sympathetic to prostitutes; Isabelle Hubert had been a prostitute. Caroline Richards had done a series of stories on the Duplessis orphans; Annie Desmarchais had been an orphan.

Okay, so maybe I was reaching. I checked my watch. Nearly seven; Ivan was working late tonight. But the casino had such excellent restaurants . . .

He wasn't in his office when I got there, so I wandered through the poker rooms, listening to the quiet riffling of clay chips, the occasional chitchat among the players. There were two tables of no limits, and I paused and watched for a few minutes, fascinated. It is a sad fact that I cannot play poker to save my life. Ivan despairs of my ever learning. It must be the math, I tell him. It's your face, he always responds.

He was deep in conversation with one of the supervisors, but smiled when he saw me. "Martine!"

"Is it a bad time?" I asked, kissing him chastely on the cheek.

"No more so than any other," he responded, and turned back to the man in the elegant suit. "We're fine on that?"

"Yes, Mr. Petrinko." He turned away and began talking very quickly to one of the dealers. I watched him. "Problem?"

"Of course there's a problem. It wouldn't be a normal day if there weren't any problems." Ivan took my arm. "You want to get something to eat?"

"I thought you'd never ask." Behind me, voices were raised

slightly, then the pit boss who had been talking to Ivan intervened to settle whatever argument was flaring. Regulars at the casino get annoyed when they're treated like everybody else; I recognized the signs.

We sat in Nuances, the casino's nicest restaurant, and didn't talk until we'd ordered: chicken Marsala and a bottle of Châteauneuf du Pape. Ivan has become French enough that he does not consider a dinner complete without wine. It's only taken me five years of marriage to get there. "So what's up, pumpkin?"

He usually only calls me pumpkin when I need reassuring. I wondered if I looked as scared as I was feeling. "Something's going on," I said. "And I think it's not about what everyone else is thinking. I don't think that it's about sex, or about some psychopath who's out there picking random victims. And I think that we're playing right into their hands by going forward with this serial killer idea."

"So what's really going on, then?"

I hesitated, and then said it. "Okay. This may be just a feeling, but . . . I think it's about the Duplessis orphans scandal."

Ivan raised his eyebrows. "The what?" I had to remember that he's only been in Canada for six years.

I took a deep breath, unwilling to begin. The Duplessis scandal was something from our collective past, something that my province and my country have tried hard to forget, even to deny ever happened. A dark shadow cast across our modern world. "Years ago, there was this guy, Maurice Duplessis, who was premier of Québec," I said. "That's a little like a governor of a state, though the premier has more power than a governor. I think." My knowledge of American government is hazy at best.

"When?" Ivan is nothing if not exact.

"In the 1950s and sixties," I said. My recollections weren't on a par with his. "Elected in the fifties, anyway. He was a social conservative. You know the deal, a return to *family values*"—I sketched air quotation marks around the term—"an emphasis on the Church, with low social spending, suppression of labor unions, that sort of thing."

"In the States, that would be called a Republican." I couldn't tell if he was joking or not.

"Whatever," I said. I didn't really understand American politics; keeping up with Québec—which was, after all, my own bread and butter—was more than enough most days. "The point with him, really, was that the Catholic Church was front and center," I said. "He gave it a lot of power, and a lot of latitude." Pull it together, Martine, you're wandering. "Anyway, what happened was that Duplessis and the Church were in each other's pockets. And the Church was running these orphanages, or asylums, or a mixture of the two, and it was—well, it was pretty horrible, Ivan."

The waiter came and uncorked the wine, Ivan went through the tasting ritual, and we were left alone again. "Tell me," Ivan commanded, pouring wine into my glass.

It seemed sacrilegious to drink liquid rubies like these when I had such a horrible story to tell. "You have to understand, in the 1940s and even through the end of the 1960s," I was trying to keep my voice steady, not looking at him at all, "it was a sin here in Québec to have a baby out of wedlock. I mean, a social sin. We were a kind of traditionalist place, especially upriver. A lot of bad things happened to the mothers."

Ivan didn't say anything. I took a deep breath. "And a lot of worse things happened to the babies. They were mostly institutionalized—put in these orphanages that were run by the Church. Oh, it wasn't just babies born to single mothers. Everyone had these huge families, and when you couldn't feed all your children, then you had to do something with them, so they went into the orphanages, too. Or if the father of the family died and the mother couldn't remarry or support her children, *they* went into the orphanage."

Ivan was watching me, his eyes concerned. He didn't know where this was going, but he knew it was hurting me; he knew that I was very aware of my Church's historical failings and that I still tried to love it. I took a quick swallow of wine. "And so there were these tremendously big orphanages, hundreds and hundreds of children in them. And *then* sometime in the 1950s the Church, probably through Duplessis himself, found out that they could get more money—you know, federal grants and support money and all that—from the Canadian government for kids in asylums than they could for kids in orphanages."

"Wait," said Ivan. "Duplessis wasn't part of the Canadian government? I thought you said he was premier—"

"He was a premier of Québec, of the province," I said. "There was also a Canadian premier. But you know there's this weird coexistence between Québec and the rest of Canada."

"Don't I ever," said Ivan with feeling. Massachusetts had never been this complicated.

"So the federal government decided that it was more expensive to support people in asylums than it was to support just regular kids in orphanages, and they upped the entitlements, so *pouff*! Suddenly a whole lot of the orphans were mentally ill, too. It was a very deliberate move. You went to sleep an orphan, you woke up an insane person. Just so the Catholic Church and the local government could save some money." Another swallow of wine. "They either renamed the orphanages as asylums, or took the kids from the orphanages to the asylums. And a lot of these kids *were* mentally ill, there's no question; but a lot of them weren't, most of them weren't, only they were all locked up together anyway. It's a wonder anyone stayed sane."

Ivan was watching me. "And the Church was in charge?" he asked, his voice carefully neutral. Like Violette, I married a Jew. It's sometimes been an issue between us; Ivan's criticisms of the Catholic Church have nearly always resulted in fights.

"Yes," I said wearily. "The Church was in charge." I hesitated, torn between not wanting to expose more of Catholicism to Ivan's critical tongue, but wanting to share what I was finding with the only person in the world who knew me, who could comfort me, who could help me think it all through. "You have to understand, *chéri*, back then, the Church ran a lot of things in Québec. Schools. Hospitals. I'm not saying that it was all bad . . ." My voice trailed off.

Ivan was gentle; he had picked up on my fear. "I'm sure it wasn't," he said. "Bad things happen, sometimes, for the best of reasons. So you're not telling me what happened?"

I didn't want to tell him. I didn't want to know. What had happened should never have happened. What had happened was a nightmare. "So the orphanages became asylums," I said, "because Québec could obtain more federal funds for healthcare facilities than for schools and orphanages. So orphans magically became mentally ill: they labeled everybody either crazy or mentally deficient and locked them away. They were called the Duplessis orphans, because this all happened under his watch and probably with his collusion, though the practice far outlived him. He died in office in 1959, but the asylums kept taking in orphans all through the sixties."

I was feeling a little queasy. I had read Caroline Richards's reports, awakening in me the memory of the original articles, the protests, the lawsuits, when the surviving orphans, now adults, had started coming out with their stories. Straitjackets. Electroshock therapy. Hydrotherapy. Excessive medication. Lobotomies. Any doctor who wanted to try something out had as many human guinea pigs available as he needed, and there would be no one to complain if the experiments failed. Better still, the medical schools were paying for the corpses. It was a win-win proposition for everyone involved.

I felt a wave of revulsion, but tried to focus. It wasn't as if Québec were alone in this. Nazis in Germany had experimented on people. Human experimentation in the United States wasn't unknown, either—Tuskegee, the Stateville Penitentiary Malaria Study, even infants injected with herpes: none of this was new. But it had happened at home, my home.

"So it turns out that she—Caroline, this reporter—was particularly interested in the experiments they were doing with chlorpromazine." I was turning my wineglass round and round in circles on the tablecloth. "In the States, you call it Thorazine," I said. "There was this guy who was working for McGill, this doctor, a psychiatrist. His name was Ewen Cameron. He was famous for doing human experimentation, combining drugs, electroshock therapy, and lobotomies." I swallowed. "Caroline wrote that he was working for the CIA, that he was part of that whole program where they used people to see what effects drugs like LSD had on them, back during the Cold War."

Ivan frowned. "So you're saying the CIA was involved with experimenting on children in Canada? And you think there's a tie-in between these stories and the murders?" he asked. "I don't know. It sounds like you might be stretching it, babe. I mean, I'm not saying that wasn't horrible, and I'm not saying that Caroline didn't make herself some enemies by writing about it, but that sounds a little too much like a conspiracy theory to me. Next thing you know, you'll be saying that the CIA had something to do with all this stuff that's happening now, with Montréal and the murders—"

"It's a possibility," I said defensively. The waiter arrived with our dinners and I looked at my plate with some dismay. I wasn't all that hungry anymore. Thinking about torture has that effect, I guess. "It's as good as the current sex fiend theory."

"Hmm." Ivan took a swallow of wine and held it in his mouth for a moment, tasting, before swallowing it. "It's a lot to take in," he said neutrally. "What does your detective friend Julian think about all this?"

"I have no idea. He's MIA." I sighed, frustrated. "Maybe you're right, maybe there's nothing here."

But, as it turned out, there was.

After a year on the farm, it appeared that I had worked my way back into the sisters' good graces. At least that was how it was expressed to me when I was brought before Mother Andrée and told that I was to begin working in the main building. "We feel that you can be trusted, Gabrielle," she said sternly, watching me closely for any signs of untrustworthiness. "You are quick and intelligent, and we will try and find tasks more suited to you henceforth."

I missed the soft breath of the animals, their warmth on cold winter mornings, the easy camaraderie that I'd shared with them and the other farm workers, all of whom were there because of some transgression or another; but there was nothing about those dark icy early mornings that I missed, nothing at all.

To my surprise, Mother Andrée hadn't been lying: I wasn't sent to scrub toilets or clean dormitories or wash dishes; instead, I was sent to the busy front office, where I was to be a messenger. The buildings at the Cité de Saint-Jean-de-Dieu were large, with long shining corridors wherever one looked; and if notes needed to go from one end of the building to another, it was one of the orphans who carried the note.

In this case, me.

I was given a new set of clothes, a light cotton pinafore for summer and a woolen one for winter, and an older girl I'd not met before showed me what I had to do.

"You'll remember it all soon," Régine assured me as we sped down a flight of stairs. "All the corridors look alike at first, so always look for the letter before you leave the stairwell. Can you read?"

"No," I acknowledged. The orphanage hadn't found reading necessary.

"Never mind," said Régine. "I'll show you the letters you need to know, and just connect them on the stairwells, and you'll be fine."

"Always the stairs? What about the elevators?" These were large noisy affairs that included two metal gates that needed to be *fought into place before the elevator would move. I was quite afraid of them.*

"Only if you're carrying something heavy or fragile," Régine said. "Not for the likes of us, the elevators aren't. So on each floor there's a sister in charge, and usually she's the one that gets the message you're carrying, yeah?"

"Yes," I confirmed, nodding.

"Or else she'll tell you where to take it. Or else they'll have given you other instructions. But if you ever don't know what to do with something, find a sister in charge of the floor, and ask her."

Régine's accent was nonexistent, not like some of the upriver accents that I struggled with out on the farm. Along with the troublemakers, they'd sensibly put children who came from farms out there to run things, and it had taken me months to understand some of them. "Where do you come from?" I asked her.

"Hush, tais-toi, we're not supposed to speak of such things," she said, alarmed, lowering her voice and looking around her. "No personal conversations."

There had been plenty of personal conversations across the road on the farm. "Tell me anyway," I urged her.

She looked seriously alarmed. "I am from Montréal," she admitted. "Do not say any more now! We'll be in bad trouble."

I was lighthearted. Bad trouble, to me, could only mean going back to the farm, and as I'd done that for a year already, it held no fears for me. She was a city girl, I thought kindly, so of course she'd be afraid of the threat of the farm.

Little did I know that she was afraid of something far worse. I had no idea, then, how bad "bad trouble" could be.

CHAPTER NINE

I went in to the office the next morning. Richard was handling everything with his usual smooth competence; I hadn't expected anything else. I found him at his desk, talking quietly into the phone, smoothing the ruffled feathers of yet another resident concerned about the proposal to make Duluth Street pedestrian-only. "I assure you, *madame*, that the mayor's office is aware of that concern. No, no one wants it to become a place for loud parties at night." He caught sight of me and grimaced. "Yes, perhaps you should write a letter to the editor. That would be most appropriate. Good-bye, *madame*."

I grinned. "She never thought to call the city councilors themselves? They're the ones debating it, not us."

He sighed. "Everyone seems to think it's a ploy on our part to make Montréal more of a tourist haven," he said.

"We *are* that devious," I agreed. "Can I see you in my office?"

We settled in and I buzzed Chantal for coffee. "Did you talk to the police yesterday?"

He nodded. "Filling in background, they called it," he said. "I got the impression that they'd have loved to find out I was the killer. Right race, right gender, and so on, and best of all, I work for you."

"Yes, well, don't worry so much about the profile. I'm not so sure that this one fits the profile."

He slanted a sharp glance at me. "You sound like one of them," he said, his voice neutral, only the hint of a question in it.

"Maybe." I waited until Chantal had delivered the coffee and closed the door behind her. I sipped; it was, of course, disappointing. Office coffee always is. Office coffee, after what I'd drunk at Violette Sobel's house, was abysmal. "Richard, I have to ask you this: did you and Danielle talk much about her work?"

He stirred his usual horrifying four cubes of sugar into his coffee before replying. "Sometimes. Not much. We talked, *bien sûr,* but not of work."

"I was in her office on Monday," I said. "She was doing some historical research, wasn't she?"

Richard frowned, thinking. "I think so," he said at last. "But it was something on the side, I'm thinking, something she was doing as an extra project. It wasn't for anybody at UQAM."

"I thought that was who she worked for," I objected.

"Yes, *bien sûr,* but there was someone from McGill there a lot, these last weeks. I met him once, when I went to take her to dinner. He didn't speak much French, I remember that. An Anglophone, and a man of a certain age. I teased her," he said and swallowed audibly, "about going over to the enemy."

More than you knew, I thought. "Do you know his name, this guy she was working for?"

"No." He shook his head. "Why? Is it important?"

I gave him my best all-purpose shrug. "I don't know. It might be. What was she researching for him, do you know?"

He leaned back in the chair, concentrating. "Let me see. We did speak of it, briefly, though not at that time. It was later . . . We were talking about human rights violations. I think that he was interested in some of the First Nations issues, and perhaps others, something that the Church had done in the 1960s."

I tried not to sound too excited. "Was it about the insane asylums? The orphanages? The Duplessis scandal?"

"Yes, yes, that could be it, Martine," Richard said. He was sounding tired. "I cannot remember exactly. You know how one listens to that sort of thing; it is a matter of courtesy only, really. But it is possible that it was about the Duplessis orphans, *oui.*"

I was going to have to find those notes—and that mysterious older gentleman from McGill. "Richard, you don't know her computer password, do you?" I asked.

He surprised me by immediately tearing up. "It is my name and my birthday," he said.

Julian caught up with me at the UQAM library. "You got the password?"

"Yes," I said, turning away from the front desk where I was still waiting for someone to notice me. "Where the hell have you been?"

"Investigating," he said, tapping the side of his nose. I wondered which late-night police show he had gotten the gesture from.

"Me, too," I said tartly. "You might have mentioned that you were going to disappear, by the way."

He leaned against the counter, his smile boyish. "Tell me you missed me."

"Hardly. Does anybody work here, do you think?"

Julian winked and wandered off. He was back almost immediately, with a flustered female graduate student. "*Je m'excuse*," she said hastily, slanting another look at him, worship in her eyes. "I'm so very sorry. You wished to go see Mademoiselle Leroux's office?"

"Yes, please," I said. I was trying to ignore the fact that she and Julian were doing everything but exchange telephone numbers on the spot.

"This way, please, *madame, monsieur.*"

The office was as I'd left it on Monday, and yet subtly changed, as well. It couldn't possibly have accumulated dust in the meantime, yet it felt dusty, as though realizing that its former occupant would not be returning. There was an emptiness that hadn't been there on Monday.

Julian was still out in the hallway talking to the grad student. If he didn't get a date out of it, I'd be disappointed in him. There was nothing left to do but look at Danielle's life and see if I could figure out why she'd died.

I booted the machine and waited; I got the password—Rousseau and the birth date—right away. I hadn't realized how close they were. That felt sad, too.

I'd been right: Danielle and I shared a number of software preferences. I looked at her computer dock and located them at once: iCal, address book, the Apple Mail client, iPhoto, Quicken. I pulled up iCal first.

On the day she died, Danielle had eaten lunch with someone named Hélène; she'd had an appointment at three with someone called Dr. Belanger, and had noted to herself that she needed to pick up tomatoes at the market. The words blurred in front of my eyes. I wondered if she'd ever gotten her tomatoes, and what recipe she had needed them for.

I'd leave the address book for Julian, I decided; he'd know best how to deal with that. I wasn't about to go into Danielle's photo album. The e-mail needed an additional password, but this time, my deputy's first name was sufficient. I dabbed at my eyes, took a deep breath, and dug in.

It has to be said: reading someone else's daily correspondence is less than thrilling. By the time Julian joined me, I was clicking through slowly, my elbows on the desk, the atmosphere in the room starting to get to me.

"Find anything?"

I didn't bother looking up. "Nothing yet," I said. "Did you get her number?"

He laughed, pushing folders out of his way and hitching one hip onto the desk. "Can't blame me for trying."

I stopped looking at the monitor and sat back in my chair. "What do you know," I asked, "about the Duplessis orphans?"

His eyes widened fractionally. "Tell me what *you* know," he said.

"I don't know much yet," I said in frustration. "But Caroline Richards was doing a series of stories on them for the newspaper—the asylums, and the experiments, and digging up that old cemetery that belongs to the provincial liquor board now. And Annie Desmarchais was an orphan—she was adopted when she was ten by Violette's family who had lost a child; plus she's the right age to be part of the Duplessis scandal. And now Richard says that Danielle was doing historical research about that period at the behest of someone from—wait for it—McGill. Which is pretty weird freelancing, since McGill and UQAM don't generally play well together. But there's more. McGill's psychiatric department was called the Allan Institute, and she's got all these notes—newspaper clippings, too—about a connection between the Allan and the Duplessis orphans. Is it a coincidence? That's a lot of connections that don't have anything to do with sex."

Julian nodded. He cleared his throat. "Isabelle Hubert was doing genealogy work, remember? The Mormons, and all that?" After I nodded, he went on. "Well, I looked at her stuff. Turns out, Isabelle's mother was in the Cité de Saint-Jean-de-Dieu asylum. The only reason she didn't end up with her brains fried, or worse, is that she escaped."

"That's the asylum that was named in the lawsuits," I said slowly. "One of them, anyway. That's where they were experimenting on the orphans and where they kept them with mentally ill adults; when their experiments went wrong, they sold the bodies for ten dollars to medical schools." I'd been learning things I didn't want to know. "That's the asylum with the hidden cemetery where there used to be a piggery, where they wanted the exhumations in 2002."

Julian nodded. "Bingo."

"Bingo," I echoed. "And if Danielle's notes are right, there's a

McGill connection to the Cité de Saint-Jean-de-Dieu asylum. But, wait, Julian, so there's a connection, but what the hell does it prove? Who on earth would want to come after them? It's not like it's a secret, you know? It's been in the papers since—oh, God, I don't know, the late nineties. The lawsuits have already been filed. Apologies have been offered. Everyone knows what happened. What's the *point*?"

"Well, Watson," said Julian, "that's what we get to find out next."

"The McGill guy, that's a lead, isn't it? Why would a researcher at UQAM do *anything* for McGill?" Another thought occurred to me: "Julian, the guy who was in charge of the medical stuff, the one connected with the CIA drug research, he was from McGill."

"Doubtful he's still alive and trying to get information out of Danielle Leroux," Julian said. "Still, it can't be ignored." He straightened up. "Okay. You keep going through her files, see if you can find anything. I'm going to try and find out more about Isabelle's mother, how she got out, what happened to her, anything that would make Isabelle a threat to somebody now."

I'd just opened my mouth to respond when his smartphone beeped. "Damn," Julian said, scowling at the text message. "Guess I have to make a detour first. Time to meet with my boss."

"Good luck," I said, my eyes returning to the screen.

I wasn't finding e-mails to or from anyone with a McGill address. I wasn't finding much at all that had any content, which on reflection made sense; my own e-mails were pretty contentless too, confirming appointments, asking questions that could be answered immediately, sending out boilerplate notices. I probably shouldn't be disappointed that there wasn't anything in Danielle's inbox that said, "Meet me at midnight and All Will Be Told."

I started looking through her documents folder, and had a little more luck. Here was her actual work: notes, Internet addresses for websites, bibliographies. Notes about the issues with the First Nations. I took a deep breath. Did that have any bearing? I frowned and read the beginning of a long file.

> *From the early 1830s to 1996, thousands of First Nation, Inuit, and Métis children were forced to attend residential schools in an attempt to assimilate them into the dominant culture. Those children suffered abuses of the mind, body, emotions, and spirit that can be almost unimaginable. Over 150,000 children, some as young as four years old, attended the government-funded and church-run residential schools. It's estimated that there are 80,000 residential school survivors alive today.*

I shook my head. Couldn't be that. What else? Notes about some court cases having to do, inexplicably, with aggravated battery. Notes about some hearings that had happened three months ago. Notes about gambling—I might come back to those, for Ivan's sake.

I almost missed the file. I was looking for anything that connected to the Duplessis name, to asylums, to orphans, and it wasn't there. What was, instead, was Largactil.

Largactil. The brand name under which, in Canada, chlorpromazine is sold.

I felt my pulse quicken as I opened the folder. File after file after file was there. Interviews. Dates. Names. But nothing, as far as I could see, that wasn't already public knowledge.

Danielle had concentrated her research work on the administration of chlorpromazine in experimental usage. She had a lot of documentation from the United States, much of which had been obtained under the Freedom of Information Act by a colleague of hers at Fordham University. Other information seemed less public domain; Danielle, a careful researcher, had noted who had spoken with her, when, and how each interview had been arranged. Her sources seemed impeccable.

There were a few interviews with survivors of the asylums, but she hadn't written much about them; it didn't seem to be particularly interesting to her. Instead, she was focusing on the medical establishment—the doctors, pharmaceutical companies, hospitals—that used the asylums as steady sources of human guinea pigs. There were notes on the use of chlorpromazine in conjunction with cold-water shock therapy, electroshock therapy, and surgery. There were notes on the resultant deaths, and on the disposals of the bodies. Everything was meticulously documented.

I took a deep breath. Danielle, it seemed, was putting together a damning dossier.

For crimes against humanity.

CHAPTER TEN

"So who would want to make that dossier disappear?" Ivan wanted to know. "Crimes against humanity. Christ, Martine, that's serious stuff."

I'd made my obligatory appearance at police headquarters, where the focus was on a couple of loners who had gotten into trouble in the Sainte-Catherine area, one of them currently being held for assault and attempted rape. The director was pleased about that. "Progress, Madame LeDuc," he said, nodding vigorously. "I think we will soon be able to say the scourge of Montréal is no more."

All I could think of was that the director had been taking the same rhetoric class the mayor had.

I then went back to the Old City where I interrupted the mayor himself; he'd been talking with still another concerned citizen's group about the possible pedestrian street, and he left the meeting gratefully: score one for Martine, I thought, as I brought him up to speed on the police inquiries. He even said good work. I nearly fainted.

For once, Ivan and I were home for dinner at the same time. He was pan-frying flounder, I was cooking green beans in garlic butter—neither of us thinks much about our cholesterol levels. "So who would want to make it disappear?" he asked.

I considered the question, pouring some of my glass of Pouilly Fumé into the beans as I did, then sipping more of it myself. "Anyone who was trying to disconnect the Duplessis affair from the drug experiments, I suppose," I said slowly. "Remember, most of what was in the news, and most of what everybody knows, is that the Church was in cahoots with the province of Québec to get federal money. Both benefitted. They're the only ones who've been sued, and it's the province that's been anteing up any restitution money, which, by the way, has been little and far between. Hope you noted the poker allusion," I added.

"Duly noted," said Ivan.

"I like slipping those in from time to time, just so you feel at home." I sipped my wine, which sat on my tongue like the harbinger of a cold frost. Like the cold of a grave. I shivered and put the glass down.

Ivan pulled up a chair and sat at the big oak kitchen table, bringing his own wine with him. "Yeah, but Martine, when did this all happen? In the fifties and sixties? Who's around anymore to even care? Most of the people involved are either dead themselves or in retirement homes." He sighed. "I mean, giving restitution is noble. Don't get me wrong. And it's probably a good thing to show the world that we take justice seriously—even if it's so far after the fact. But isn't it a circus? Parading some senile person around who may not have a clue what's happening, just for the sake of delayed justice. Taking them into the courtroom in a wheelchair. Look at the Allende trial. Look at those Nazis they brought to trial: one was wheeled into court in a hospital bed, for Christ's sake. It was a circus."

I was staring at him. "A necessary circus," I said slowly. "You surprise me, Ivan."

"Why?"

I raised my eyebrows. "You of all people? Don't you *want* to see Nazis going to trial? Isn't that sacrosanct for you? Never forget, and all that sort of thing?"

He flushed. "You're saying that just because I'm Jewish."

"Well, yes," I said. "Come on, Ivan. You've got a pretty big stake in this justice-is-justice-whenever-it-happens thing. Don't you? Because your ancestors died in pogroms and concentration camps in Russia? Your family was almost wiped out during the Holocaust because someone else saw them as less than human. I'd think that you'd have it encoded in your DNA, some sort of desire for justice. Better late than never."

He shook his head. He's a pragmatist, Ivan. "People spend too much time looking back," he said quietly. "It's about making sure that it doesn't happen again."

I lost patience then. "How can we be sure it won't happen again, if we don't understand why it happened in the first place? If people get away with treating other people like objects, no matter where or when or for what reason, then it can always happen again, and it *will* always happen again!"

He looked at me soberly. "And is that what your Danielle was doing? Making sure that somebody didn't get away with it?"

"Yes!" I was pretty sure, anyway; I just had to figure out who, and how. And what. And why the drug angle. Minor details. "This guy from McGill that Richard met in her office, he has to be part of it," I said. "No way UQAM and McGill are going to collaborate on anything. It's just not in their nature. They don't speak the same language, literally *or* figuratively. So that has to be a link, a connection of some sort . . . I just don't know how."

"And you said that one of the original experimenters was from McGill, right?" Ivan got up and checked the flounder. It smelled heavenly. "Babe, how close are the green beans?"

I waved the question away as irrelevant. I was on a roll. "Exactly! Ewen—Ewen Something-or-other. The shrink, the guy with ties to the CIA. Listen, Ivan: that whole crew up at the Allan Institute, they were part of McGill: the institute was McGill's psychiatric department. And McGill had to know they were doing CIA experiments there, too, but hey, funding is funding, isn't it, and CIA money spends just as well as any other currency."

He shook his head. "McGill's a respected university, Martine," he objected. "They weren't going to jeopardize their reputation with something like this."

"Why not? Who knew how bad it was? I mean, the sensory deprivation experiments, they were public, they had volunteers coming in to work with them. It was all aboveboard. No one needed to know about the rest."

"The flounder's done."

"Wait, Ivan! Maybe there's *still* a connection there and McGill doesn't want it made public! Take it from me, that's a great recipe for a public relations nightmare, if a Canadian university were *still* holding hands with an American intelligence agency.

Maybe all of this is a big cover-up that's continuing now. Maybe . . ."

Ivan shook his head. "McGill University and the Central Intelligence Agency? Nowadays?" His skepticism couldn't have been clearer.

"I don't know," I conceded. "Maybe not anymore. But I'm going to find out."

"Uh-huh. And those beans?"

"Maybe UQAM is in on it somehow," I said slowly. "That's not impossible, right? We already know McGill was in on it, and maybe—if anything—UQAM wanted to expose McGill's involvement. That's why Danielle was involved, why she was interested. There's a long history tying universities to government agencies. At least I think there is." I made a mental note to find out. "There has to be: it's probably one of the ways that universities get their funding, and the government gets its results. I really think that we're onto something with this." I was feeling giddy with anticipation and Pouilly Fumé. If there was a conspiracy here—and I was starting to believe that there really was—I was going to get to the bottom of it. And bring justice down on those who deserved it. Martine LeDuc as Joan of Arc. Or Erin Brockovich. Heady stuff indeed.

And then I smelled something and was brought back down to earth with a thud. "Oh, damn, check the beans, will you, sweetheart?"

CHAPTER ELEVEN

The next morning there was an e-mail from Julian waiting for me at the office. "Confirmed that Annie Desmarchais was at Cité de Saint-Jean-de-Dieu," he wrote. "I'm still looking into Isabelle's mom. Lunch at one to compare notes?"

I stared at the computer monitor, feeling as if someone had hit me in the stomach. Annie Desmarchais hadn't merely been an orphan. Annie Desmarchais had lived for the first ten years of her life in one of the worst hellholes in the world; she had, if what I had been reading was true, been subjected to humiliation, to sexual abuse; she had spent her days scrubbing floors, doing laundry, cleaning kitchens; and that was only if the drugs she was injected with hadn't made her too incapacitated to work. She had not been to school. She had not been exposed to any kind of culture.

Violette Sobel, I thought, had a hell of a lot of questions to answer.

I took the Métro up to Sherbrooke and walked the rest of the way to the Desmarchais mansion. I was dressed for the Pekinese this time, in jeans, sweater, and jacket: armor of sorts.

Again, Violette answered the door, though I had the sense of another presence hovering. "Madame LeDuc, how nice to see you again," she said sweetly and insincerely, and opened the door. The Peke caught sight of me and growled. I narrowed my eyes and would have growled back if I'd dared.

This time, there was no exquisite coffee waiting. The front room was chilly and felt disused, and I shivered as I walked in. "I'm really not sure what else I can tell you," Violette said, gesturing gracefully for me to be seated.

I looked around for the Pekinese, but he was nowhere in sight; probably lurking somewhere, waiting to attack. I had more important fish to fry. "Madame Sobel, you did not tell me where your sister had lived before your family adopted her."

She sighed. "I thought I had made that clear to you, *madame*," she said, a thread of irritation tracing through her voice. "As far as we were concerned, Annie had no life before she came to us. She was part of our family. We did not speak of any time when we were not together."

"But she did," I pointed out, "have a life. Ten years of it."

She straightened her spine even more than it was already, and I remembered that she taught yoga. I simply couldn't imagine it. "May I ask, *madame*, what is your point? Surely nothing that happened to my sister in her past had anything to do with her death. I am assured by the police that it was an instance of random violence."

I sat and didn't say anything. I just looked at her, willing myself to focus, hoping to make her uncomfortable. I'd heard that was how you did it: by just staying silent. Ivan had told me that most people get uncomfortable with silence. Ivan knew a lot about making people uncomfortable.

It didn't seem to be working very well.

The Peke decided at that moment to make his appearance, slinking under Violette's chair and glaring at me from the protection it afforded. I ignored him and he whined loudly. We both ignored him. Violette seemed completely prepared to outwait me. It was a pity, I thought, that Julian hadn't given me lessons in interrogation techniques.

I finally gave in, and there was a gleam in her eye when I did. I was beginning to dislike this woman . . . and her little dog, too.

"*Madame*," I said carefully, "Annie was in an insane asylum. How was it that your family selected someone from a hospital, rather than a school or orphanage?"

"She was an orphan," she replied, her words measured. She, too, was treading carefully. "That is all that matters, surely? She was given a good home."

"I'm sure she was," I said. "But now she's dead."

She looked at me. The Peke looked at me. He whined again, and this time she made a small gesture and he jumped into her lap. Busying her hands in his hair, she cleared her throat. "As I've said, I think I told you everything I know."

"I doubt it," I said.

There was a frigid silence, and then her wrist moved infinitesimally; somewhere in the back of the house a bell rang. I had been correct about someone else being about; the door opened and a man, dressed in a dark suit, appeared silently. "Madame LeDuc is just leaving," said Violette.

I stood up. Everyone's eyes were on me. "Don't you care?" I asked in desperation. "She was your sister! Don't you want to know why she was murdered?"

"Show her out, please, Pierre," she said, and her voice was tinged with frost. "As you have noted, *madame*, this is a house of grief. Please do not bother us again."

As I was going through the door, the Pekinese snarled.

"Well, that was thoroughly useless," I said, sliding into the booth across from Julian. "She's either scared, or hiding something, or both; but she's not talking."

He had ordered poutine for two. A boy after my own heart. Poutine is Québec's unique contribution to the hardening of the world's arteries: crisp French fries, mixed with cheese curds and smothered in chicken gravy. It's horrible. It's heavenly.

His mouth full of food, Julian shook his head. "What did you expect?" He swallowed and washed the bite down with cider. "She's not going to give up a secret they've kept for decades, and certainly not to someone without a name."

"I beg your pardon?" I stared at him, a gravy-coated French fry halfway to my mouth.

He gestured dismissively. "Not a Name," he said, "with a capital N."

I nodded slowly. "Ah, I see. Not like a Fletcher. One of *the* Fletchers."

"Got it in one." He nodded approvingly.

"Okay, so I'll bow out gracefully and let you take her on.

What about Isabelle's mother?" I asked. "What's going on there?"

He swallowed more cider, wiped his mouth, and nodded. "Well, one of us had to be successful," he said as he pulled out his notebook and flipped through the pages. "And I found out about Isabelle's mother. Here's the scoop: Juliette Hubert was barely out of diapers when her father was killed in a farm accident." He looked at me. "What's a 'farm accident'?"

I shrugged. "What do I look like—an agricultural expert? Who knows? The machinery they use looks terrifying, maybe that was it."

"Hmm." He returned to his notes. "Mother couldn't support the five children on her own. Enter the parish priest. 'We'll take good care of the little ones for you, don't worry about them.' She, of course, believed him."

"Not sure she had a lot of other options."

"True enough," he conceded. "So off went Juliette, along with"—he flipped a page back—"Thérèse, Lysette, Marie-Claire, and Frédérique-Aimée."

"All girls," I said. "Maybe it wouldn't have happened if she'd had boys instead. Farms need boys."

"Maybe not," said Julian. "Anyway, needless to say, Mom never saw any of them again. She didn't even know where they were. Probably thought they were living in clean, happy convents somewhere, learning to read and write."

"What happened to her?"

"Juliette's mother? Died," he said. "Don't know where, don't know when, don't know how."

It didn't matter, I thought. What a bleak life. She lost the farm and her children when her husband died; she probably left Québec altogether and went down into New England to work the mills, thinking her children were safe and cared for. Poor woman, at least she had the fantasy. "And Juliette?"

"Ah, Juliette," he said. "She went into the asylum and didn't know much outside that life. But she was feisty, that's for sure. What records there are—and, mind you, they're few and far between—show that she was in trouble most of the time. And being in trouble was big. Really big."

All of the lightness had drained from his face. "Hell, Martine," Julian said. "Freezing water. They put little kids' heads into freezing water to punish them. Juliette spent a lot of time being cold."

We were both quiet then, thinking about this. It was Dickensian, I thought, pictures from a horrible past that happened not all that long before I was born. That was part of the horror, I realized: its immediacy. A small child, alone and afraid, the nuns, the doctors.

The water.

I pushed my poutine away, nauseated. At this rate, I was going to lose a lot of weight.

Julian rallied. "So she grew up. And who knows what happened to her, but it was bad—nothing good happened in those places. No records of the so-called medical stuff that went on—I think that was all through the Allan—but you can imagine they were probably more likely to use the difficult children for the experiments. It's one way to keep everyone in line." His voice was grim. "Anyway, Juliette didn't stay in line. She survived longer than many of the other kids—she was a survivor, our Juliette. And when she was sixteen years old, she scaled the walls. Literally. Not knowing what was on the other side. You have to admire that."

I couldn't begin to imagine what kind of courage that took.

Julian shook his head. "Over the wall and out into the city."

"Wait," I interrupted. "Where was she?"

He looked surprised. "The Cité de Saint-Jean-de-Dieu asylum."

"Where Annie Desmarchais lived until *she* was ten years old."

We stared at each other. "It means something," Julian said.

"Yeah," I said, nodding. "But what?"

Juliette Hubert had not fared particularly well once she was free in Montréal; but perhaps that didn't matter. Perhaps, after where she'd been, *anything* was better. Possessing no skills, social or otherwise, she drifted into the life of the night, worked the streets and the brothels of the Sainte-Catherine area. She survived; she survived longer than most. Thinking herself sterile, she was astonished when, in her forties, she became pregnant. Juliette had the child, and at a time when it was nearly impossible to be a single mother, she kept the child, making a life for the two of them in a one-room convenience flat in Chinatown, taking her daughter to school every day, leaving her to the owner of a local noodle shop to feed and supervise in the evenings, coming home late to sing lullabies and tuck her into the one single bed they shared.

Like Victor Hugo's Fantine, she sickened and died, but not until Isabelle was in her teens and had her own ideas about the world. Isabelle finished school, finished university even; and though she returned to her mother's profession, it wasn't because she had no other options. It would be interesting, I thought, to analyze why Isabelle had taken to prostitution; but she had, and in a way that justified all her mother's sacrifices, at least if making a lot of money is a justification.

I looked across the table at Julian, exhausted. "What's the point?"

"Hmm?" He finished his poutine and pushed the bowl away. "The point of what?"

I gestured toward his notebook. "All that. So her mother was in the asylum. Her mother's dead, Julian, she's been dead for years. Why would the killer go after Isabelle?"

"Isabelle did something," he reasoned, "that made her a danger to someone. That's what we're saying, isn't it?" I nodded. "And we have to think that it was connected to her mother, to her mother's early life. So what did she do? That's what we have to find out. For twenty-some years she did whatever she was doing, and no one cared about her. This summer she did something else, and she had to die."

I sighed. "Julian, what we're saying is that out of the blue, suddenly *this summer,* all of these women did something, learned something, said something that meant they had to die. All of them at once. How big a coincidence is that?"

"Exactly." Julian nodded. "So it's not a coincidence." He sat forward in his chair. "They aren't just connected," he said slowly, "they also connected, somehow, *with each other.* They had to have connected, it's the only way it can work. So we have to figure out how they did. And when. And why."

And that was the hundred-thousand-dollar question.

* * *

Julian wasn't ready to descend on Violette Sobel yet. "Let me make a few calls first," he said. "Smooth the way. We saw how well she reacted to your impromptu visit."

"Ah," I said. "That's not the way *it's done*." I sketched quotation marks in the air.

"Precisely, Watson, you know my ways." He beamed as he held the door for me and we left the poutine place. "In the meantime, you've got to check in with *monsieur le directeur*. And I'm going to play connect the dots."

"E-mail?" It's what I had been thinking about.

He shook his head. "You're better at that than I am," he said, and his voice grew brisk. "I'm going to see how Caroline Richards fits in. She's the only English one in the lot."

"She was a reporter," I pointed out. "She was writing about the asylums, about the drug experiments. I'd say that her involvement is obvious."

Again, the finger on the side of the nose. "We'll see," he said, then switched his attention to the street. "I don't believe it! Did you see that? Some idiot cop ticketed me!"

I looked at the TT, double-parked as usual. "What a surprise."

"Methinks you mock me, lady." He jumped up, made a sweeping bow, then hopped into the car. "Catch you later."

Speaking of drugs, I thought facetiously as I hurried toward the Métro, *that* level of energy just had to be chemically induced.

I had a feeling I could use some of them myself.

CHAPTER TWELVE

Monsieur le directeur de la police was pleased. He was brilliant, and didn't mind, for once, sharing his exuberance over his brilliance with me. "We're very close," he told me unctuously that afternoon. "Very close indeed." Uriah Heep–like, he rubbed his hands together. Had he been able to dance a jig, I had no doubt that he would.

"Close?" I asked.

"To solving the murders, of course!" He beamed. Even though Richard did most of the liaison work with the police, I knew the director well. I'd never, in seven years at this job, seen him beam before.

It was a little scary.

"I see," I said cautiously. "What have you found?"

He kept rubbing his hands together. It was getting irritating. "We have a viable suspect in custody." He nodded, pleased. "Very viable indeed."

"That's good news," I said automatically. And it was, of course; but it also seemed very convenient. Not that I was going to teach the director his job, and I certainly didn't want to spend my time going off on tangents if they weren't going to lead to the truth, but still. Still. "Um . . . You're sure about him? What evidence do you have? The—mayor will want to know," I added hastily.

"But of course, *madame*. He is a *clochard*, a homeless man. He had, in his possession, belongings of two of the victims."

Yikes. That could throw a curveball into my investigation. But it still wasn't necessarily proof of murder. Homeless people picked up anything they saw lying around. I cleared my throat. "*Monsieur le directeur—*"

"There is more, of course," he said briskly. "And we're not ready to charge him yet. But it is looking good, *madame*, very good."

Very circumstantially good, I thought. Of course he was going to jump on the first and easiest answer that came along. Julian had better be making progress, and so had I, or else they were going to railroad some poor, possibly mentally ill, homeless man— "How old is your suspect, *monsieur*?" I asked suddenly.

"*Comment?* His age?"

"The mayor will wish to know all the details you are free to share," I said apologetically.

"Ah. Yes. *Bien sûr.* The suspect, he is in his fifties."

I wrote it down dutifully. "Thank you, *monsieur le directeur.*"

He beamed again. "It is my pleasure, *madame*."

It was all enough to make you sick.

* * *

I walked down to the river after I left the director's office. The news, such as it was, would wait; and Montréal was experiencing one of its few perfect fall days, the sun bright and warm, the leaves starting to turn, the air slightly crisp but far from cold. The cold would come soon enough.

I got as far as the Old City and sat on a bench, though not without a shiver. The river walk was filled with people, some of them in suits and dresses, playing hooky from their offices; others were in the traditional tourist garb—mismatched clothing, souvenir hats, and cameras—that made my heart glad. A horse-drawn carriage clip-clopped lazily past, and two young men on roller skates did intricate circles in front of the Labyrinth. Even the ducks at the fountain at my back seemed joyous.

It wasn't a time to think about murder, but the reality was that there were four women who should have been there with me, enjoying the people, drinking in the sun. That was the perspective one had to keep.

That it was preplanned murder, and not random sexually motivated serial killings, I was now convinced. Yeah, okay, so it wasn't as if I were drawing on years of experience in criminal investigation. But I'm intelligent, and any intelligent person—it seemed to me—would be thinking the same thing. It was premeditated, planned, carefully calculated murder.

Restless, I got up after a few minutes and walked back through the Old City, dodging the inevitable tourists, buskers, and double-parked cars along the way, glad I was wearing my flats to navigate the cobblestones. Maybe I wasn't ready to go back inside on such a brilliant day, or maybe I was just curious, but I found myself heading toward the Boulevard de Maison-

neuve, and soon enough was staring at one of the city's remaining convents, big brick institutional buildings that still speak of
the past. A past that's best forgotten.

I felt a sudden stab of guilt: I've been a Catholic all my life. I
went to a Catholic school and wore the Catholic uniform and at
the bottom of my purse even now there's a rosary that I may not
use with any regularity, but that my fingers seek out every time
I need to feel grounded, every time I need some sort of physical
touchstone to an otherworldly reality. The nuns who taught me
were extraordinary women, smart and connected to the world,
interested and involved and—most important—not at all convinced that they had all the answers. "We all have our own
roads to God," Sister Evangeline told me once. "He doesn't care
how you get there, only that you do."

And truth be told, I'm not crazy about a lot of aspects of my
church—who could be? But it's still my family. You don't leave
your family just because your uncle Jean-Louis was arrested, or
because your father's too authoritarian, or because your mother's too remote. You criticize them; you try to change them; but
you don't leave them.

Some days, that was harder than others.

Here I was, looking at one of my family's worst transgres-
sions, its abandonment of its own code regarding the sanctity
of life. Unborn children are supposed to have rights, at least in
my church's view, but apparently the ones that *had* been born
through "sin" had none. I took a deep breath. The guilt would
have to wait, I told myself: the injustice had to be righted first.
No matter where it led.

Where it led, I decided, was to McGill. That's where the

experimentation started, not in the wretched dark orphanages–cum–torture chambers, but in the laboratories where fortunes were being made—or not made—when a drug proved itself to be effective.

McGill University's Allan Memorial Institute of Psychiatry lived in a massive gothic building called Ravenscrag on McTavish Street that would be scary even if you *didn't* know what had happened inside. I'd looked it up online when I was in my office and had found all sorts of interesting—and probably irrelevant—information about the place.

Everything in the photos looked green and beautiful: the manicured lawns that sweep down the flank of the mountain, the trees behind the edifice, the very permanency of the building itself, solid and imposing, with its tower and craggy windows and bits of additions peppered throughout. It hadn't been built to be a psychiatric hospital, I knew: it was a mansion, a castle meant to impress—but to me it screamed out that it was an asylum, belonging to the "pauper's palaces" school of architecture.

Ravenscrag had been originally built in the late 1800s by Sir Charles Allan, one of the shipping magnates who were Montréal's first *nouveaux-riches*. There had once been a sumptuous interior—a place for laughter and parties, girls giggling prettily behind fans, men taking port and smoking cigars in the library. There had been a greenhouse, a ballroom, a billiards room, and bedrooms enough for the nineteen servants the Allan family employed as well as the family and any guests who might be staying with them at any given time. It was the magnate's son who donated the property to the Royal Victoria Hospital, and it didn't need the rumors of ghosts to make it seem haunted after that. Frankly, it gave me the creeps.

But reading ghost stories wasn't going to help me: I needed to find out from the university itself what it was willing to tell me. I stopped by the mews to pick up my car and headed west.

My first stop was the department of psychiatry downtown on McGill's main campus. Parked illegally, of course. Maybe I should invest in a moped.

I smiled at the receptionist. "I'm Martine LeDuc," I said in the informal manner of the city's English speakers. "I work for the tourist department, and I'm doing some historical research."

She was blandly pleasant. "How can we help you?"

"Well, it's just information for a brochure . . . I understand that back in the 1940s, McGill was doing a lot of pharmaceutical research, working in cooperation with the Americans. It sounds like something important, something that would be a feather in the city's cap, so to speak." I'd heard Ivan using that expression, but she was looking at me blankly, so maybe I hadn't used it correctly. I tried again. "We're trying to promote Montréal's role in scientific work."

"Oh, of course," she said, clearly still not catching on, but brightening as a thought occurred. "I know! You'll want to talk to Dr. MacDougal. He knows all about that."

"Great!" I said, my voice as perky as I could manage. "How do I get in touch with him?"

She consulted her computer. "He's got postdocs all day," she said, her voice doubtful. "That's at his office here, just upstairs and down the hall. Maybe you could try and catch him in between them this afternoon? Or would you like to make an appointment? I can get his secretary on the phone for you."

Neither option seemed useful. I didn't want him to be able to dismiss me because I was there at an inconvenient time; but neither did I want to make an appointment and give him time to put on a public face. *If* this was the guy I was after, which was by no means certain. "What time's his last student today?" I asked instead.

She scanned the monitor. "It looks like five thirty."

I frowned. "That's not good for me. You know, I left my appointment book behind. Can I have his secretary's number? I'll call myself, tomorrow."

"Sure thing." She gave me the number and a sunny smile. "Have a nice day!"

Five thirty, I reflected as I left the building, would do just fine. I couldn't wait to see what Dr. MacDougal had to say.

I cannot even begin to recount how many different sorts of people lived there, hundreds of them. The vast majority were children with nothing wrong with them other than that no one really cared. A few still had families; a few still had visits; and if we thought that the visiting parlor at the orphanage had been constructed for show, it was nothing like the show that went on when someone's family came here to see them.

There were adults, too, who mostly lived in different areas of the building from us, different floors, different wings, and they were the ones who were truly insane, who stripped naked in the dayrooms and dribbled on the furniture, who ran screaming down the hallways and caught you up to ask, breathlessly, "Are you the king?"

And, as is true, I think, in any place where a lot of people live together, be it city or asylum, there were the strong who preyed on the weak.

We'd all been through it, our first few days and weeks and months there: food stolen, blankets stolen, and no one to complain to. There was more gratuitous violence, as well: bare toes stepped upon, hair pulled, arms twisted. Later, there was even more, darker things, deeper pain, and even though I understand that people do what they feel they must do to survive, I found some of what happened difficult to forgive. You'd think, wouldn't you, that we'd have had the sense to all band together against our common enemy, the sisters and the orderlies and the doctors; but we did not, and what we did to each other was in its own way as bad as what they did to us.

Back from the farm and working in communications, I listened to Régine and learned from her, and I obediently took the elevator when I was sent to Sister Lise. If you didn't know where someone was, there was a chart in Sister Marguerite's office; but since I couldn't read it, I had to ask her for help.

"Sister Lise," Sister Béatrice said, and looked sharply at me. "That's down in the basement. Have you been there?"

"No, Sister."

"All right then," she said. "You have to take the elevator in the east wing; that staircase doesn't go down to Sister Lise's department."

"Yes, Sister."

"There will probably be an orderly around when you step off the elevator. If there isn't, then just stand there and wait by the desk. Under no circumstances do you go anywhere in the basement alone, do you understand?"

"Yes, Sister."

"Very well. Off you go."

And off I went, down the creaking and shuddering elevator and into the basement. I felt a wave of relief when the elevator stopped and I could wrestle the two screeching metal gates open and step out of the infernal machine.

There was no one in the basement to greet me, and I heeded Sister's words, staying precisely where I was. The elevator opened into a lobby of sorts, an ill-lit one with a particularly low ceiling; there was a desk and chair and lamp, and three of the walls held closed doors.

At first, nothing happened. I stood and waited. The electric clock on the wall ticked loudly.

One of the doors burst open, thrown against the wall and with a loud thud, bounced back—it was made of steel, so it suffered no ill effects. An orderly, wearing the white shirt and trousers of his profession, his hair cut short close to the skull, came through and yanked a drawer completely out of the desk, grabbing something inside. A pair of handcuff restraints.

I moved then, and caught his eye. "Yeah?"

"I'm here with a message for Sister Lise," I said, trying to look anywhere but at the restraints. More than two years since I'd last been in them, and there were still scars on my wrists. Automatically, I tugged at my cuffs to cover the marks.

"Stay here," he said, and went back through the door, pulling it closed behind him. A moment later I heard a scream, horrible in its intensity, long and drawn out, a sound no human should make.

The door opened again, more gently this time. A nun came

through, briskly, pushing the door shut behind her. "You have something for me?"

It was as though nothing had happened. As though we were conversing on a normal day, in a normal set of circumstances. "Yes, Sister."

No mention of what I'd heard. No mention of the blood I'd seen on the sleeve of her habit. I wrestled with the accordion doors on the elevator, desperate to put as much space as possible between myself and that place.

CHAPTER THIRTEEN

The McGill corridor wasn't so different from the ones I remembered from my own days at university—long, dusty, with professors' offices lined up on either side. This wasn't where the labs were, I noted, reviewing my campus map; just where offices and classrooms were located, where academic discussions took place.

Well, I was up for one of those.

The afternoon sun slanted in through the two windows at the end of the hallway, making dust motes dance in the air; and, taking my cue from the few students around, I sat down cross-legged on the floor and pretended to study my notebook. I was still wearing the jeans from my unfortunate interview with Violette Sobel; with any luck, I, too, could look like a postdoc student. Or so I fervently hoped.

From the tone of the voices within, it sounded like Dr. Mac-Dougal and his current student were winding down. I thrust my notebook into my bag and stretched, ready to spring when the door opened. It did at last, two long shadows casting themselves across the corridor, and I clambered ungracefully to my feet. The student was speaking. "Thanks, I'll get back to you with those results."

"Best of luck with them."

I waited until the younger man had departed and turned to the professor. MacDougal was tall, with red hair and freckles and a puzzled look about him. "Hello? Can I help you?"

I stuck out my hand for him to shake. "Professor, my name is Martine LeDuc. I work for the city's tourism board."

He shook my hand, bemused. "Pleased to meet you, *madame*. What can I do for the tourism board?" He was not, I noticed, inviting me in.

"I was told you were the best person to talk to about some of the experiments that were going on at Ravenscrag in the 1970s," I said.

"Really? You were told that?" He looked vaguely amused. "Do I look old enough to have been a faculty member in 1970?"

"You look old enough to try to deflect my questions."

This time the smile was condescending. "Well, Martine LeDuc, you should probably make an appointment. Why don't you leave me a card?" He waited while I fished one out of my purse. "It will be interesting to understand precisely why the tourism board wants to talk about old history."

"It's an old city," I said.

"With some old stories that are best left buried," the professor warned. "Good day, Martine LeDuc."

I could almost hear my husband's voice. *That went well . . .*

* * *

Ivan was working late at the casino so I made myself a grilled cheese sandwich and curled up with a novel. Maybe a connection would come to me unconsciously if I didn't concentrate so hard.

Or maybe I just wanted to get my mind off the investigation.

The phone rang at nine: Julian, my partner in crime. "What are you doing right now?"

"You sound like an obscene phone caller," I said. "Next you'll ask what I'm wearing. I'm enriching my mind, that's what I'm doing. What's up?"

"Checking in on your visit to the corridors of academia." He listened to my narrative of my oh-so-brief encounter at McGill. "Bullshit," he said. "I'll take his picture over to UQAM, I'll bet you anything that's the guy your deputy saw."

"Where did you get his picture?" I asked, curious. Police procedures still baffled me.

"He's published articles, his face has got to be somewhere. I don't know all that much about it but I'll have someone do a search through our databases. If that fails, there's always Google. Maybe you can show it to Mr. Rousseau, too. But in the meantime, let's assume that he's the guy we need."

"I think that's reasonable," I conceded.

"He's clearly scared, otherwise he wouldn't have fobbed you off like that. Maybe you need someone with a little more pull to get him to talk."

"Not my boss," I said immediately. "If this is a real lead, Julian, then the mayor is in over his head. He postures nicely, but the reality is that McGill has clout, and not just in the city or the province, and he knows that: he's not going to do anything to alienate them. We need somebody bigger than McGill if we want to put pressure on them."

"Right," said Julian. "I know what we need. We need entrée into the federal government. That's what we need. Someone in Ottawa."

I smiled; I couldn't help but smile. I hadn't thought of going that way; but now that Julian had pointed it out, the next step was obvious. "I know just the person," I told him.

As soon as we hung up, I called the capital; and thirteen hours later I was in our Volvo, driving west and aware of a growing sense of dread in the pit of my stomach.

Julian called before I was even out of the province. "It's MacDougal," he confirmed. "He and Danielle working together, they were the ones doing the research. Wow. McGill and UQAM working together, who would've thought? Talk about sleeping with the enemy!"

"The enemy of my enemy is my friend," I reminded him. But part of me wished I could see where this all was going.

Because it was going higher than any of us had ever imagined.

I'd met Elodie Maréchal in graduate school. She was my closest friend back then; we went on the occasional vacation together, drank coffee daily, and told each other everything. After we each got our degrees, though, we'd gone our separate ways: I to city government—or at least a reasonable facsimile thereof—in Montréal, Elodie to join the big cheeses in Ottawa.

We'd both gotten married; I had an instant family with Lukas and Claudia while Elodie decided to have her child the old-fashioned way, with her husband taking time off for paternity leave while Elodie continued to work. I can't imagine him ever considering doing anything else: one simply doesn't say no to Elodie.

She worked for the Deputy Minister of National Defense; I wasn't sure exactly *what* it was that she did, but she had whole departments reporting to her at the National Defense Headquarters in the Major-General George R. Pearkes Building on Colonel By Drive; even the names echoed with stiff military bearing.

Elodie wasn't in the military herself but that didn't seem to matter much; she had the authority she deserved and didn't much care what people thought about her beyond that.

I asked for her at the front desk, where security was a major concern; but as it turned out I hadn't needed to as she was already in the lobby. I saw her long before she saw me, across the foyer, talking with some animation to a cluster of men in dark suits around her, gesturing dramatically as she always did. Elodie had started out as the government's nod to the French speakers of Québec and now practically ran the place, her short dark hair framing a pixie face that belied her true spitfire nature. I smiled.

She caught sight of me as the group broke up, doing a rapid scan of the room, like an admiral checking to see that no armada was creeping up on her. "Martine!"

I smiled and gave her the requisite French kisses on each cheek. "Thought I might take you to lunch, *chérie*."

She stared at me. "You came all the way to Ottawa to take me to lunch," she said flatly. "*Bon*. You want something. What exactly is it?"

I shrugged. "Conversation. Some ideas," I said.

She started walking toward the entrance and I kept close. A young man came up with a clipboard; she scanned it and put her initials at the bottom without breaking stride. "Montréal is already the third most popular tourist destination in Canada," she said cheerfully. "Don't know how to move you up farther on the list, Martine."

"It's not about tourists."

Something in my tone must have gotten to her, because she stopped altogether and looked at me. "*Bon*," she said again, still staring, but in an abstracted way as if she were doing sums in her head. "Let's eat."

We went to one of the pubs at the nearby ByWard Market and made small talk as we ordered. Elodie barely waited until the waiter had left the table; she'd always been direct. "You're involved in something," she said. "Are you all right?"

I flushed. "I feel as if I'm going in circles," I admitted. "Maybe I need someone to give me perspective."

There was a twinkle in her pixie face. "Oh, I can do that, all right," she said. "Remember our Government and the Family course?"

"I can't believe you brought that up," I said stiffly, mock-serious. "I told you, I was missing two pages of the assignment."

"Uh-huh. And if I hadn't read your final paper you'd have been laughed off campus. Talk about perspective." She leaned forward. "*Alors*, what is it, Martine? Is it Ivan?"

I stared at her. "Oh, lord, no." But she was right to ask: it *had* been about Ivan for the first two years of our marriage, when I struggled with the complexities, the sheer unfairness, the difficulties, the expectations of being a stepmother. There had been a lot of late-night phone calls to Elodie back then. A lot of electronic wailing. Me sitting on the telephone and drinking too many glasses of red wine and, yes, complaining because my neat little life was getting messed up by someone else's children. Of course that's what she would remember. "No, not Ivan," I said. "It's sort of about work."

"Sort of?" The dark eyebrows rose gracefully. "Speak, Martine," she commanded.

I took a deep breath. "Okay. There have been four murders this summer in Montréal," I said. "Two in July, one in August, one last week. All women. There was a sexual component in each case. The bodies were all left in public places, on benches located in different parts of the city."

She was listening. "I've read about it," she commented, nodding.

"The police think it's a serial sex killer. They think the victims have been chosen either randomly or through some psychosexual pattern that the profilers haven't figured out yet. They have someone in custody—a homeless man who was in the area and who was found with clothing that belonged to two of the women."

"Very circumstantial," observed Elodie, who is married to a lawyer. "Very *convenient.*"

The waiter arrived with drinks and an appetizer. I waited until he departed before continuing. "One of the detectives assigned to the case and I, we've been working on a different theory," I said. "All of the women were connected in some way to the Cité de Saint-Jean-de-Dieu asylum. One of them actually lived there back in the day herself. One's mother lived there.

One was doing research on some medical experiments being performed at the asylum, and another was a reporter who was writing about the whole Duplessis orphans scandal."

Elodie took a swallow of her diet cola and gestured. "Go on."

"So," I said, "we wondered if *that* might be the connection. At first, I thought it was because of the crimes-against-humanity issue. That maybe, either individually or together, they might have been threatening someone who doesn't want to be connected to the past, threatening to take it to trial."

"No one's taking it to trial," she said briskly. Elodie knew all about the orphans. "There's enough evidence against the Church, but the Church isn't going to do anything. They're still talking about 'isolated individual events,' the morons. And the Québec government already paid restitution to the Duplessis gang, back in 2002. Ten thousand dollars per person, and an additional one thousand for every year they were in the asylum; came out to about twenty-five thousand dollars for every orphan involved in the settlement." I didn't ask how she had that information at her mental fingertips; Elodie always seems to know everything. "That wasn't enough, of course, but they were all getting older, and that was the way it was shaking out; so they took the money. At this point it's old news, Martine. No one's going to trial."

"Maybe not," I said. "Or maybe."

The dark eyes were sharp. She put down the glass. "Tell me what you think," she said.

What did I think? It had all seemed so clear, back at McGill. How was I going to make the case to the one person who might be able to help me? I swallowed. "Elodie, I don't think it's about the misappropriation of federal funds or the classification of orphans as mentally ill or even about burying them in unmarked graves, though God knows that's all bad enough." I took a deep breath. "I think it's about the drugs," I said.

She put her elbows on the table and took a deep breath. "The drugs?"

I nodded. "Part of the experiments at the asylum had to do with drugs. Some didn't, the lobotomies and all that—that was different. But they were experimenting with drugs, too, and where there are drugs, there's money."

She was frowning. "Martine," she said, "it's horrifying, I know, we all know, but it's over, it was over a long time ago, most of the people involved are dead, and no one's going to come after—"

"They were working for the CIA," I said flatly. "The experiments were connected to McGill, to the Allan Institute. They had permission to do what they were doing. They had permission from the highest levels of the government. And" —I paused— "this year's an election year."

She stared at me, aghast. "And you think that after all this time—"

"I do," I confirmed. "It's been a busy year for the archives. At least two of the murdered women signed in to them this spring. And we think that a scientist at McGill's been looking into it—discreetly, by using a researcher at UQAM. No one would ever suspect she was working for him: UQAM and McGill are like chalk and cheese. The researcher's one of the victims. The reporter—another one of the victims—has been burning up the lines to the States, getting old classified documents through the Freedom of Information Act." I hesitated. "The only reason I have the researcher's notes is because the killer couldn't get into her system in time. Two of the other victims had computers. Julian told me their hard drives had been wiped. Someone went in and did that, someone who wasn't a serial sex killer." A shiver of fear traveled up my spine. "Elodie, no one could do that unless they weren't working alone. I think MacDougal's involved, but—"

"MacDougal?" she interrupted. "*Christopher* MacDougal?"

"Yes," I said, surprised. "He's the scientist I just mentioned, the one at McGill."

"*Merde, alors*," she muttered, gesturing for the waiter, who came right over. "Your sandwiches will be right up," he assured her. "Never mind," Elodie said briskly, standing up, tossing money on the table. "We have to go."

I was staring at her. "What is it? What's wrong?"

"We have a problem," she said.

CHAPTER FOURTEEN

Elodie's office overlooked the Rideau Canal. I know, because I stood at her window for a very long time looking at it while she was closeted with some highly placed government official in the next room over. I heard the occasional bit of conversation when they raised their voices at each other, Elodie's voice in a higher register than the man's, but just as emphatic.

I stared across the canal. This was making less and less sense to me.

It was another twenty minutes before the door opened and she stormed into the room, slamming it behind her. "Morons," she said, slapping her desk for emphasis. "This administration is staffed by morons."

"What's going on?" I asked, turning away from the view that was by now imprinted on my retinas. "You have to tell me, Elodie. We've got people dying. We've got the wrong person locked up. You *have* to tell me."

"Not if *that* moron has his say, I don't," she said, tossing her head in the direction of the next office. She rummaged around in her desk drawer until she located a package of cigarettes and a lighter. She took one out, lit it, threw the lighter down on the desk with some force, and did a rapid inhale-exhale. "Okay. You're right, the premier is up for reelection. Happy happy joy joy. But his campaign chest isn't what it should be. His campaign chest isn't what it could be. So this past year he's been going after deeper pockets. Corporations."

I sat down on the closest chair. "Drug companies," I said.

She nodded, puffed again on the cigarette. "Specifically, Lansbury Pharmaceuticals."

I could feel a headache building. "They synthesize chlorpromazine," I said, remembering from reading Danielle's research.

She shrugged. "Maybe. Maybe not. Even if they did, they're probably on to more lucrative and cutting-edge drugs now. But you can bet that they were underwriting some of the work done at the Allan Institute, and they knew what was going on in the asylums."

Yep: the headache was there. "What does Dr. MacDougal have to do with it? I don't understand. What's the problem, Elodie?"

"Who do you think finances his work? Gives him grants?" She went over to the television, a flat-screen mounted on the wall. People in public relations *always* have televisions in their offices. Hers, I noted, was far nicer than mine.

Elodie had a tablet computer and was sliding her way through several screens; when she finally found what she was looking for and put it up on the big monitor, I was thinking that it was a very good thing that tablets are virtually indestructible. "A campaign spot," she said tersely, standing back and touching the tablet.

The scene was some city hospital, where parents hovered anxiously over a child in a hospital bed. A doctor came in, peered at a chart, and checked the child's chest with a stethoscope, before turning, beaming, to the parents. "She's going to be just fine," he said, and they burst into cries of delight. He patted the patient reassuringly, stood, and the camera backed up, filming as he walked out the door. "Two years ago, that little girl would have died," he said, looking directly into the lens. "Today, she's going to live, thanks to Lansbury Pharmaceuticals."

He looked off camera to the right, and was joined by the Canadian premier. "It is the government of Jean Callas that has enabled companies such as ours to develop medications that save lives. A vote for Callas is a vote for progress, a vote for life." Appropriate music closed the scene as the two men, beaming at each other, shook hands. The background ran blue.

Elodie clicked it off. "*That's* the problem," she said. I saw just what she meant.

The "doctor" on the tape was Christopher MacDougal.

"Okay," I said. "Let's think about this. Let's not get ahead of ourselves. The premier of Canada has *not* been creeping around Montréal killing off researchers."

Elodie slumped back in her desk chair and rubbed her forehead. "He's got nothing to do with it," she said tiredly. "He probably doesn't even know about it."

I was less sure of that than she was but I let it slide. "Who, then?"

"You're kidding, right? It could be anybody." She frowned. "I don't get it, Martine. This was a political ad financed by Lansbury that used a spokesman from McGill to give it gravitas. That's all, at least, that's all I thought it was. But—I still don't get it. If Christopher MacDougal is working with the government, then why would he be stirring up the past? You know that if the ad works, there will be lucrative returns for both Lansbury and McGill, government grants, subsidies, the whole nine yards. Shouldn't he just be letting things lie?"

"Maybe he's a researcher with a conscience," I said idly. "Elodie, the only way to find out is to pinpoint who they were getting close to."

"They?"

"The murder victims," I reminded her. "That's where it all started, isn't it?"

"No," she said grimly. "It started a long time ago, Martine. And it's not over yet."

"We'll talk as we walk," Julian said, meeting me down on the riverfront.

"You getting paranoid?" I certainly knew that *I* was. Tired from the trip out to Ottawa, and feeling like we were getting close but without a clear direction to take. "They're arraigning the guy they've arrested," I said in frustration.

"I know. Come on, let's go to the pier and look at the boats."

I peered at him. "Are you all right?"

He nodded, resting his arms on the rail, looking down at the high-end yachts clustered around the dock. Directly below us was a yacht larger than my house with a tremendous hot tub on the fantail. Every inch of it was sparkling in the sunlight.

"Nice," I commented, more out of awe than appreciation.

"*Nouveau-riche*," said Julian, who came from the not-so-*nouveau* rich part of town.

A woman in dark glasses, jeans, and a Himalayan jacket strolled over and paused at the railing on the other side of Julian, looking down at the yacht. "A little overdone," she commented to no one in particular; but she said it in English. Julian glanced at her and then looked back at the boat himself. "Francine?"

I gaped, then leaned in to listen as well as I could. Behind us, a group of Japanese tourists had been decanted from a tour bus, their voices high and excited and, for my purposes, far too loud. Who the hell was Francine?

She shook Julian's hand, though she did so furtively. "You will see that no one knows?" she asked.

"I'll make it part of the routine," he said soothingly. "Just to ask them questions. Not as suspects, just part of the fabric of the investigation. I told you. I don't care about anything else. I'm not connected to Vice in any way."

I was starting to get a good idea of who this Francine was. I reached past Julian. "*Bonjour*," I interrupted. "I'm Martine LeDuc."

She looked flustered, but took my hand gracefully enough. Julian cleared his throat. "This is Francine Lescaut," he said to me. "She is—she was—Isabelle Hubert's employer."

The madam. I should have realized that Julian would find her. I smiled encouragingly. "You were saying?"

She glanced over her shoulder, but there was nothing to see but Japanese tourists taking a tremendous interest in the yacht and ignoring us altogether. "I don't want any trouble for my clients," Francine said, her voice anxious, leaning closer to Julian and me.

"There won't be any," he assured her. "You have my word."

She looked from him to me, compressing her lips, and then nodded. Reaching into her bag, she pulled out a thumb drive. "Here," she said. "For Isabelle."

Julian took the drive and slid it into his pocket in one smooth motion. "For Isabelle," he agreed. "You won't regret it."

She nodded again, then turned and shouldered her way past the tourists clustered around us, disappearing almost immediately into the flow of people walking along the waterfront. I jabbed Julian with my elbow. "Clients?"

He nodded. "Let's walk." We moved away from the railing, and the Japanese visitors crowded eagerly to take our place, cameras clicking and whirring.

"It occurred to me," Julian explained, "to think about how Isabelle got involved in all of this. She didn't just start thinking about her mother out of the blue. She didn't do whatever it was that scared somebody without *something* starting her down that road. Something, or someone." He took my arm to steady me as a couple of overenthusiastic Rollerbladers swept by. "And who did she know? Remember, she wasn't one of the girls up on Sainte-Catherine, cruising the losers."

"She was expensive."

"She had clients," Julian said carefully, "at the tops of their professions. All sorts of professions."

My stomach gave a sudden lurch. "Politicians?"

He shrugged lightly, and touched his jacket. "Let's find out."

Three hours later, I was ready to jump out the window. We were sitting in my office, and I'd long since replaced the coffee Chantal had brought us with the bottle of single-malt Scotch I kept in the cupboard under the TV. Nearly everyone had left the building, and the periodic footsteps in the corridor echoed eerily.

It turned out that the question wasn't so much about who was on the list, but who *wasn't*.

I pulled gently on my hair. "This is going nowhere."

Julian sighed, rubbing his eyes. "It's here, somewhere," he said, frustration in his voice. "I know it is."

"It *isn't!*" I sounded petulant and I knew it. "Julian, we've been looking at these names for hours. We don't even know for sure which ones were Isabelle's." Francine had asterisked the names of Isabelle's regular clients, put question marks next to the ones she thought Isabelle might have seen. It wasn't so much that the list was long, it was that we had to stop, go online, and look up every name that we couldn't immediately identify. There had been a number of very long searches.

I was tired and cranky and more than a little scared. It occurred to me that for all we knew, there could be a fifth person out there who was still at risk. And unless we figured this out soon, we could have another death on our hands.

I wish I never had to go to the basement again, I wish that no one ever had to go to the basement again.

"Did you know?" I asked Régine. "Have you been down there?"

She was having none of it. "Hush! Can't you see, we can't speak of that!"

Marie-Rose knew about it, too, but she wasn't talking, as if articulating something made it more real. "Don't talk about it, Gabrielle," she urged me when I asked her what she knew. "Just don't talk about it."

"But the doctors—"

She looked scared. "They hurt people," she said softly. "That's all I know. The other kids say that they hurt people down there."

I heard her say it, but I didn't want to believe it. Oh, not because I thought everyone at the asylum was too kind to hurt anybody—far from it. After all, the sisters hurt people, too. They put us in restraints. They hit us when we were impertinent, or too slow, or too loud. What could go on downstairs that was worse than the howls I'd heard my first night in restraints?

I finally gathered up my courage one day and put my question to Sister Lise. By then I was more confident in my position at the asylum: Sister Marguerite had begun remarking on how responsible I was, how quick, how discreet.

"Sister, what do you do down here?"

"It's not so mysterious," Sister Lise said briskly, as though telling me something perfectly ordinary. "Down here, we try to make people better."

One of the doors to the anteroom opened and a boy stood there. It took me a moment to recognize him: he was taller and stronger than he'd been before.

Bobby.

"Sister," he said, "Dr. Desmarchais is asking for you." He saw me then, and smiled. "Hey, salut, Gabrielle."

"Salut," I responded, not knowing if I should answer or not. If it was allowed.

Sister Lise didn't seem to mind. "Tell him I'll be right there," she said to Bobby, and turned back to me. "It's all for the good of humanity, everything we do is for the greater good. And you're helping, you see, you're all helping to make progress. Now off you go. Sister Marguerite will be needing you."

All for the greater good. I looked at Robert before I left, but all I saw in his eyes was that same dark light that had started the day he stole the cake for me.

I ran into him from time to time after that in the basement. He was impressively smart; he could read and do arithmetic and sometimes he'd grab my hand and drag me outside with him where he produced a packet of cigarettes.

The first time I saw Bobby smoking, I was terrified. "What are you doing?" I breathed in horror. "You'll get in trouble for sure!"

"Not me," he said with a casual smile, putting the cigarette in his mouth, lighting a match and holding it to the end until there was a faint orange glow. He sucked in, then expelled the smoke in one long controlled breath. "Who d'you think gave them to me, anyway?"

"I don't know." All I knew was that my heart was pounding with fear. And excitement.

"The sisters and the doctors," Robert said carelessly.

My eyes widened. "Why?"

He held it out to me. "Want to try?"

I shook my head. "Sister'll know for sure," I said, fighting an impulse to bless myself at the thought. It didn't even matter which sister: one of them would know, and then I'd be in trouble.

"Won't happen. The doctors like me. I help them out," he said carelessly but with a quick glance at me to make sure I was suitably impressed. "I'm their best assistant."

"Bobby," I said, frowning, "everyone knows that they're hurting people down there. How can you do that? How can you help them?"

He took my arm, and I shook his hand off. "Listen, Gabrielle," he said, his voice low and intense. "Do you really want to be nobody for the rest of your life? Nobody, like we were back at the orphanage?"

"Of course not, but sometimes," I stammered, "sometimes parents came to adopt someone. Those kids became somebody."

"Not me," Bobby said. "They never came to adopt me. Or you, Gabrielle." He paused. "Listen, the way to survive here, it's to be useful. I learned that, I learned how to play the game, it's not that hard. And it works. They know my name: all the doctors know my name. They talk to me. They ask me how I am, they ask what I think about things, they want to know my opinion, can you believe that? One of them was talking about sending me to school, he said I'm that smart."

"Good for you."

"It could be good for you, too," and his voice was persuasive again. "Gabrielle, everyone knows you're smart. Sister Lise said so to Dr. Maginot, I heard her. You could have a better life."

"By staying in the basement all the time?"

"By working with them." His eyes were filled with clouds. "When one of the kids is sent down here, I know what to say, I know how to calm them down. And I know a lot of the kids, I can tell the doctors all about them. They appreciate that. You could do that too, Gabrielle."

"I won't." I turned to face him. "I think that maybe if you do something bad all the time, you turn a little bit bad yourself." I pushed myself off the building where I'd been leaning. "I have to go."

Nearly every time I went downstairs after that I saw Bobby, living out his choice, his voice filled with honey and respect as he said, "yes, Doctor," and "no, Doctor," and I wondered if they really were going to send him to school, give him another life, or if they were using him the way they used us all. When I saw him in the basement, we smiled and nodded to each other, him because he could and me because I was starting to get a little scared of him; but inside I just felt cold.

CHAPTER FIFTEEN

Julian went home armed with the thumb drive and prepared to continue the search. I kicked off my shoes and stayed in the office, not ready to face the Métro, not willing to call Ivan and have him pick me up. There was something pricking the back of my brain; a little time alone doing mechanical tasks like answering the e-mails that were piling up might, I thought, be able to jar it loose.

After about half an hour, I slipped my office key in my pocket and padded down the back corridor to use the restroom. I washed my hands and dampened my cheeks, repositioning my chignon, which had slipped a little, blotting a place where my mascara had smudged. On my way back to the office I heard a door shut, somewhere close.

Curious, when it was clear that everybody—on my floor at least—was out of the building. Probably a security guard, I decided. Yes: it had to be a security guard.

As I put the key in my office door, the hallway lights went out.

My pulse started racing. I got the key to turn, slipped in, and closed the door, locking it behind me faster than I'd ever done before. The lights were still on in my office; everything was the way I'd left it. There was a logical explanation for this, there must be.

But it was on tiptoe that I made my way across to the other door, the one that connected with Chantal's office and the main entrance to our suite. I opened it slowly, just a crack; the lights were turned off out there, too.

Had they been on when Julian left?

I couldn't remember. I closed the door again, silently, and forced myself to take several deep breaths. I am fervently anti-handgun so obviously that wasn't an option. The closest thing I had to a weapon was the hairspray I kept in my desk drawer.

I remembered the police reports describing the women who had been killed, how they'd been raped, how they'd been mutilated. My mouth went dry.

I padded back across to my desk, reaching for the telephone. I heard some footsteps in the hallway and the door handle turned.

I screamed. I'll admit it. I am no Nancy Drew; I'm not accustomed to anything more frightening than the child support checks in my life. Screaming is probably not the best response to an emergency situation. I can't say I ran through a whole lot of other options in my mind before I did it.

There was a pause, then someone rapped on the door. "Mrs. LeDuc! Are you all right?"

I froze. Deer-in-the-headlights time. I think I had my hand over my own mouth to keep myself from screaming again.

"Mrs. LeDuc? Please open the door. I know you're there. I don't wish you any harm." This time, I recognized the voice.

Dr. Christopher MacDougal.

I woke up then, I think. Realized that if I was going to handle this, I was going to have to start handling it. I picked up the telephone, checked for a dial tone, and started punching in Julian's number. At the same time, I called out, "I'm fine, thank you, Professor. What are you doing here so late?"

He cleared his throat. "We need to talk, Mrs. LeDuc."

Julian's answering machine. Great. "Professor MacDougal," I said clearly, for both of them to hear, "it's late. I've had a long day and I'd like to go home. Maybe we can talk tomorrow."

"Mrs. LeDuc, really, even *you* must see that it's impossible to carry on a conversation through this door." The condescending tone that I remembered so well.

"I'm sorry," I said. "But it's late and I have promised my husband to take precautions these days." This was sounding really stupid, the cat and the mouse bickering back and forth at each other through a closed door. I found the extension for security and punched it in. "I'm calling security now."

He laughed, a thoroughly unpleasant sound. "Who do you think let me in?"

There was a click in my ear and a voice, blessed, wonderful, human. "*Sécurité.*"

"*Ici Madame* LeDuc," I said, crisply and loudly. "I desire an escort to the street, please, and a taxi." To hell with the cost. "Please send someone to my office now."

"*Bien, madame.*"

Silence from the corridor. I didn't hear any steps receding down the hallway, didn't hear anything at all for a good two to three minutes, when there was an authoritative rap on the door. "Madame LeDuc? *Sécurité.*"

I grabbed my jacket and purse, thrust my feet hurriedly back into my shoes, then opened the door. The navy blue of the uniform and the vaguely familiar face were reassuring. The lights, I noted, were turned on. "Did you let someone in the building to see me?"

He looked surprised. "*Non, madame.* No one has come in since six o'clock."

"I see." I didn't say anything else until he'd flagged down a cab for me and I thanked him and gave the driver my destination. I sat in the back and didn't think, didn't cry, didn't do anything but shake.

Ivan wasn't home. There was a note on the kitchen table: "Went to play racquetball with André," it said. "Page me if you need me."

I paged him, then called Julian's mobile. "Hey, Martine, what's up?" He sounded as if he were at a party.

"Have you checked your voice mail?"

"No, why, what's wrong?"

I shivered, looking around me again for reassurance. As soon as I'd gotten in I'd made sure all the doors and windows were locked, all the drapes drawn, and I still felt a long way from safe. The Scotch I'd drunk earlier was turning sour in my stomach. "MacDougal was at my office."

"When? Tonight?"

"Yeah. He—it creeped me out, Julian. I think it was meant to."

"Probably." Somewhere in the background there was laughter, quickly smothered. "Where are you now?"

"I'm home. I'd better get off the line, Ivan's probably trying to call me. Check him out, Julian, will you?"

Ivan called as soon as I'd hung up. "Hey, babe, what's up?" He sounded slightly breathless.

"Get here," I said tersely. I think I was about to collapse.

He didn't waste time asking questions. There are many things I love about my husband, and his ability to read me—and respond—is one of the best of them.

By the time he got home, I was drinking Côtes du Rhône, wrapped in a wool shawl, and still shivering. I couldn't seem to get warm enough. As soon as Ivan walked into the room, I burst into tears.

Another thing I love about Ivan is that he knows when to talk and when to shut up. That night, he held me, and rocked me, and didn't say a single word for an hour. I love my husband.

Julian was delighted.

I have to say I was less than thrilled with his reaction. "Someone's getting nervous," he said the next morning, back at my office. "It means we're getting close."

I observed sourly, "The last time someone got close, she also got dead."

He was undaunted. "If they wanted you dead, you'd be dead," he said. "That was a warning."

I shivered. "I could do without another one. Are we making any progress? Did you go through Francine's lists last night?"

He looked at me, grinned, looked out my office window, and looked back at me. "You and *Francine* went through Francine's lists last night," I concluded. "Julian, stop looking so damned pleased with yourself. You can't flirt your way through this investigation. Did you find anything?"

He was unabashed. "Got a couple of options," he said.

I gestured him into the seat across from my desk. I was feeling like pulling rank on him. "Tell me."

He didn't sit down. He came around the desk and put his hand on my shoulder gently. "I'm sorry I wasn't there for you last night, Martine," he said softly. It was oddly touching. I looked at the picture of Ivan and Lukas and Claudia at the amusement park and swallowed hard. "It's okay," I said. "I'm okay. Tell me what you found."

He sat on the edge of my desk. "Francine left a page off the list," he said. "For what seemed to her to be obvious reasons. I guess we'd call it the political page."

"That alone could get anyone hurt; I understand her reticence."

"Ah, but it's hard to stand up to my boyish charm," Julian pointed out, feigning innocence. "Anyway, we've got an embarrassment—and I use the term advisedly—of riches. People in politics. People in entertainment. People in business." He took a deep breath and a mischievous smile played with the corners of his mouth. "Fletchers."

"*Oh, là, là,*" I commented under my breath. "But that just means they were seeing a call girl—it doesn't mean there was any connection to the drug experiments. Wait," I said, noticing his look. "You're holding something back, aren't you?"

He nodded, almost gleeful. "Last two names on the list," he said. "My boss . . . and yours."

"The mayor and the *directeur du service*?" It was almost comical. "Good thing she didn't work out of a bordello. Those two would have killed each other if they'd ever crossed paths . . ." My voice trailed off. "Julian, the director is still holding that *clochard*, that homeless man."

"Don't jump to conclusions," he said. "Our work isn't done. Let's file these for now. I'm going to see Mrs. Sobel. My mother gave her a call."

"Your *mother*?"

He shrugged. "Told you my family connections would come in handy. When my mother calls, people listen. And obey."

I spared a brief thought for what *his* childhood must have been like.

Julian was looking at me. "What are you going to do about MacDougal?"

"I should probably beard him in his lair," I said, "but frankly, I'm too scared to do it." Also, I had promised Ivan the night before that I would not. "I'm not sure what he's up to, Julian. Last night . . . well, yeah, it was scary, but it was a little obvious, wasn't it?"

"A warning," he said again.

"But what's he warning me to do? Keep investigating? Stop investigating? He could have been just a bit clearer, you know."

There was a knock on the door, and Richard stuck his head in. "I'm sorry to interrupt, Martine," he said formally.

I waved him in. "Richard, this is *détective-lieutenant* Julian Fletcher from the SPVM."

He nodded and they shook hands; they'd obviously met before. Richard turned back to me. "I wanted to remind you that I'll be in late tomorrow. It's Danielle Leroux's funeral."

Something caught in my throat. "*Bien sûr*," I said automatically. I'd completely forgotten the other rituals in my single-mindedness about Danielle's death. "Is there a wake tonight?"

He nodded. "At the funeral home. Then tomorrow at Saint-Denis church."

I glanced at Julian. "I'll go to the wake," I said. "Thanks, Richard. Take all the time you need." And if something didn't get done because we were both paying our respects, well, that was fine. Francine's list had, if nothing else, given me something to keep in my back pocket for when the mayor next chose to blame me for Montréal's lapses in perfection.

As the door closed behind my deputy, Julian said, "While I'm talking to Violette, you might want to take on the Providence Foundation. Could be that something came up in conjunction with Annie's work that sparked her interest."

I shook my head in frustration. "You said her computer there was wiped. Nothing on the hard drive."

"Yes, well, it's not all about computers, Martine," Julian said cheerfully, pushing himself off my desk and heading toward the door. "You can actually talk to real people too, you know." He sketched a salute and was gone.

Real people. Now there's a quaint concept.

I called Ivan to tell him where I was going, part of the agreement we'd made the night before. "What if you're in a meeting?" I'd asked when he made me promise to keep him informed of my whereabouts.

"Screw the meetings, my wife's welfare is more important."
He hesitated. "I don't suppose I can talk you out of any of this,
can I? Get you to hand all your information over to the police
and have them do their job, instead of you doing it for them?"

"They're not doing their job," I said. "Except for Julian. And
nobody over there takes him very seriously."

"I just wish it didn't have to be you, babe."

You and me both, I thought.

CHAPTER SIXTEEN

It took me about twenty minutes on the Métro to get to Sherbrooke and another ten to walk to the foundation where Annie had worked. The building that housed it was old and imposing: it had been one of the fur trader's mansions, with the requisite stone lions flanking the impressive front doors. If you didn't know that philanthropy went on inside, you'd never dare ring the bell.

It was answered after a lapse of a minute or so by a young woman dressed in a little black nothing dress and a string of pearls. Probably real ones, and that dress was a Harvé Benard.

Apparently people who gave money away had a decent amount of it to keep, as well.

She was friendlier than she looked, though, and within minutes I was ensconced in a comfortable leather chair in a more than comfortable library-cum-drawing room, with tea being ordered. No one in these high places did anything without first serving beverages of some sort, it seemed.

Presently an elderly man shuffled in, apparently oblivious to my presence, and began perusing books on one of the shelves behind me. Innocent enough, but the hairs on the back of my neck were standing up all the same. After last night, the last thing I needed was someone creeping up on me from behind. Never mind that this particular guy didn't seem to be the creeping sort.

It was a relief when the door opened and a middle-aged woman came in. Neat conservative suit, glasses, hair that—like mine—seemed to defy hairpins. "Madame LeDuc? My name is Elizabeth Romfield. I understand that you are investigating Annie Desmarchais's death."

"Yes," I acknowledged, standing to shake her hand, sitting again as she indicated I should. "I have a few questions—"

"I am at your disposal," she said pleasantly, sitting in a matching leather chair across from mine. "Annie was my closest friend for the past twenty years," she added, her voice quiet and echoing with loss. "Anything that I can do to help, I will."

"I appreciate that," I said, awkwardly. "And I'm so sorry for your loss, *madame*."

There was a moment of silence while I slid my ever-present notebook from my bag, trying to organize my thoughts as I did. I still uncomfortably felt the presence of the old man at my back. "*Madame*, what can you tell me about Annie's work here at the Providence Foundation?"

"In general?"

I shrugged. "In general, in specific. Everything can be useful."

"I see." She smoothed an already-smooth skirt, then met my eyes. "Well, as you probably know, she was one of the founders. I don't know where the name came from. It was established initially with a grant made by Annie and Violette Sobel, her sister. The money was inherited from their father, though I believe each of them was left well off by their respective husbands. Violette has little interest in the day-to-day functioning of the foundation, though she attends board meetings, as is proper. But from the beginning, Annie wanted to be a part of it, and I believe that her involvement was a prerequisite of the grant. She reviewed applications and did the first level of triage."

I looked up. "Triage?"

"Not all grant applications can be accepted," Elizabeth explained. "Not all, in fact, are appropriate. Annie decided which ones to deny right off and which ones to pass on to the committee for review. Beyond that, she also did her own research, bringing possible recipients to our attention, candidates who in many cases had not heard of the Providence Foundation but could benefit from it."

"I see." I hesitated. "I'm afraid you'll have to start at the beginning. What sorts of grants are offered? For what, exactly? And what kind of money is involved?"

Elizabeth got up and went to the far end of the room, where she removed a binder from a shelf. Taking a glossy folder from the binder, she resumed her seat, passing it over to me. "Here is general information you can take with you," she said.

I took the brochure. "I've actually seen this already, on the website," I said, half apologetically. "I just wanted to hear the more personal side of the foundation work."

"Well then, to answer your question, we have a wide range of grants. We start at a thousand dollars and go up into the hundred-thousands on some rare occasions. Most grants are for between ten and twenty thousand dollars. We give only to institutional recipients, not individuals. While we consider any proposal based on its merit, we have traditionally put a lot of money into the private mental health system."

I watched her. "That seems logical," I said.

She raised her eyebrows. "Logical, Mrs. LeDuc?"

"In view of Annie Desmarchais's own past."

There was a moment of silence. "I'm not sure I understand," Elizabeth said, more stiffly.

I exhaled in exasperation. "Why is this the best-kept secret around? Honestly, you'd think it was something that everyone's ashamed of! Ms. Romfield, Annie lived for the first ten years of her life in a mental institution, one where mental health was the least expected outcome. Children there were little more than test subjects for some sort of shadow medical establishment. And she got out of there, and she managed to get an education, she managed to do well, and give back to others. That's something that she—and everyone who knew and cared about her—should have been trumpeting from the rooftops! And instead, everyone's acting like it's something awful, something to be ashamed of. If there's something here that I'm not understanding, I'd appreciate it if you'd explain it to me."

She stayed quiet for a moment after my outburst, and in the silence, the old man behind me dropped a book. I'd forgotten his presence altogether.

Elizabeth smoothed her skirt again. "Mrs. LeDuc—may I call you Martine? So much easier . . . You have to understand, that's a part of Québec's past that we'd all like to forget."

"I know the rhetoric," I said. "Believe me, I know. Don't forget that I'm the *directrice de publicité*: I even helped write part of it myself. So don't bother going through the paces with me now." I leaned forward. "You say that you were her best friend. Then do something for her now, Elizabeth. Find out why she died. Make sure that whoever did this to her pays."

A flicker of a glance over my shoulder, so quick that I might have imagined it. But I hadn't. "Annie didn't like to discuss her past," she said quietly. "It was a horrible experience that she did her best to eradicate from her memory." She looked directly at me. "You seem to know what was going on in the asylums. If that had happened to you, would you want to remember it? Or even think of it again? It's the stuff of nightmares."

"The nightmares caught up to her," I said.

A sharp intake of breath. "Surely that had nothing to do with her death! I read in the newspaper that they've arrested the killer."

"They've made an arrest," I acknowledged. "Did Annie participate in any of the lawsuits against the government? Was she part of any of the orphans' groups?" She hesitated, and I added, as gently as I could, "It's a matter of public record, you know. I'll find it out anyway—you might as well tell me."

Again that flicker, no more, of attention to the man who was now silent behind me. For all I knew, he'd gone to sleep, or died, or I was getting paranoid. I cleared my throat and Elizabeth Romfield made her decision. "Annie spoke rarely of her past," she said, as though acknowledging a defeat at chess. "It was, for her, like looking back into a dark cave. An apt simile, as I'm sure you'll agree." She smoothed her skirt again. "When she was adopted, she was given tutors. Round the clock, practically;

all she remembers is studying. And doctors, doctors of all sorts, asking interminable questions."

"It seems extraordinary that she could have caught up like that," I murmured, since she seemed to be waiting for me to say something.

"It was," she agreed. "Annie Desmarchais was an extraordinary woman."

She examined her nails for a moment. I reread my notes. No one in the room moved or made a sound. Finally, she spoke again. "Her father was himself a doctor," she said. "He had inherited wealth, so he had no need to work. But he was fascinated by mental illness and how it could be overcome."

I stared at her. "Then adopting Annie was a kind of *experiment*?" I asked, aghast.

She shrugged, looking at her hands as though not knowing what to do with them. She ended up clasping them in her lap. "I cannot speak to his motivations," she said, still looking at her hands, her voice precise and careful. "There had been a death in the family. That seemed reason enough to adopt. I'm sure that he meant nothing but the best for both his daughters." She looked up at me. "He arranged for their education. He arranged for good marriages for both of them."

"He *arranged* for their marriages?" I asked. "Wasn't that a little old-fashioned?" A man who sends his daughters to college but arranges their marriages, I thought. Was I the only one who found that a little weird?

She tipped her head, considering. "Perhaps. But the old families have old-fashioned values. It certainly didn't seem to shock anyone at the time."

I looked at her sharply. "At the time? You knew Annie then?" I'd assumed they'd met through the foundation.

"Of course," she said. "Annie and I were in school together. She was enrolled starting in sixth form; I remember us all thinking that was a little odd, but she only said she'd been abroad. And we accepted that, of course."

I readjusted my thinking to accommodate this new information. "Did she ever discuss her past with you?"

A shadow crossed Elizabeth's face. Annie had talked about it, all right. "Occasionally," she said, flicking an imaginary piece of lint off her sleeve. "Once we were adults. But mostly we talked about the future."

"What about her father? You said he was a doctor; was he a psychiatrist?"

She looked pained. "I don't see how sullying his memory is going to do any good!" she exclaimed. "Martine, really, I want to help you, but—"

"Then help me," I said. "Help Annie."

Another stretch of silence. "He *was* a psychiatrist," she conceded at last. "He was in private practice, but he had some sort of affiliation—don't ask me, I honestly don't know what—with the asylum where Annie had been living. And with the Allan Institute, through some work he'd done at McGill. Even when she was in her teens, he still went back there occasionally. Maybe regularly." She looked again at her pristine fingernails. "Please understand, this was the seventies. We are all a product of our times."

Just get on with it, I pleaded silently.

She took a deep breath. "We were, all of us, very concerned

about what was happening in the Soviet Union, about the spread of Communism," she said at last. "Dr. Desmarchais was passionately anti-communist. Well, so many people were in those days, weren't they? He felt that we should all do our part to help keep the free world free."

"And what was his part?" I asked, my voice barely above a whisper. I thought I already knew.

She shrugged and used my own expression. "You can make the inferences."

"He was involved with the experiments," I said. "With the mind-altering drugs."

She nodded. "He thought that there could be some use for a drug that would incapacitate a subject's ability to think and to remember. It was all so very convenient. You see, no court of law can rule against psychological warfare because of the difficulty in prosecuting psychologically induced states of mind as proof of assassinations and other orchestrated events."

"Uh-huh."

"And, you know, everyone back then was so concerned about what was happening in the United States," she said. "Take Robert Kennedy's assassination. Let's face it, nobody just picks up a gun on some sunny day and decides that all of a sudden they're going to start shooting people. The precision and cold, calculating nature of the shooter has to be thoroughly ingrained into a subject with rigorous conditioning and mind control."

"Uh-huh," I said again.

She looked up then and met my eyes, sensing my withdrawal. "It's irrelevant, anyway," she said briskly. "He wasn't the only one doing the experiments, and he died a long time ago. I cannot see that this has any connection with a murder that happened over half a century later."

"Was Annie one of his subjects?"

She looked me straight in the eyes. "I don't know."

I shook my head. "With all due respect, Elizabeth, I don't believe you. She was your best friend for years. You can't tell me she didn't tell you."

"She didn't know!" Her hands went into a frenzy of straightening her already-perfect clothing. "She didn't know. Once she was older, once she went to university and started understanding what he'd done, she wondered, yes. She asked him! But he denied it, he always denied it."

"She came to his attention for some reason," I pointed out. "Why did he adopt *her*, out of all the children in that place?"

"We wondered that, too," Elizabeth replied. "Annie was sure that there was something dark behind it all; but her parents would never tell her, and Violette was too young to know, so she never found out."

"Maybe she did," I said.

The look she gave me was pure anguish. "I hope you're wrong," Elizabeth Romfield said. "I pray to God that you're wrong."

When I looked to see what had become of our audience, the old man was gone. There was no one there. I wondered if there ever had been.

I grabbed a coffee and a sandwich at the closest St. Hubert, and headed back to the Old Port. Chantal was typing, Richard's door was closed, everything was fine. "You've had three calls from Ottawa," Chantal said. "You know that smartphone the office bought you? You're supposed to keep it turned on."

"What's the problem?"

"Don't know. Someone named Elodie Maréchal. Said you'd know who she was."

I was already looking at the pink slips. "Thanks, Chantal," I said. "Can you get her on the phone for me now, please?"

I shut my door and waited at my desk for the call to go through. I knew that I'd upset Elodie. Let's see if anything had come of it.

Chantal buzzed her through almost immediately. "Martine?" Elodie asked plaintively. "When are you going to learn to answer your mobile?"

I sighed, cradling the telephone against my shoulder as I removed my shoes. "*Et tu, Brute*," I murmured. "I was busy."

"So it seems. Okay, here's what I've got for you. This guy is willing to talk, but *only* if you don't know who he is."

"Talk about . . . ?"

"The drugs. The experiments. The whole thing."

I could feel my heart rate quicken. "Does he know of a connection between that and the murders?" I asked.

"If anybody knows, he will," Elodie predicted. "He's high up, Martine. I mean, *really* high up." There was a burst of static. "Can he call you tonight?"

This was a call that I didn't particularly want to be traceable to my home telephone, and after last night, I wasn't staying late at the office for a while. Besides, I had plans. "I have to go to a wake tonight, Elodie. Can he call tomorrow?"

"I'll check." She sighed. "You may have opened a big can of worms here, *mon amie*."

"Better to have left it a secret?" I countered.

"You make a good point. Be in your office in the morning, *chérie*. I'll tell him you'll be there."

"Thanks, Elodie." I knew that if this all blew up, heads would roll, and hers could well be on the chopping block. She probably knew it, too.

"Yes, well, let's wait and see how it all shakes out." Oh, yeah: she knew.

I sighed and called Julian. No answer. He was starting to become as elusive as the ghosts we were chasing.

Ivan, on the other hand, was at his desk. "I'm going to Danielle Leroux's wake tonight," I told him. "Can you come along?"

He thought about it. "Bad guys going to be there?"

"I wish I knew."

"Okay, sure. Let me just put out a couple of fires here and I can get away. Want to get a bite to eat first?"

"Is that an invitation?"

"Of course." He yawned. "Gotta go play some poker, babe. Where and when?"

I thought quickly. "Meet me at La Raclette on Saint-Denis at six-thirty. Can you? That's close enough to the funeral home to walk over after." And I hadn't had fondue in ages.

He groaned. Ivan has a very American approach to walking: he doesn't do it much. "That means it's about sixteen blocks away," he said.

"Ah, but every one of them in my scintillating company," I reminded him. "Thanks, sweetheart."

"No problem. Watch yourself until then, okay?"

"Doing my best." I hung up and wondered if that were true, then eased back into my shoes. It was time to go talk to the police director, and see if he'd extracted a confession from his prisoner.

I fully expected that he had.

I worked with Régine, but my closest friend at the asylum was Marie-Rose. She'd come with me from the orphanage, on the same bus even, but we really only got to know each other once we'd worked on the farm together. She was younger than me, though by how much—who could say? As I said before, we didn't celebrate birthdays.

We didn't celebrate anything at all.

Marie-Rose and I contrived to have beds next to each other in the dormitory, which gave us the opportunity to whisper together when Sister's back was turned. Those conversations, I have to say, kept me going for a long time. They assured me that I was not, in fact, going crazy myself.

It was an easy enough belief to espouse. People were mean and then said they did it to be kind. People treated one like an animal and then said it was for one's own good. People hurt other people—children, even—and then said it was to make the world a better place. Who wouldn't sometimes feel a little crazy?

"Maybe we're the crazy ones," said Marie-Rose.

"No!" I said it fiercely; but sometimes, in the night, it was something that I wondered, too. Who was crazy here?

Sometimes as I went about my work, bringing notes to disparate parts of the building, I caught a glimpse of the occasional—and rare—*visitor being ushered into the large bright parlor that the sisters reserved for outsiders. What did they think of the place, I wondered. What did they think of the scrubbed walls and gleaming floors, the fresh flowers that were always in the entrance hall, the smiling faces of the sisters who met with them? Did they think that good things happened here?*

Once I carried a message to the sister in the hydrotherapy room. Here they tried to make people less crazy by putting them in baths of cold water, adding ice cubes to make sure it stayed cold, keeping them there for hours. I was no doctor, I said once to Régine, but I didn't see how cold water made crazy people less so. She did her usual quick scan around to make sure that no one could hear us. "They only send the women there," she said.

"What does that mean?"

"Experiments," was all she'd say, and I never really understood what she meant. But there was so much at the asylum that I didn't understand. "Keep your head down and pray it doesn't happen to you," was Régine's counsel, and it was good advice.

There was so much there that I prayed would never happen to me. But I suspected that everyone in the building was praying the same thing, and it didn't work for a whole lot of them, did it?

CHAPTER SEVENTEEN

Ivan was late. Ivan is often late. It's one of the few things that I *don't* love about my husband.

I flipped through my notebook while I was waiting. Julian had been right: there was no way that I would ever have kept any of this straight in my head if I hadn't written it down. As it was, I was *still* having trouble keeping everything straight in my head.

My wine arrived and I sipped it slowly, reflectively, looking to see if there was some connecting thread I had missed. I got to the interview with Violette Sobel and wondered if Julian had had more luck with her, and if so, when exactly he planned to share that information with me. I read a little aimlessly, my hand turning the pages automatically . . .

And stopped. Violette had said that Annie and her husband had tried to have children, but they hadn't been able to. Okay, I know, so a lot of people have infertility problems. But let's pair that with Annie's past and the percentages start rising. I didn't know if the Duplessis orphans were infertile, but with what had gone on at the asylum, I wouldn't ignore the possibility.

It was a poker hand, I thought, that Ivan would surely bet on.

Annie must have been part of the experiments, part of the program. She had been adopted, I thought, either out of guilt or—I would bet—because Dr. Desmarchais was conducting a little experiment of his own. Take a damaged child and put her in an optimum environment. Does she survive?

I shook my head. No: he'd been interested in drugs, in using pharmaceuticals to combat Communism and make the world safe for democracy. Annie had nothing to do with that, surely.

By the time Ivan arrived I was more puzzled than ever.

He was in high spirits. "Getting closer to tournament approval," he said. The Montréal Casino was applying to be a stop on a number of world poker tours; it would be important for Ivan to secure its status. The question had been occupying him, off and on, for over a year.

I raised my glass. "Congratulations, sweetheart."

"Thanks." He looked around for a waiter. "What are you drinking?"

"Côtes du Rhône," I said. "But don't get a bottle unless you want to drink it yourself; we have a wake to go to, and I probably shouldn't be tipsy for it."

"Ah, yes. Danielle Leroux." He put his hand over mine. "I'm unaccustomed to being married to an investigator, my love. Sorry." He paused. "I won't tell you how worried I am about you," he resumed conversationally. "Because I know how little you'd appreciate it."

"I'll consider it said." I smiled. "Thanks for caring, Ivan."

He squeezed my hand before releasing it. "My pleasure, babe."

The funeral home was filled to overflowing. There were snacks in the front room, Danielle's coffin in the back, flowers and insipid piped-in music surrounding us. The coffin was closed, and I remembered the photographs I'd looked at, that first day, at the police station.

I found her brother sitting near the coffin, a faded-looking overweight woman in a tight black dress sitting next to him, a glass of wine untouched and perhaps even forgotten in her hand. "Monsieur Leroux?" I asked in French. "I don't know if you remember me, we spoke a couple of days ago. My name is Martine LeDuc." I gestured behind me. "*Je vous présente mon mari*, Ivan Petrinko." The two men shook hands gravely. "Monsieur Leroux, again, I'd like to say that I'm very sorry for your loss."

He raised mournful eyes. "The police have caught her killer," he said, his voice dull. "Thank you for your help."

I exchanged glances with Ivan; he nodded and turned to the woman sitting next to Jacques. "Madame Leroux," he said, extending his hand to her. "Please accept the expression of our most sincere condolences." Okay, so it sounds better in French, even with Ivan's accent.

She started murmuring a reply in her upriver accent that Ivan would never understand and I turned to her husband. "Will you be staying on in Montréal to settle your sister's affairs?" I asked.

He shrugged. "There is little to settle," he said. "The funeral is tomorrow. We will clean her apartment and we will go home."

His callused hand sought and found that of his wife and closed around it, whether for support or to support her, it was hard to say. It was a curiously touching gesture.

I wasn't about to shatter what little peace they were finding here. I gave him my card. "Please, *monsieur*, if you need any assistance, call on me."

He looked at it and then looked back to me. "I thought you were with the police," he said dully.

Oops. "Not officially," I said, "though I have been helping them with their inquiries." A phrase that could cover a plethora of situations. "*Monsieur*, if there is anything in your sister's affairs that strikes you as unusual, will you call me then, too?"

He laboriously put the card in a pocket without letting go of his wife's hand. I knew how that felt, I knew how many times Ivan's touch had been a lifeline for me. "But they caught the man," he said again.

I shrugged. "There are always details," I said cryptically. "And he has yet to go to trial."

"*Bien, alors.*" Our audience was clearly over. Ivan was still saying nice things to Madame Leroux and receiving incomprehensible replies in return. I shook her hand and we walked away.

"What now?" Ivan was eyeing the sweets table. "Besides the pastries, I mean."

It was a good question. I saw Richard, across the room, deep in conversation with the woman I'd met the first day I went to the UQAM library; but it was Ivan who suddenly pulled me aside. "Shit. Who *was* this woman, anyway?" he asked, his voice low and intense.

"What? Why? What do you mean?"

He turned his back to the other people. "The three guys over there? In the expensive suits? *Don't look*," he added quickly. "They're Americans. *Persona non grata* at the casino. Lots of money, lots of connections, got thrown out and asked not to return because they were trying to take over some of the action."

He was talking like somebody in a Rat Pack movie, and I said so. "What does that mean, anyway, take over the action?"

"I don't have time to give you gambling lessons, Martine," Ivan said impatiently. "I'll be happy to explain at length later. What you need to be asking yourself is why they're here, at the wake of a relatively unimportant librarian."

I leaned up to kiss his cheek, and glanced at the three men he had indicated. He was right, of course. "Do they have government connections?" I asked softly.

Ivan shrugged. "Who doesn't, these days?"

It was a non-answer. I looked around again. Maybe Richard had an idea of who was who in the room; it appeared he was the closest thing Danielle had to a friend. "Okay," I said, "wish me luck."

Ivan started to say something but I was already halfway across the room. The three suits were blending in well, on the whole, without getting too far from one another. They were all in their mid-forties: the one closest to me had an acne-scarred face and eyes that never seemed to stay still. The other two were slightly older, slightly more florid; one of them was engaged in conversation with a familiar-looking woman. Ah, yes: the landlady; she'd let Julian and me into Danielle's apartment.

Fools rush in, I thought, mentally blessing myself with the

sign of the cross. I had a feeling I was going to need all the help I could get. I went over to acne-face with my hand outstretched. "Good heavens, it's Christian!" I exclaimed in French. "What are you doing here? I didn't know you were a friend of Danielle's!"

He wasn't flustered in the least. "You have me confused with someone else," he said, his voice flat, his accent American, his French surprisingly accurate.

I frowned, and raised my voice ever so slightly. "But I'm sure of it! We met at the party at the consulate!" I managed a flirtatious giggle. "Don't tell me you don't remember me, Christian!"

Now he was looking slightly uncomfortable. "You're mistaken," he said, glancing at me and then away.

"Hard to believe. We had such a good time that night. Of course, if you'd rather *pretend* you don't know me . . ." My voice trailed off and I glanced around with a rueful smile. Several people gave uneasy smiles back, no doubt wondering if I planned to make a scene.

Good: I was hoping he was wondering the same thing.

One of his colleagues drifted over. "Is there a problem?" he asked in English, his smile pleasant, his eyes hard.

Before Acne-Face could respond, I had turned to the new arrival. "I am so sure that Christian and I met," I said, my English as heavily accented as I could manage. "Were you at the party at the consulate, too?"

He looked blandly from Acne-Face to me. "I don't believe we've ever met." Another American accent. "Will you excuse us, Miss–er—?"

"LeDuc," I said automatically, then mentally kicked myself.

I was way too naïve to be playing this game. Lying was *not* second nature.

He nodded, clearly filing the name away for future reference, while I mentally used up every swear word I knew. "Excuse us, Miss LeDuc," he said pleasantly and led Acne-Face away.

Ivan was at my elbow. "That went well," he remarked. "Remind me to change the locks when we get home."

"*Merde,*" I said miserably. "I had a chance there—"

"To find out what?" he asked. "We have files on them at the casino, babe. I'll bet the police do too. We can find out anything you need without making yourself a target."

"Maybe he'll forget," I said hopefully.

"And maybe you'll win the World Series of Poker. Anyway, onward and upward. Hey look, your boss is here."

And indeed he was, the mayor looking distinguished in a dark suit, his wife elegant in her usual designer clothes. Their son was with them, a twenty-something with a gargantuan ego who was attending UQAM and playing in a local rock band with an improbable name. Patrick, that was his name.

I waited until the trio had gone through the motions by the coffin and murmured the required platitudes to the family, and then I drifted over. "*Monsieur le maire,*" I said pleasantly. "How thoughtful of you to be here."

"Ah, Madame LeDuc," he said. "So sad, of course. *La pauvre petite.* Good news about the arrest, though, a fitting end to a sad chapter in the city's history."

"Indeed," I said noncommittally, and offered my hand to his wife. "Madame Boulanger."

Estelle Boulanger received me as the wife of a landowner

might have noticed a tenant-farmer. "Madame LeDuc," she said, her hand limp in mine, her gaze fixed somewhere just slightly over my head. Patrick, their son, offered me a sneer. I concluded that he didn't want to shake hands. "*Bonsoir*, Patrick."

He turned to his father. "I'm getting something to eat," he said, and walked away. Big loss. I cleared my throat. "*Monsieur*, do you know the gentlemen over there—"

But they were gone.

CHAPTER EIGHTEEN

I slept fitfully, dreaming about endless corridors and doctors with bleeding scalpels in their hands.

Ivan was doing his usual routine of reading e-mails and news from his tablet over breakfast, but I caught him sneaking glances at me. "What is it?" I exclaimed at last, impatient.

He mumbled something incoherent and went back to staring at the screen, and a few moments later he was stealing glances again. "Oh, I give up," I muttered, and left early for the office.

Theoretically, my job was done. There had been an arrest: the homeless man they'd arrested was going to a preliminary hearing; I didn't have to keep playing go-between. But until I was officially told to, I wasn't about to stop. I'd just stop meeting with the director of police, which wasn't going to exactly ruin my day. Nor his, come to think of it.

Richard was out for the funeral and Chantal had a toothache. "Go ahead." I waved her away and called downstairs to get someone out of the secretarial pool to help. I called Julian, who didn't answer—there was a surprise. I was beginning to think he'd left the planet altogether.

I dealt with e-mails for a while and got myself a second coffee before leafing through my notebook again. Julian called in. "Hey, there, what's up?"

"Where the hell are you?" I asked crossly.

"Nice to talk to you, too, Martine," he said cheerfully. "I'm on my way to Danielle's funeral, actually."

"Watch for three middle-aged Americans in fancy suits," I said, forgetting for a moment that I was mad at him. "They were at the wake last night. Ivan says they're connected in some way; Connected with a capital C, that is."

"In what way? And what's their interest in Danielle?"

"I don't know. Maybe something, maybe nothing, who knows. I'm waiting for a call from Ottawa and then I'm heading over to the casino—Ivan says he'll get security there to let me look at their files."

He raised his eyebrows. "How does Ivan know them?"

I sighed. "The thing about a casino is that nothing's private. There are cameras everywhere, and files open on the most amazing people. Or so I gather." I shrugged. "Confidentiality's a big thing, too."

"Meet me afterward, then," he said. "We'll compare notes." There was a pause, and I heard him swearing at someone and informing them that they could not drive. I deduced that he was in traffic, probably weaving in and out of it in his TT. I was beginning to think that he wasn't going to live long enough to finish this investigation. "Listen, Martine, meet me over in the Plateau, okay? Two o'clock at McKibbins?"

"Fine," I said, and hung up. Almost immediately the phone rang again.

"Mrs. LeDuc? Christopher MacDougal here."

My stomach turned over slowly. "Hello, Professor," I said.

"I'd like to clear up a misunderstanding. Detective Fletcher seems to think that I had ulterior motives in coming to see you in your office the other night."

Well, at least Julian had done something about *that*. "What do you want?" I asked. And then, as another thought struck me, "I'd have thought you'd be on your way to Danielle Leroux's funeral now. Apparently you knew her quite well."

There was a slight pause. "We seem to have gotten off on the wrong foot here. I have a suspicion that we're on the same side."

"People on my side don't turn out lights and creep down corridors trying to break into offices at night," I said. "I don't think I have anything to say to you."

"Perhaps not. But I would very much like to talk to you, Mrs. LeDuc. It could be—mutually beneficial."

I gave up. The problem was that he was right. "Fine. In a public place. In the daytime."

"Absolutely. Today?"

"I'll be on the Plateau this afternoon," I said. "Meet me in the Parc Lafontaine at four o'clock, all right? In front of the bistro." I disconnected before he had the chance to respond.

Who *was* this guy, anyway?

I'd had three cups of coffee and was wondering when the

hell the secretarial pool was going to send someone so that I could go to the bathroom when the call finally came through. "Mrs. Martine LeDuc?"

"Yes, this is she," I said, adding automatically, "Who is this?"

A discreet cough. "Mrs. Maréchal assured me there would be no need to give you a name."

"Right," I said, quickly opening the notebook to a new page and searching frantically with one hand for a pen. "I'm sorry. Elodie said that you could help me?"

"You are interested in the MK-Ultra work," he said. The name was new to me. I wrote it down. "Whatever you can tell me would be helpful."

"Very well. The work conducted in the Québec asylums during the 1940s, the 1950s, and particularly in the 1960s, through the Allan Memorial Institute, was done for Section Nine of the Canadian government," he said, his voice pedantic. "They were associated with the CIA's MK-Ultra program. Mrs. Maréchal seems to think that there is a connection with some murders you are investigating in Montréal."

"There may be," I said slowly. This was sounding like a spy novel now. Section Nine? "What can you tell me—um—sir?"

There was another pause, during which I heard him lighting a cigarette. "We were contacted in 1949 by an officer in the Central Intelligence Agency of the United States," he explained. "Several of our universities were doing pharmaceutical research, McGill among them. The thinking at the time was that it was necessary for a truth serum to be developed." He cleared his throat. "You have to remember that at the time we were very concerned about espionage and how to conduct the Cold

War. By 1952 the United States was alarmed enough to institute official congressional hearings, driven by the House Committee on Un-American Activities. Here in Canada, I regret to
say, we shared many of the same priorities." Yeah, that was just
the sort of thing that Duplessis would get on board with: right-
wing paranoid thinking.

He'd paused to inhale on his cigarette again. I seized on the
one new menu item. "A truth serum?"

"It began with just that," he said. "But there were a number
of other ideas being circulated—in the strictest privacy, you understand. Ultra-classified."

He cleared his throat, and then finally came to some inter-
nal decision and said it. "There was a question as to how far
drugs could go in controlling a person's behavior while at the
same time keeping that person unaware of what he was doing."

There was a moment of silence, spinning out taut and fine
between us. I thought for a moment that I was going to throw
up. I could hear echoes of Elizabeth Romfield's voice. I had been
ready to write her off as a complete nutter, with her thinly veiled
accusation of the CIA being behind the second Kennedy assassination. "Please tell me," I said, as steadily as I could, "precisely
what you mean."

He was lighting another cigarette. Good thing I'd gotten to
him before the cancer did. "As I said, the CIA program was
called MK-Ultra. We never had an equivalent program. There
was no need: we just piggybacked off theirs. Ewen Cameron, an
American, came up to supervise the experiments." He paused.
"It was felt that the work should be done outside of the United
States, for a number of reasons which are probably obvious.

So Ewen used to commute up to Montréal from his home in Vermont." He cleared his throat. "Dr. Cameron believed that he could erase existing memories and replace the erased memories with ones suggested to his patients, completely rebuilding their psyches. In other words, he could create a different person."

I was struggling to breathe. This had happened. Here. In Montréal. My beloved city. "How was this supposed to help with the Cold War issue?" I asked.

"My dear young lady," the disembodied voice said, "it was believed in certain circles that people could be programmed to do whatever one wished them to do. And then, if necessary, they could be reprogrammed to forget anything that had happened. The possibilities for any agency relying on secrecy, undercover work, and assassination—well, they're endless."

I closed my eyes, but that didn't blur the images his words had evoked. "Oh, God," I murmured.

"God," he said, "had nothing to do with it at all."

CHAPTER NINETEEN

There was a lot of e-mail in my in box, and I didn't feel like going through it. Doing a fast triage, I found an address I didn't know, and before chucking it, decided to check the contents: it was a photograph, an old one in black and white, of a group of people standing in front of another nineteenth-century institutional building, facing the camera.

The accompanying text was unsigned:

This is a photo of Doctors Ewen Cameron and Heinz Lehmann standing with a group of other doctors outside the Miséricorde hospital in Montréal in 1959. This was a hospital for unwed mothers and also an orphanage. At the time Lehmann was directing the research institute of the Allan Memorial. What are two McGill psychiatrists doing in a group photo on the steps of this hospital? What legitimate reason would they have to be there?

What a really good question. One I wasn't sure I even *wanted* to know the answer to.

I checked the e-mail address, but it was a free Gmail account; anyone can be anyone they want to be with web-based e-mail accounts. I sighed and squinted at the page. Was this my anonymous friend in Ottawa?

Suddenly I just needed to be out of the office. I was feeling restless and, besides, I always think more clearly when I'm moving. I got my car out of the underground garage and set the GPS to Rue Hochelaga.

It was time to see exactly what it was we'd been talking about.

The buildings that were once the infamous Cité de St.-Jean-de-Dieu orphanage/mental hospital/child abattoir were now sanitized and operating efficiently—and presumably correctly—as the Louis-Hippolyte Lafontaine Mental Health Hospital, with some long-term facilities located in adjoining buildings. I'd already read everything online that I could about it and just wanted to take a look myself.

What struck me first was that it was a very long drive to get out there from downtown, and all the way I kept thinking: if it seems long now, it must have seemed even longer sixty or seventy years ago, when these children were being brought out here. It would have been all farmland, then, even though it was officially part of the city.

The place seemed somehow distant—isolated and apart, even now; I couldn't imagine what it had felt like then. It's as far east as you can go, and it feels very much like you have left Montréal—and indeed all of civilization—behind.

As, in fact, they had.

No one was around looking at me curiously, and so I drove in slowly, taking in the imposing façade, gray stone, with—and why was I shocked?—the inscription still in large letters over the entrance: *Hôpital Cité de St.-Jean-de-Dieu.*

I'd have thought they'd have gotten rid of the words. As though they'd have wanted to hide it, hide the past, hide the pain.

I took a deep breath. I parked the car and walked around slowly, awed and more than a little amazed by the sheer size of the place. Building after building, all of them with five or six floors, and all of them, sixty years ago, filled with the demented, the schizophrenic, the bipolar . . . the orphans. And the nuns.

I took another deep breath and released it slowly. Breathe, Martine. It was such a jarring bit of cognitive dissonance: I'd gone to a convent school myself. I had learned to read and write— and *think*—from nuns, and I loved and admired them so much that for a period of more than a year I seriously contemplated joining the order, becoming a *soeur grise*, one of the Gray Sisters, teaching others as they had taught me. There had been nothing there but love and caring and generosity. Discipline, yes; but discipline in moderation. And never cruelty. If anything, I'd escaped my home life to the peace and calm of the convent school with relief. I loved the sisters, and I had never, not for one moment, doubted that they loved me. Had so much changed in—what? Twenty years? From what it had been?

And, I wondered, how could these women have sold off those children's bodies to the medical school for ten dollars each? How could they have stood by—or, worse, taken part—when it came to experiments such as sterilization, lobotomies, electroshock, drugs, ice water, straitjackets, isolation?

It was beyond understanding. I stood there and felt the wind tugging at my skirt and jacket and looked away from the imposing gray stone buildings, out across the road, my eyes tearing from the wind and the connection I was suddenly feeling with the past. There wasn't much to see. Somewhere out there had been the farm, also run by the nuns, which had supplied meat and vegetables to the asylum.

I imagined myself standing there as a child, a little girl, seeing my new world for the first time, and an immediate feeling of panic closed in. I started breathing faster, feeling like I couldn't get enough air. I would have been small and frail and surrounded by miles and miles of nothingness, only this tremendous building at my back ready to swallow and devour me, only the piggery for escape, the place where the bodies that didn't go to medical schools had been buried. In 1960, there was nothing else out here. No one to help me. No one to save me.

I swung back to look at the hospital again, and noticed the small building off to the side where a *garderie*—child care—was apparently being run. A large cheerful giraffe was holding a sign. "*Attention à nos enfants*," it said. Watch out for our children.

The irony of that sign was the last straw. I got back in my car and peeled out of there, but I didn't leave alone: the images came flooding after me. Why so many orphans? Mothers dying in childbirth, unwed mothers shamed into giving their children to the Church, large families unable to feed every mouth, even in such a Catholic area and time it seemed impossible that there were so many unclaimed children. Hundreds of them.

That wasn't all. There was, according to my anonymous e-mail correspondent, a connection between the Miséricorde orphanage—which surely was one of the ones to send orphans to Cité de St.-Jean-de-Dieu—and McGill. Ravenscrag. MK-Ultra. The CIA's fierce desire to be able to brainwash the world. If another place like Miséricorde had been involved, then how many others were there? Ten? Fifteen? Fifty?

I punched an address into the GPS and the ghosts dissipated as I drove, and within half an hour found myself on the other end of town . . . in every possible sense of the term. Sherbrooke Street became Côte-des-Neiges as it climbed up the side of the mountain and then I was driving through an upscale neighborhood, the fur traders' mansions, the homes of the railroad kings, the carefully Anglophone section of the city, so high on a hill that you expected your ears to pop.

The Allan, still housed in the mansion called Ravenscrag, isn't what *it* used to be, either. The interior of the mansion had been stripped once its wealthy owners had died off; it was only impressive from the outside. Montréal's done a grand job of erasing the parts of its past it wants to hide. Now the building houses the psychiatry department of the Royal Victoria Hospital, part of the McGill University Health Center, and if anyone finds the house creepy now, it's only because—well, frankly, because it's a creepy looking place. Nothing bad happens here.

Not anymore.

Here there was a guard shack, but I talked my way past its somnolent inhabitant easily enough—thank you, city ID. I drove up a long, very long, gently curving driveway . . . and, right at the top, right on cue, there it was. Ravenscrag.

Crazy ornate Italianate style. If the Addams family had had a house at the top of a hill overlooking the city and the St. Lawrence Seaway, it would be this one. I drew in another deep breath.

Allan's son had wanted none of it, though, and he donated it to the Royal Victoria. The inside was gutted, and it morphed into the first of its several hospital incarnations, eventually becoming the psychiatric department of McGill University.

According to my caller from Ottawa, Cameron had commuted here, every day, from his home in Vermont to do his experiments on "biological systems" (that's *people*, to you and me). He treated his patients with hallucinogenic drugs, long periods in the sleep room, and testing in something he called the Radio Telemetry Laboratory—I really didn't want to know what that last bit was. I shivered just at the name.

Montréal native musician Leonard Cohen came here as a paid volunteer when he was seventeen. He talked later about the sensory-deprivation experiments, said that he liked them because he learned to dissociate, leave his body, go on long voyages through the universe. I even found a photograph online showing him wearing a blindfold, with his ears, fingers, and hands encased in padded restraints that prevent movement and cut off sensory stimulation.

It's eerie, Ravenscrag. And what happened inside was eerier still. The words of my anonymous e-mail correspondent came back to me: *What are two McGill psychiatrists doing in a group photo on the steps of this hospital?*

My smartphone alarm went off, and I jumped. Just a reminder of my meeting with Julian, but my nerves were pretty frayed by now. Conscious of my heartbeat, conscious of blood in my ears and veins—how did mere proximity to this place make me so acutely aware of my body?—I turned around and headed back down the hill.

After my afternoon's travels and the thoughts they'd provoked, I felt that I really, really needed a shower.

I settled for a glass of beer with Julian at his Anglophone pub. "Well?"

"You don't look very chipper," he said. He, of course, looked as perfectly put together as ever.

"Been on a sightseeing tour," I responded, and took a rather large swallow of the lager in front of me.

He politely waited a moment for me to elucidate, then shrugged lightly when I didn't. "Well, I think we're on the right track," he said. "For a couple of reasons." He numbered them on his fingers. "One. Violette Sobel is scared out of her wits. She knows damned well where her adopted sister lived before coming into the heart of the Desmarchais family, and she knows damned well how it happened. Father caught sight of Annie when he was working over at Saint-Jean-de-Dieu and she haunted him, until he pulled her out and took her home. Or at least that's the story Violette got; I wouldn't stake anything on its veracity. Maybe he thought that bringing one of 'em home would balance things out. Violette says that Annie spent the first half of her life grateful to him and the second half blaming him for his role in it all."

"Lots of mixed feelings there," I said, nodding.

"Less mixed as time passed, it seems. Annie'd been looking at death for a while." He hesitated. "She had a cancer scare last year, and it came back this winter. Violette says she wanted to do something important before she died."

"Such as?" I took another hefty swallow of beer.

"Such as trying to get an equitable settlement for the remaining orphans," he said. "They're organized, you know, you must have seen it in the news. They call themselves the Duplessis Orphans—and you know that the government gave them something back in 2002, some restitution money, right?"

I nodded. I'd heard that, of course, from Elodie.

Julian cleared his throat. He'd been reading up on things. "It's all been desperately horrible for them," he said. "They'd been trying to get some sort of settlement since 1988. In 1999, the Church pretty much refused all responsibility, the archbishop of Montréal said they'd have to present case-by-case proof before he'd so much as issue an apology—oh, and that has still not happened, by the way. The Sisters of Providence said they'd do their own investigation, but ended up saying there'd been no abuse. Premier Bernard Landry finally put together an apology and an offer in 2002: each of the orphans received a ten thousand dollar lump sum and an additional thousand dollars for every year they spent in the asylum, which translates into roughly twenty-five thousand dollars per person."

Someone had already given me those figures. Elodie? "Is that a lot?" I asked.

He shook his head. "No other government concession in history has ever been so low. And it seems Annie wanted to do something about that."

"Why?" Annie Desmarchais was beyond wealthy.

He smiled quizzically. "For justice, Violette said. Incidentally, *she* approved not one little bit. The past should stay in the past, all that sort of thing, that's Violette's take on it all."

"Violette didn't spend the first ten years of her life in a hellhole."

"There is that," Julian acknowledged. "Anyway, it's all Annie talked about, ever since the cancer came back. She wanted to do something for the other orphans. She remembered a lot of them, kids that were tortured, kids buried out on the farm. She had names, names of the dead. She said everyone should know about them."

"That wasn't good news for somebody," I said.

"It simply isn't done at their level of society, you see." He managed a smile at his halfhearted attempt at levity. "Violette's husband was Jewish, and Annie pointed out that in Canada, what happened to those kids should be as well known as the Holocaust. She said that if she had her way, Canadians wouldn't ever forget, either."

He paused. I was thinking it over. "And number two?"

"Sorry?"

"You were naming reasons we're on the right track," I reminded him. "Violette Sobel was number one. What's number two?"

"Ah." He grinned vividly, wickedly. "My boss has taken me off the case."

I stared at him, aghast. "You're not serious."

"*Au contraire.* I'm very serious. They're arraigning their homeless suspect down on Rue Notre-Dame as we speak, or they will be tomorrow."

I closed my eyes. I suddenly felt exhausted. We were up

against something so gigantic . . . I could see the superior court building, its massive columns, the sheer size of the place daunting. Justice, one felt, was being meted out there. But without Julian . . . "*Merde*," I said with feeling.

"Not to worry," he assured me. "While it seems that my extraordinary skills are apparently needed, or so I am told, in solving a case that was clearly a matter of domestic abuse drawn to its logical if tragic conclusion, I have informed the powers-that-be that I am indisposed. I require a week's holiday, as from now."

"But—"

"But nothing. We're getting there, Martine, don't you see that? Come on, think about it. Why do you think I was put on the case? I'm the resident bad boy. And when *you* decided to investigate, they probably thought you were harmless, you've never solved a crime in your life. Do you really think they imagined we'd figure anything out? They don't think much of either of us, they don't expect anything from us, and that's a good thing, it really is." He paused and took a breath. "And I'm damned if I'm going to let some poor homeless fellow do a man in the iron mask and rot in prison for the rest of his life so that, once again, Québec's sins can be swept under the carpet."

"That's a lot of metaphors," I said with admiration.

"I pride myself on my metaphors," he said, grinning. "So glad you noticed. Now, here's the thing. Annie Desmarchais wasn't expecting the government to pony up all the settlement money she wanted."

"Then who was she targeting? The Church?"

"Not that Violette noticed," he said. "Though they sure as hell *should* pay, if you ask me."

"Which, of course, I didn't," I murmured.

"Which you didn't," he confirmed. "Here's the thing. Violette knew that Annie had been meeting with a professor from McGill—"

"Christopher MacDougal," I said, reaching his wavelength with a click that must have been audible.

"None other than," Julian agreed. He took a sip of Guinness and looked out approvingly over the stream of pedestrians passing by. "A solid connection, that, I'd say, wouldn't you?"

"She wanted *McGill* to pay?" I must have sounded as disbelieving as I felt. "Julian, listen, that means she had proof of a connection between the Allan Institute and the Cité de Saint-Jean-de-Dieu! I mean, everything that we have, it can be explained away. We don't have anything concrete. She *had* to have proof, she was a businesswoman, she knew damned well that it would have to stand up in court."

"And that, my little chickadee, is exactly what you're going to talk to Dr. MacDougal about."

I was doggedly following my own thread of thought. "We still have to connect the other women," I said. "Danielle is easy, she was doing MacDougal's research for him. But the other two?"

Julian finished his Guinness and, putting some money on the table, stood up. "That," he said, "is what *I'm* going to find out next."

I was to learn to read and write.

It was a privilege, everyone said, and I agreed: when I was learning to read and write, I wasn't running all over the institution with messages, I didn't have to go down to the basement or out to the farm. They needed me to help with recordkeeping, Sister Béatrice said. That was why I was to learn.

And it was easy, really. Figuring out which symbols stood for which sounds. Seeing my own name take shape under my pen. Beginning to read the signs that seemed to be everywhere at the asylum. "Private." "Hydrotherapy." "Locked ward." There was magic in what I was doing, unlocking an understanding of the building around me.

Marie-Rose told me about books. She couldn't read them herself, of course; but back at the orphanage sometimes one of the older girls used to read books to her. "Stories," she said wistfully. "Stories of days gone by, and princesses and kings. And saints, too"—she blessed herself—"and foxes that could talk. Will you be able to read the books, Gabrielle? Will you be able to tell stories?"

I would be able to read books, I thought. Someday, I would leave the asylum, and I would read a book. And another. And another.

Sister Béatrice was not offering books, and I knew better than to ask for them. I concentrated hard during our lessons, and practiced with every word I encountered, wherever I went, and she seemed surprised by—and pleased with—my progress. "You're a clever girl, Gabrielle."

Finally I was put in a room with a long shiny table and rows and rows of filing drawers and given a task. "We will bring you a list of names," said Sister Béatrice. "You will look them up in the files. You will write down next to each name whether or not that person has family, and if so, what family there is. Father, mother, uncle, cousin, do you understand? And the family's address."

"Yes, Sister." There was a time when I would have asked why, but I didn't want to go back into restraints, and Sister Béatrice was famous for putting you in them for the most minor of infractions. I could feel the cuffs cutting my wrists just thinking about it. Nothing was worth that.

"Bien." She looked at me suspiciously, as though she could read my thoughts, and I arranged my features into the most bland of all possible expressions. She was back in a very short while, the promised list in her hand. "These are the files you will use," she told me, indicating three or four of the file cabinets. "When you've finished, come find me in the dayroom on the third floor. You can find that, can't you?"

"Yes, Sister."

"All right, then." And she was gone.

I worked hard on the list, but when I brought them to Sister Béatrice, she barely glanced at them. Names and names and names and names—the latitude and longitude of our lives . . . What I hadn't expected was to recognize them.

The names were nearly all those of children who had been brought there from my orphanage. Names I knew; faces I knew; stories I knew.

"You'll have to work more quickly in the future," she said. "All right. You'll need to take this directly to the basement clinic yourself, I don't have time to have Sister Marguerite send someone."

No one was in the small antechamber, but one of the doors stood open. I stood and waited, watching the clock's hands move around. Wasn't Bobby down here anymore? I was going to get in very bad trouble if I didn't return to Sister Béatrice, and soon.

I kept looking at the open door until finally, hesitantly, I went through it. There was very little light in the corridor, just some *bulbs placed at what seemed to be long intervals along the hallway, and I stood there for a moment, trying to get my bearings. A door was open, but the doorway was covered with thick strips of clear plastic hanging vertically from the door, and I stopped there, indecisive about what to do.*

Voices inside. "Disconnecting the frontal lobe didn't seem to help the last time."

"That's true, Doctor."

"But we need to know why. And whether it would happen again."

Calm voices, it was always a relief to hear calm voices, or so I'd come to understand. In a place like Cité de Saint-Jean-de-Dieu, calmness was a rare commodity. Taking a deep breath, I pushed the vertical strips of heavy plastic away.

I was looking at a table with lights pointing down toward it, and a body lying on the table, and blood everywhere. People standing around it. The doctor said something sharply when he saw me, an expression of irritation. The nun—Sister Lise—strode over to me, blocking my view of the table. "What are you doing here?"

I held up the paper that was still, miraculously, in my hand. "I'm supposed to give this to you. From Sister Béatrice." I couldn't work out how words were coming out of my mouth: my lips felt as though they were covered with something heavy and fuzzy, as though they could scarcely work. And my stomach was heaving.

She snatched the paper from my hands. "Bien. You may go now."

I turned, and in that moment I saw Bobby, standing off to

the side holding something in his hands. He didn't look at me. He'd made his choice: cigarettes and a place where he could be respected, a place where he could be somebody.

I ran.

CHAPTER TWENTY

Christopher MacDougal was early.

I saw him from a distance as I was walking through the park, a vast, beautiful bit of nature in the middle of the Plateau, with an "*espace*"—space—in the center, run as a nonprofit that included a bistro and an amphitheater for plays, films, and so on. Mixing culture and nature. I hadn't personally come up with the idea, but I sure as hell made certain everybody knew about it: it's a great PR angle.

My phone rang just as I was heading down the path toward the *espace*. "Martine LeDuc," I said, keeping my voice down even though MacDougal couldn't possibly hear me from this distance.

"Babe? What's going on?"

"Not much," I said, mystified that Ivan should be calling me. "Why?"

"You were supposed to be here at lunchtime to look at some security tapes."

Oh, *merde*, yes. The people at Danielle's funeral. I'd completely forgotten. "Oh, Ivan, I'm sorry. I got busy and—"

"Forgot," he finished for me. "No big deal, but I'm heading downtown for a couple of meetings, so if you come now—"

"I probably won't get to it today, *chéri*," I said apologetically.

"All right then. No worries. I'll see you tonight. Take care."

"You, too," I said automatically, already clicking off the smartphone. MacDougal had caught sight of me and was walking in my direction. My gut remembered the night in my office even if my head knew how safe I was here, and I felt it twist in fear. Standing next to him was making my skin crawl.

"Mrs. LeDuc," he said, offering his hand.

I shook it firmly. "Professor MacDougal."

He half turned, gesturing toward the bistro, people flowing in and out of the indoor serving area, others settling in at the tables grouped under the trees. "Perhaps something to drink? An *apéritif?*"

I'd already had a glass of beer I'd drunk far too quickly, and I needed my wits about me. "An espresso," I agreed, and we found a small zinc table outside. Around us, voices in a babble of French and English, though mostly French. We did the pretend-you're-looking-around-while-feeling-awkward thing that people who don't know each other do when they're first together, and I wondered for a moment where the little train was that took children around the *espace*. Only on weekends, I remembered.

A server appeared and the professor ordered for us in atrocious French, and once she'd left we finally looked at each other, as though her presence and the fact of ordering had made the meeting real; it gave us the signal to begin. "I want to know," I said to him, "what you and Annie Desmarchais were talking about before she was murdered."

"Of course you do." He was unperturbed. "Aren't we supposed to have some lubricating small-talk conversation first? Talk about the upcoming elections? Do you think the Parti Québécois stands a chance this time around? Or perhaps the weather—it's been fine, but I hear there are clouds moving in for tomorrow."

I stared at him, using my best you've-got-to-be-kidding look. It worked. He sighed and crossed one leg elegantly over the other. He was wearing a pale gray suit with a white shirt and a red tie: academia meets big business. As, I suspected, he was about to tell me.

He didn't disappoint. "We're both aware of the MK-Ultra experiments at the Allan," he said finally. I nodded. "I was not directly involved. I was in medical school before I knew anything about them, to be honest, and that was in the seventies. It was all over by then. But my advisor—my mentor in every possible way—worked at the Allan in those years."

"So you cut him some slack." Using the pronoun was a safe enough bet; I hadn't yet heard a woman's name associated with the project.

"Of course I didn't," MacDougal snapped. He stopped as the server—a young woman with the best complexion I've ever seen anywhere—put our coffees down. "*Non, merci, rien d'autre,*" I said impatiently when she asked if we wanted anything else. I just wanted her to go away.

MacDougal stirred sugar into his coffee. "There was no need

for me to gloss over any of the project with Dr. Schmidt," he said. "It was never presented to me as anything but good medicine, and it was a very long time before I was able to think for myself on that score."

He sipped his coffee. I ignored mine. "What happened?" I asked.

"You must understand, the Allan was seen as one of the best places in the country to work," he said. "A premier placement. I was honored to be taken on there. And of course, by the time I was there, the—excesses—had stopped."

"Excesses?" I raised my eyebrows. "That's a funny way of talking about torture. Or murder."

"It wasn't murder!"

"No?" I leaned forward, nearly across the small table. "What do you call it then, Professor?"

He put down his cup with a thump that made me jump. "Why don't I just tell you what you need to know?" he asked. "I don't appreciate the third degree, or the attitude. If you want information, then by God have the courtesy to ask for it without a layer of contempt."

I leaned back, took a sip of coffee, and nodded. "You're right," I said, gesturing. "Go ahead."

He drew in a deep breath, let it out slowly. "Very well. I first saw the Allan in 1982. You have to understand, back then, it was legendary in the psychiatric community. I felt I was lucky to be there, and lucky to have the mentor I had. There were rumors, even then—but there are always rumors in hospitals. One even had Dr. Mengele himself escaping from Germany at the end of World War Two and continuing Nazi experimentation at

212 JEANNETTE DE BEAUVOIR

the Allan. It was laughable." He glanced at me. "I still don't believe that particular bit of the story." He paused. "But the rest . . .
well, it's credible."

He dampened his lips before continuing. "Drugs were being
used in a big way in the eighties," he said. "ECT—electroshock
therapy—had gone out of vogue, but the drugs were very cutting-
edge." There was some bitterness in his voice, now. "And Lansbury Pharmaceuticals was the major supplier. Whatever we
wanted, they seemed to be able to get, sometimes at great rates,
sometimes for free. And when you're prescribing . . . well, you
have to understand, and I don't say this easily, but the truth is
that doctors don't know as much as the general populace gives
them credit for knowing. Doing medicine is always a little hit-
or-miss, some times more than others. What people don't get is
that the brain is a very complicated organ, and there's a lot to be
understood about it, even today. A lot that no one knows yet. So
we learn by experimentation."

Somehow I'd finished my coffee without being aware of
drinking it. I brought the empty cup to my mouth and then set
it down again. Still I didn't say anything.

"The experimentation," said Dr. MacDougal, "must, however,
be rigorous, ethical, and conducted always with the patient's permission and with their best interests in mind. A formula that
I began to discover had not always been the Allan's practice. It
had particularly been lacking when there was American funding coming in. Consent was not always required. No: I lie—
consent was never required. The Americans saw that sort of
thing differently than we did."

"The CIA," I said.

He nodded. "The CIA. They gave us everything: money, expertise, they kept the government off our backs, no inspections . . . just left the doctors free to do whatever medicine they thought would be best. As long as the CIA got the results they wanted." He sighed, rubbing his wrist, his eyes going past me, past the park, into some darkness I was only skirting the edge of. "And then the plug got pulled. When the Americans ended MK-Ultra, the psychiatry department started hurting for funding. There was panic. The Allan needed a knight in shining armor to rescue it and—lo and behold, as if by magic, one appeared. That was when Lansbury upped its part of the ante." He glanced at me. "Don't misunderstand: Lansbury was part of the Allan before the CIA ever was. But since the seventies, it's been the major funding source. And I was grateful. So grateful, in fact, that I agreed to help them with PR campaigns."

"Yes," I said. "I know about the videos you did."

"Yes," he said bleakly. "I expect that you do. And I don't know about you, Mrs. LeDuc, but I need something a little stronger than coffee just now." He signaled for the server. "Will you share a bottle of cider with me?"

I nodded. I didn't trust my voice.

He ordered the cider and then took in another deep breath. This couldn't have been easy for him, and despite my anger, I found myself feeling sorry for him, too.

But not too much.

We didn't say much of anything for a few moments. The server brought the cider and poured us each a glass before leaving again; MacDougal drank thirstily and then put his glass down; it made an odd sound on the zinc tabletop. "So there we were," he said. "The Allan humming along, Lansbury money matching funds with the McGill money coming in, and everything was perfect. Then last year I happened to be attending a fundraiser and found that I was sitting beside Annie Desmarchais."

Aha. I was wondering when we'd get to her.

"I didn't know that much about MK-Ultra, to be perfectly honest," MacDougal said. "But she did—and she told me. She told me about her own past, before she was adopted by the Desmarchais family, and how orphans had been reclassified by the Church so that the asylums could get the federal mental-health money."

I hated to interrupt him, but I had to. "Was it really that much more money? I've never seen any figures. Were there enough children to justify it?"

He smiled bleakly. "It was," he said softly, "a perfect storm of possibilities for abuse. You had a governmental system trying to save money, and turning orphans into psychiatric patients saved on education. You had nuns working ten- to twelve-hour days, day after day, without any kind of preparation for the task, each one of them responsible for between ten and twenty children. Boys were cared for by men hired out of the community— and we're not talking urban Montréal here, the Cité de Saint-Jean-de-Dieu was out in a village back then, it didn't become part of Montréal proper until later—so whomever they hired was also undereducated and underprepared."

He took a swallow of cider. Thus reminded, I took a quick sip too, feeling the tartness on my tongue. He cleared his throat. "And, yes, to answer your question . . . Québec at the beginning

of the last century was the cradle of the Western world, quite literally the cradle, with more births for a period of about thirty years
than *anywhere else* in the western hemisphere. There was no
birth control, and unwed mothers were shamed into giving their
children to the Church; they were told that their own bad traits
would rub off on their children otherwise. They thought they
were saving the children." He shook his head. "Like I said, a perfect storm for abuse. And abuse there was, tremendous abuse.
All of that would have been terrible enough, all by itself."

"And then there was MK-Ultra," I said.

He nodded. "And then there was MK-Ultra."

We both drank in silence for a moment. He wasn't finished.
"Annie told me she was one of the Duplessis orphans. She told
me that she felt guilt, immense guilt, for not being able to go
back and help every other child in that hellhole. And then she
told me about the basement—that was where they did the experiments. Only on children with no family. Only on children
no one would miss. I'd like to think that they believed they were
working toward the greater good, trying to discover what might
and might not help a patient."

"It doesn't matter what they believed," I said.

He shrugged. "Perhaps. Perhaps not. In any case, the point
is that both the Allan and Lansbury were deeply involved in
what happened in that basement for all those years. So you can
imagine how deeply affected I was, how desperate to do something to make right what had happened, not that anyone ever
could. Annie and I became, well, friends, of a sort. She was determined that it all should come to light, that McGill and Lansbury should both not only acknowledge the part they played in

the situation, but that they should also provide financial compensation to the remaining living victims. I agreed to help. We needed a researcher, someone impartial, and so I enlisted the assistance of—"

"Danielle Leroux," I said. I knew this part already, but seeing it fit so neatly into the jigsaw puzzle of information was powerful.

"Yes," he said, and his gaze went unhappily around the immediate area, looking at the family seated next to us, the little boy blowing bubbles in his soda with his straw.

He knew, I thought. He knew that asking Danielle for help was ultimately the reason she died. "It wasn't your fault," I said suddenly. "You didn't kill her."

"I may as well have."

I waved that away. He'd have to come to terms with it on his own. "What about the others?"

He didn't pretend to misunderstand me. "I only know about Caroline Richards," he said. "Annie had contacted her, asked her to help with her investigation, help get the word out. Who better than an investigative journalist? The CBC had done a series some time ago on the Duplessis orphans. Annie thought that Caroline could do something similar. Put it on public display, put pressure on the university and Lansbury to ante up. Caroline was excited about it—if she could've carried it off, it would have been a major coup for her. Awards. Who knows what."

"Did you meet her?"

"Caroline? No, never. She met with Annie, and they were careful. Never at the foundation or the newspaper, always a different place, always careful."

"Not careful enough."

He looked at me. "I suppose not."

I sighed and finished my cider, watched him refill my glass. I really didn't need any more. "You know where this is all leading," I said. "Someone, probably either at McGill or Lansbury—and my money's on McGill—found out. They realized these women were the driving force behind the investigation. They wanted them dead and they were willing to do it in such a sensational way that no one would look beyond the how as to the why."

"That's my understanding of it as well." He was staring into his glass.

"And you have no idea how Isabelle Hubert fits in?"

He shook his head. "I don't. She seems to have moved in some powerful circles, however, and it's possible . . ." His voice trailed off delicately.

Yes. It was possible. But I had something even better: I had the motive. "Her mother was at the asylum," I said. "At the Cité de Saint-Jean-de-Dieu. She went over the wall, ran away, managed to escape. She was just a teenager. Isabelle was doing genealogical research, she was finding out about her mother's story. I expect that's the connection you didn't know about." I blew out a sigh and stood up. "Thank you, Professor."

He politely stood up with me. "You will continue to—er—pursue the matter?"

"In conjunction with the police," I said smoothly. Yeah, right. You never know.

CHAPTER TWENTY-ONE

"It's all well and good to know what," said Ivan on Saturday morning. "And even why. That doesn't do much to tell you the *who*, though, does it?"

"I know," I said, frustrated. Upstairs, the kids were quarreling over the use of the computer they shared when they were at our house; they didn't have to share, apparently, at their mom's. I didn't have the energy to go play referee, and Ivan had his hands full making sandwiches for lunch. Creative sandwiches; Claudia had just informed us that she'd turned vegetarian and that anyone who ate meat was, ipso facto, contributing to murder.

Reason number four hundred why I'd never really wanted children: I just didn't have the patience. I was dealing with enough mayhem already: it was annoying, on top of everything else, to be told—and in the most patronizing voice imaginable—that I should be worrying about where my ham came from.

I slumped down in my chair at the kitchen table. "Julian's off the case," I said miserably. "*Monsieur le directeur* having concluded that they were all sex killings and that the perpetrator is locked up."

"Won't he change his mind if there's another?" asked Ivan.

I stared at him. "What did you say?"

He shrugged; somehow he always looks more Russian when he's shrugging, making hand gestures. His body in movement is different from his body at rest. I don't know what that's about. Genetics? DNA?

It's not like he's ever spent time in the cafés of St. Petersburg.

"Martine, just because you've found these connections between the victims doesn't mean that there's not somebody else out there who's still in danger from this guy, whoever he is," he said, and immediately got distracted. "Oh, damn. Vegetarians eat eggs, don't they?"

"You mean that someone else—"

"Look," he said, pulling out a chair and sitting across from me. "Whoever this is, he's going around eliminating women who he feels are putting him in some sort of danger because of their investigations into the Allan and the asylum, right? So who's to say that these are the only four? Maybe there's someone else, someone who's not even on your radar. Maybe even a man."

A man. That was a thought. How would they pass off a man's murder as the work of a psychotic rapist? Then I had a thought. "Dr. MacDougal?"

Ivan shook his head. "If they wanted to keep him from talking, wouldn't they have done it by now?"

"I don't know." The professor *did* seem to have all the facts, I thought, and maybe a dawning willingness to share them; yet the killer hadn't even considered eliminating him. What was the difference? Or was he the killer? He could have, after all, just been been putting on some act in front of me. I stared into space, biting my bottom lip. There was still too much that we didn't know.

Ivan got up again and bustled around the counter. "Lunch is ready!" he called out, then turned to me. "Let's not talk about it now," he said. "There's no reason for the kids to hear this."

I nodded, still thinking, dazed by the revelation. We had to narrow all this down to a person, I thought; not the Allan, or the asylum, or even McGill or Lansbury Pharmaceuticals. A *person* had raped and killed these women, not a corporation, not an institution. Who was it?

Claudia was not happy with the egg salad that Ivan had determined was the only nutritious non-meat we had in the refrigerator, and sulked. Lukas, happily tearing into his ham-and-brie on baguette, made piggy noises at her. "Stop it!" I said, rather more sharply than I'd meant to. "Claudia, eat the egg salad. We'll go out for crêpes tonight. And Lukas, stop teasing your sister."

"I'll be hungry all afternoon!" she wailed.

"Not if you eat the egg salad."

"Eat it, Claudia," Ivan intervened, his voice brooking no nonsense. "We're going to be walking a lot this afternoon, you need to have something in your stomach."

"Why are we walking a lot this afternoon?"

"Because we're going to Notre-Dame-des-Neiges to see your *belle-maman's* mother."

"Oh, yuck," said Claudia. "I hate going to the stupid cemetery."

"You make it sound like we're going to have tea with her or something," said Lukas to Ivan, watching his sister, enjoying the show. "She's dead," he added loudly, for Claudia's benefit.

Every month Ivan and I visit my mother's grave in the cemetery high up on the hill—the "*mont*" or "mount" part of Montréal. If the kids are spending that particular weekend with us, they come along. We trim the grass and weeds that seem to always be springing up, we plant bulbs if it's fall, we whisk the snow away if it's winter, we add fresh flowers in the summer.

I'd had a fairly—okay, *very*—problematic relationship with my mother when she was alive, but I'm nothing if not dutiful now that she's dead. It's guilt, no doubt. But it has to be said that interactions with her now are certainly a lot easier than they were before.

"Well, we're going, anyway," said Ivan.

"I vote that we don't," said Claudia.

"Me, too," added Lukas, for once with his sister.

"This isn't a democracy," I said calmly. "There are no votes. So eat your lunch, or you'll have the same thing for dinner." I took a prosaic approach to meals. I had no idea whether it was good psychology or not. You didn't eat it at lunch, that's what you got for dinner. You didn't eat it at dinner, it would be waiting for you at breakfast. After the first two days of howling and slamming doors, the system continued to work well.

"I thought we were going to the *crêperie* tonight. You said we were going to the *crêperie!*"

"And go to the *crêperie* we shall," Ivan agreed. "But if you don't eat your sandwich now, you'll be eating egg salad at the *crêperie*."

"This is so unfair!"

"Yes," Ivan and I agreed in unison.

Notre-Dame-des-Neiges—our Lady of the Snows—is one of the most beautiful places in the world, at least of the places I've ever been. Maybe it takes the edge off dying, if you know that forever you'll be in this gorgeous quiet place. Comparable to Cambridge's Victorian-era Mount Auburn cemetery, Notre-Dame-des-Neiges is the third-largest cemetery in North America and part of the historic register. People come for many reasons: to visit the graves and mausoleums, to bird-watch, to see the plant and tree and animal species, to feel calm and reflective. I come because I am a daughter.

Maman's stone isn't as imposing as many of the others, but it's in a nice place under a tree on the upper slopes of the cemetery, and as always, as soon as we arrived I put my hand on it and murmured something that was part prayer, part conversation, part incantation.

"You miss her?" Ivan's voice was light in my ear.

"Of course," I said automatically, though the reality was far more complicated than that. My connection with my mother had been intense: we'd alternately passionately loved and passionately hated each other, *maman* and I, all throughout my childhood; the feelings, as could be expected, gained both momentum and intensity once I hit adolescence.

Unpleasant memories, most of them. There was no overt abuse; she never, ever laid a hand on me; but she did manage to make me feel awkward and unintelligent for most of my life. I'd had to fight it to get where I was now. Most of the time I was pretty damned successful.

"At least," he said, as though following my thoughts, "your relationship was never boring." His, apparently, had been.

"No," I agreed. "It was never boring." I watched as Lukas and Claudia pretended to embrace a nearby weeping statue; they were giggling, and I could almost hear what my mother would have said about that. "But she ruined kids for me," I said.

"What do you mean?"

I shrugged. "Thanks to her, I was absolutely terrified of not being an adequate stepmother, and I'm still not sure I'm getting this whole parenting thing right." I sighed and looked past her grave, out into the middle distance. "I never told you this, but I almost didn't marry you, because of your kids, because of those feelings."

Ivan shook his head. "Stop it. You're doing better than ninety-five percent of the parents out there. You know that. Stepmothers have a difficult act to follow. By definition, you entered a house of grief. And you've done wonders with it. The kids love you, you get along better with Margery than I do, and you make it look easy."

I stared at him, aghast. "Easy?"

He shrugged. "You bring your own style to it. You bring your own self to it. And sometimes it explodes, because that's what parenting is all about. Just realize I know that this stepmother gig isn't exactly a walk in the *parc*. And whether your mother would realize that or not is strictly irrelevant."

I grinned and kissed him. Some day Ivan isn't going to say exactly the right thing at the right moment and I'm going to faint.

Maybe.

We got to work. The kids, easily bored, wandered off together, arguing fiercely about something they weren't going to remember ten minutes later. The afternoon was warm, one of those long autumn days that make you believe you can hold off the winter just a little longer, that fill your heart and lungs with sunshine and hope. We trimmed and polished and put some flowers in the vase in front of the stone, then just sat there with our backs to the stone and looked off together into the distance, the city below us, each of us immersed in thought—or not. In my case, my mind was pretty much a blank, I wasn't thinking about anything in particular. "What a perfect day," I said on a sigh.

"It is that," Ivan agreed. "Lucky to stay forever in such a perfect place."

And that was when it hit me.

The sheer privilege of this place, the luxury of space and beauty, the option of remembrance, of having your name on a stone, even when there was no family left to tend the grave, even when one hundred years had passed, that reminder that you had once been here, breathed this air, walked these streets.

He was right: there was memory here.

Something the orphans buried without tombstones would never have. No beauty, no names, no remembrance. It was as if they had never lived or breathed or suffered or died. People write books, compose music, make discoveries, become saints or murderers, and all of it ensuring that, for a little while at least, their names will not be forgotten. Parents have children so that their names, their genetic code, their fortunes will live on after them. Vast cemeteries are built so that someone walking through them can happen on a name, read the dates and the inscriptions, maybe say something out loud, and for that brief moment the person can live again.

I looked around me at the beauty, the tranquility, the peace of all these monuments, the thousands and thousands of people whose names are still read, still remembered, still wondered about, and I thought of that unmarked burial ground by the pig farm, of those small bodies taken from the asylum morgue in the dead of night and buried together, no markers, no memories of names or faces or anything that proved they had lived short unhappy lives and died in terror and pain. The lobotomies. The electroshock. The injections. The drugs.

"What's going on?" Ivan's voice interrupted my thinking, his concern clear. "Martine, are you all right?"

I shook my head as though I could rid it of all those thoughts. "Everyone should get a chance to be buried along with their name," I said, feeling my throat closing up. "Everyone should at least get that chance."

He reached over and took my hand. He didn't say anything.

"Whoever it is," I said, not even realizing how savage I sounded, "I'm going to get him."

Julian shared my resolution.

"It's about narrowing it down to a person rather than a company," I told him after mass on Sunday. The kids and Ivan were playing Monopoly in the living room, and I was sitting on the edge of my bed, talking quietly into the telephone so no one would hear. Ivan's one request was that the kids not know anything of what I was doing. It seemed a small enough favor. "It's either McGill University or Lansbury Pharmaceuticals, there's little doubt of that. But a company didn't rape those women. A university didn't kill those women. Someone real, someone flesh-and-blood did. But who?"

"You're sounding strident," Julian observed.

"*Pardonne-moi*," I snapped. "It's not a topic I can be completely calm about. And I find the fact that you *can* be so calm particularly disturbing."

"Stop it," he said without heat. "You're too emotionally connected here, Martine. Stand back. We have to be rational."

"I'll be rational," I said grimly, "when we can put this person behind bars—and expose everything, make it all public, say whatever it is they don't want said."

"That's all well and good, but there's no particular need to make a target of yourself," Julian said mildly. "Why don't you say all that about Lansbury a little louder? I don't think they can hear you all the way to City Hall. You really want to show your hand before we know what's going on?"

City Hall. And my job. He was right; it had to be considered. But my job was small potatoes compared with people's *lives*. "Wait," I said. Some of my synapses were finally firing. Dancing, actually. "I *know* someone from one of the pharma companies! Well, that is to say, at least I've *met* him, he's an attorney." That City Hall association . . . and I remembered the amused eyes, the connection I'd felt with him. "He said his company's a big donor to my boss."

"Is he Lansbury?"

I hesitated, trying to remember. I thought he was from Lansbury, but I couldn't remember. "Maybe."

"Doesn't let McGill off the hook," he said.

"But listen. Think about it for a second. There's a lot more oversight at the university. McGill's been making a show of putting the past behind them. They need the city's goodwill. But Lansbury's only responsible to their shareholders."

"You think someone from Lansbury . . . ?"

"I mean, maybe." I hesitated. "Oh, hell, Julian, it can't be. There's a limit to how committed anyone is to their company, right? Raping women, torturing them, posing them? Nobody would ever do that for an employer."

"Exactly," said Julian.

I ignored him. I was on a roll. "But what if it *is* Lansbury, and they hired someone to actually do the—you know, to do it for them? Think about it: if I'm right, then we're hitting all the high notes. Everyone says that you'd have to be a psychopath to do this kind of violence, right?"

"Hmm." There was still an undercurrent of objection in his voice.

"Well, so maybe Lansbury has a very rational reason to want the women out of the way, and it's really just coincidence that it's all women, but that works in Lansbury's favor, because now they can hire this murderer-rapist-psychopath to carry it out. Just because a crazy person did it doesn't mean that there's not a sane reason *behind* it." My words were all tumbling together and I wasn't at all sure I was making myself clear.

"And Lansbury doesn't want anyone to know about their role in MK-Ultra?" asked Julian. "Hate to tell you, but that ship has sailed. It's pretty much common knowledge."

"For anyone who knows about MK-Ultra," I agreed. "But seriously, how many people do? Who cares anymore? Who's even heard of it? I hadn't, not before this all started. I'll bet you hadn't. Nobody who knows is talking, and every year it gets more and more remote, it's ancient history, it's over, we've all moved on. It's of academic interest. And, anyway, that's not the worst part, not from Lansbury's PR point of view." I knew a thing or two about PR myself: this was familiar territory. "There's that crossover between MK-Ultra and the asylums, and that part's trickier because there's money involved. Restitution money. Money and reputation. Nobody wants the headlines to point out that the friendly company that makes your pain reliever also assisted in strapping down children and injecting them with drugs. The social networks would be all over this if it ever came out."

"Perhaps," Julian conceded. "But we're getting ahead of ourselves here, Martine. If Lansbury's really behind this, then why go to the risk of killing anyone? Why go to the risk of a court case? They could just pay everybody off and make it go away without publicity."

"I don't think Annie Desmarchais or Caroline Richards were looking to get paid off," I said. "Oh, my God, Julian, that has to be it. Isn't that how this all started? Remember what we said at the beginning, that *something* changed this summer, something that made it necessary to start killing now? The only reason that he had to make his move, whoever he is, was because something changed. And that's what changed. It was all this interest from people who weren't susceptible to getting paid off."

"I still think it's implausible that a corporation was willing to put out a hit," he said.

"Maybe the corporation didn't—put out the hit, as you say. Maybe just a couple of people knew. Maybe some others turned a blind eye. Or maybe they just said to shut the women up and didn't care how it happened. We'll have to find out."

"Okay," Julian said. "I give in. You're right: we'll have to find out. Who's this guy you know?"

I'd been thinking about that. "Carrigan. Something Carrigan. Richard, was it?" I wondered out loud. "But I can't talk to him. Not about this. He's connected to my boss, and I'll be called out before I've had time to ask one question." It was an impasse. I swore eloquently in French.

"All right. Here's what we'll do. We'll find out who's in Lansbury's Montréal office," said Julian. "We'll narrow it down from there. We'll ask questions. We won't give up."

"Fine," I said. "But I still don't see it happening. You're off the case, Julian, you can't be asking official questions."

"Leave that to me," he said comfortably. "I'll see you tomorrow."

"When? What?" But he'd already hung up.

Huddled underneath our sheets that night, Marie-Rose and I consulted. "Sister Béatrice told me, the next time, to draw a line through the names where there's a family," I whispered into the darkness. "They're only interested in children who don't have anybody."

Marie-Rose shivered. "What does that mean?"

I took a deep breath. "I think it means there's nobody who will come and ask questions if something bad happens to them," I said. I was scared out of my wits.

"What bad things will happen?"

I remembered that scene in the basement. "I'm scared," I said instead of answering.

"I am, too," Marie-Rose whispered. "Jean-Loup works in the basement sometimes."

Jean-Loup was another one of "our" orphans. "What does he do? What did he tell you?"

"He has to take dead kids to the morgue sometimes. They do operations, but a lot of times the little kids don't survive. They die, and he takes them to the morgue, and sometimes he takes them out to the farm to bury them. Right turns his stomach, it does."

I thought of Bobby, whose stomach didn't turn anymore. He reassured the children, I remembered him telling me. He kept them calm.

I lived with the names, all the time, the names of children, some of them older than I was, many of them younger, and each name represented a person, someone like me, someone who breathed and thought and cried and felt things.

I swallowed hard against what was rising in my throat. "What are we going to do?" I asked her.

"I'm going to be good," said Marie-Rose. "I'm going to be so good that they'll never want to punish me. I'm going to make sure they never send me to the basement."

"It's not about being good," I whispered. "It's about no one knowing what happens here. Do you have family, Marie-Rose?"

"What?"

"Did anybody come to visit you at the orphanage? Do they send you cards for Christmas?"

I could feel rather than see her nod in the darkness. "I have my uncle Théophile," she said. "Sister Louise used to read his letters to me. He lives on a big farm."

"Then you're safe," I said. It was the first time I'd actually articulated what I knew in my heart to be true. I paused, the enormity of it crushing me. "I'm not."

"Of course you are, Gaby! They need you, don't they, to keep the records?"

"Only until they teach somebody else to do it." I knew I wasn't safe, yet something compelled me to ask questions. Jean-Loup was of little help, as horrified as he was about what he saw downstairs. "It's not just the operations," he said to me when I consulted him a few days later. "It's the room where they're in restraints."

"Like we are, sometimes," I said, nodding.

He gave me a somber look. "Nothing like us, Gabrielle," he said. "They give the kids shots, with needles, and watch them to see what they do. Sometimes they put electricity through their bodies, and sometimes they do it too much and I have to take them to the morgue, too."

Electricity through their bodies? "I don't understand. How is it they let you see all this? They're always careful when I go downstairs."

"They know that I know I could be next," he said simply. "Besides, who am I going to tell? Qui? I never see anyone from the outside, and everyone inside already knows."

And that was the end of that.

CHAPTER TWENTY-TWO

As it turned out, I was the one to get into Lansbury Pharmaceuticals first.

Sunday night we drove the kids to the airport, said goodbye, and watched them through the gate.

"It could be worse," said Ivan philosophically. "Claudia could be vegan."

"Funny man."

"Glad you noticed," he said. "Let's get going."

We got the car out of the airport's short-term parking and weren't going anywhere near home. "Um, Ivan, you do remember where we live, right?"

"Ah, but we're not going there."

My eyes widened as I saw the casino sign. "No. You're not going to work. You're not taking me to work with you."

"Of course I am, my little butterfly. But observe how I'm not dressed as the director of poker tonight." True enough: Ivan never went to work in jeans.

"I have a feeling I'm not going to like this." I find gambling intensely boring, poker more so than anything else.

"Ah, but that's where you're wrong, love of my life," he said. "This trip's entirely for you."

I was still grumbling when we got there. Montréal's casino looks like a giant spaceship decked out in bright, colorful neon lights perched precariously on the edge of the St. Lawrence. I always felt I should be putting on dark glasses when I got there.

Ivan took my hand and we went, perhaps predictably, to his office. He shut the door behind us and offered me a seat. "The tapes?" I asked, trying to make some connection. "The guys in the suits from the funeral?" I'd completely dismissed them from my mind, as they didn't fit in with our theory. I think Julian forgot about them, too.

"Don't think they're the problem," Ivan said, his voice distracted. "They left for New York that afternoon. Nothing to do with you—but something for the casino to worry about. They were at the funeral because of me. Sorry for the dead end. But I think I can just about make it up to you here."

I was still not happy. When we drop the kids off at the airport on Sunday nights, all I can usually think of is a bubble bath and a brandy, and not necessarily in that order. "Ivan, what's going on?"

He went to the wall and flicked on the monitor affixed to it: standard casino issue, views of the poker tables, the image alternating from one section to the next. He fiddled with the controls and zoomed in on one of the players. "He's here," he said with satisfaction, and pressed a button on his desk. A woman's voice floated out of the intercom. "*Oui?*"

"Sylvie, would you ask Pierre Lambert to come see me when he has a minute, please?"

"*Bien sûr,*" the faceless Sylvie responded and clicked off.

Ivan grinned at me. "Don't worry, I haven't lost my mind. I thought of this today at the cemetery."

"Uh-huh," I said slowly.

He laughed. "Really. It'll be worth it, I promise."

We watched the monitor as a young blonde woman dressed in elegant casino black approached the table and murmured something in the ear of one of the poker players. He glanced up at the camera, so that it seemed he was looking directly at Ivan and me, and nodded. Almost immediately after that he put his cards in and stood up. "Who is this?" I asked Ivan.

"A regular."

"Yeah, I kind of figured that out already. You knowing his name, and all." I smiled to take the bite out of the sarcasm.

"Funny woman," he said, not without appreciation.

The door opened and the man from the monitor appeared. In his thirties, I'd guess; well dressed in a city that prides itself on dressing well, with a Gallic hooked nose and dark hair, dark eyes. "*Salut,* Ivan," he said easily.

"*Salut,* Pierre." Ivan shook his hand perfunctorily and gestured in my direction. "This is my wife, Martine LeDuc. Martine, Pierre Lambert."

We shook hands, and Pierre sat down on Ivan's office sofa, crossing one leg over the other, elegantly, completely at ease. "How can I help you?" he asked in accented English; if his name hadn't given him away as a Francophone, his voice certainly would have.

Ivan sat down also. "Martine is the *directrice de publicité* for the city. She has a project she's working on, and she needs an introduction over at Lansbury Pharmaceuticals, and I remembered that your partner works there."

"Ah, yes." He nodded. "For almost ten years now."

I was staring at Ivan. He'd pulled a rabbit out of a hat and was looking inordinately pleased with himself, though how he'd managed not to blurt it out and give the secret away was beyond me. Unplumbed depths, my husband has. Great self-restraint. He smiled innocently in my direction and addressed himself to Pierre. "So I was wondering . . ." He let his voice trail off expectantly.

Pierre nodded. "Nothing is easier. We will speak of it when I go home tonight, and perhaps a meeting can be arranged."

I found my voice. "That would be most appreciated," I said. "Um, *monsieur*—I need for it to be soon."

"If time is of the essence, then of course," he said, nodding. "Perhaps tomorrow. I will see." He stood up. "If that is all . . ."

Ivan stood with him and held out his hand again. "*Merci*, Pierre."

"*De rien, mon ami.*" He turned to me. "*Madame*," he said formally, shaking my hand. "We will call you tomorrow."

"Thank you very much," I said again, and watched him exit and the door close behind him. "When were you going to tell me about Pierre?" I asked Ivan.

He laughed. "I wouldn't have lasted much longer," he confessed. "Honestly, I only started thinking about who I might know when we were at the cemetery, and Pierre's name came to me on the way to the airport. Pierre's only here on weekends, mostly, except in the summertime when it's pretty much any night. He's good at getting the tourist trade to share some of their vacation dollars with him."

"He's professional?"

"One of the best." Ivan was unperturbed.

I knew about professionals. If you go to a casino and count cards at blackjack, you'll be invited to leave pretty damned fast: you're cheating the casino itself when you cheat at blackjack. But poker's a different story. Poker is the only casino game where you don't play against the house, so the house has no stakes in who wins and who loses. Professionals are ejected from every other game, but welcomed at the poker tables.

There were always a few who were there hour after hour, winning a little, losing a little, then waiting and winning big when they'd finally landed a whale. It looked to me like an infinitely boring way of making a living, but then again, I didn't make nearly as much as they did.

And, some days, I could use a little boredom in my job.

The next morning I was at my desk early. There was a message from the mayor: the crown prosecutor was looking into the police's suspect and, until a decision was made, I didn't need to check in with the police director. The phone rang at half past eight—an unheard-of hour for normal people to be doing business in a city that stayed up late—and Chantal buzzed me. "It's for you."

"Who is it?" I felt cross; I had a lot on my plate and my deputy was supposed to be fielding calls when he was there.

"Asked for you specifically, not Richard. It's someone called Jean-Louis Montrachet. Francophone."

"You think?" Then I shook my head: it wasn't Chantal's fault, and I had a feeling that she was coping with some of Richard's load these days as well as her own. "*Merci*, Chantal, I'll take it." I pushed the appropriate button on the telephone. "Good morning, *ici* Martine LeDuc, how can I help you?"

"*Bonjour, madame.* I understand that it is I who can help you."

I wasn't in the mood for games. I'd slept badly, dreaming of long polished convent corridors and children crying in the dark. "Monsieur—er—Montrachet, that's it? I don't know—"

He cut in briskly. "My partner is Pierre Lambert," he said. "I work for Lansbury Pharmaceuticals. He told me that he spoke to you and your husband last night, and that you wished to speak to someone from my company."

Oh. *That* kind of partner. One never knew. I cleared my throat. "Monsieur Montrachet, forgive me. Yes. Thank you for calling." I tried to gather my thoughts; I'd thought I'd have time to consult with Julian before speaking to him. Useless to ask for an introduction to the C-level suite; those people would as soon admit malfeasance as shoot themselves. "Forgive the intrusion, and my curiosity, but what is it that you do at the company?"

If he thought the question odd he didn't say so. "I am in the marketing department," he said.

That didn't help, or really mean anything at all. I felt stuck: now that I had the fish on the line, so to speak, I had no idea what to do with it. There were probably clever questions to ask, but I didn't know what they were. And without knowing what to ask . . . "*Monsieur,*" I said, finally, "may I take you to lunch today?" There was a silence, and I added quickly, "I would not ask, but it's very important."

"Very well, *madame*. My partner respects your husband very much, and would like to do him a favor." There was a slight pause. "Let us say one o'clock at l'Orignal. My secretary will make the reservation."

I swallowed hard: he'd just made sure I wasn't wasting time by naming one of Montréal's more expensive restaurants. "*Bien*," I managed to croak. There was no way I could justify expensing this. "Please make it for three people."

"I will see you then," Jean-Louis said and was gone.

Okay. It doesn't matter. You're getting close. Maybe, I thought hopefully, I could get Julian to pick up the tab for lunch. I looked up his number and pressed the digits. Surprisingly, he answered. "We're having lunch with someone from Lansbury's marketing department," I said cheerfully. "Aren't you impressed?"

"I am," he said, sounding bemused.

"One o'clock at l'Orignal," I said, trying to make it sound like I went there all the time. "Name of Montrachet."

"Aren't you going to tell me anything else about this?"

I sighed. "Nothing more to tell, really," I confessed. "He's the partner of one of Ivan's regulars—I mean, my husband. He's the director of—"

"I know who Ivan is," Julian interrupted, amusement in his voice now.

"Oh. *Bien*. So there's this regular poker player, and he's married to this other guy who works in marketing at Lansbury." It didn't sound like much when it was put that way.

"Well done," said Julian unexpectedly. "Is Lansbury paying for lunch?"

"No," I said. "You and I get to argue over the check."

He laughed. "See you then, Martine."

I should mention that the restaurant in question—whose name roughly translates as "the moose"—is probably worth every penny one spends there. It specializes in the freshest high-end game, fresh fish, and oysters, and if Jean-Louis could get a same-day reservation there for lunch, then he had some pull. I was beginning to feel more cheerful about the whole thing.

Julian and I arrived at about the same time and were shown quickly to a table where a man was already seated. He rose to greet us, and I made the introductions. He dressed every bit as well and expensively as his husband, and even resembled him slightly; maybe that happens with couples who have been together a lot of years. We sat down and Jean-Louis turned to Julian. "Would you prefer that we speak in English, *monsieur*?"

Julian said blandly and in French, "It doesn't matter to me. If you are more comfortable in French, then *allons-y*."

I stared at him. He'd always made *me* speak English. He kicked me, almost gently, under the table, and I smiled at them both. "We wanted to ask you some questions about your company," I began.

Jean-Louis held up a hand. "Perhaps," he said gently, "we can order first?"

"Of course." I was overeager and knew better than to be this rude: this whole situation was getting to me. Deep breath, Martine. I smiled blandly at the two men and for a few moments we all pored over our menus. They ordered the grilled venison steak; I settled for two appetizers—oysters and elk tartare. Lots of protein. I had a feeling I'd need to keep up my strength. We agreed on a bottle of wine and finally the niceties were finished.

"So," Jean-Louis said, "please tell me what this is about."

"It's rather a long story," I began, but Julian put up his hand. "I am with the *service de police de la ville de Montréal*," he said, pulling out his credentials. "It is important that you understand that from the beginning."

He looked from one of us to the other. "Have I done something?"

"No, not you," I said quickly, though for all I knew perhaps he had. "It's about the past, actually."

He was confused, and not hiding it too well. Julian cleared his throat and began. "We've learned that from the 1950s through the 1970s, Lansbury Pharmaceuticals was under contract to supply various drugs to a number of psychiatric facilities in the province," he said, leaving out the fact that the company was also supplying drugs quite innocently to a whole lot of other hospitals. Maybe he just wanted to scare Jean-Louis. "These facilities included the Allan Institute and a psychiatric asylum called the Cité de Saint-Jean-de-Dieu, both of them here in Montréal."

I was watching Jean-Louis, and there was no reaction at all, no obvious change in blood pressure, no eye movement, no flush of recognition. If he knew anything about what Julian was saying, he was a better actor than most actors.

Julian went on smoothly, "It has come to our attention that there is a possible link between what happened at those facilities and some more recent crimes in the city, and of course, we must follow up on these possibilities." He accompanied the last bit with a hand gesture that said, it's nothing, you know how these things are. Well done, Julian, I thought. He managed to do what the true bilingual does: adapt not only his words, but his means of expression, his gestures and facial expressions, to the pattern of the other language.

He stopped to allow the server to put our plates in front of us and there were the usual few moments of confusion as the server asked if we wanted anything else and I wished he'd get the hell away and Julian gave him a Fletcher look and he did in fact go away. I needed to learn how to do that look.

"Will you tell me the connection?" asked Jean-Louis.

Julian didn't hesitate. "I'm sorry, that's impossible," he said, with regret in his voice. "Police matters, you understand—"

"Yet you expect me to understand enough to answer your questions."

"Look," I said, urgently, ignoring Julian's pained expression. These two could play mind games all day, and if I was paying for this lunch, I was going to get my money's worth. "You've heard of the Duplessis orphans." He nodded. "That's what we're talking about," I said, drawing in a deep breath. "Lansbury was supplying the asylums, or at least one of them, that the children were sent to. No one's innocent in this affair, not the government, not the Church, not the nuns, not the doctors; but it happened, and we think that someone's trying to cover it up now."

"But, *madame*," objected Jean-Louis, "that affair is resolved. The government settled with the Duplessis orphans. It was on the news, in the newspapers. It was some time ago—ten years maybe? Fifteen? More? I cannot remember."

"And then there's the Allan Institute," I went on doggedly.

"Again, it was Lansbury that supplied the drugs for the CIA program MK-Ultra, for the experiments going on at the Allan. You've heard of MK-Ultra?"

He nodded, his mouth full of venison.

"We think that the two are connected. We think that orphans from the asylum were being used as subjects at the Allan. We think that Lansbury supplied the drugs in return for the asylum's use as an experimental lab to see what worked and what didn't . . . and in return received a hefty amount of what the CIA was spending on MK-Ultra. We think that the unifying factor was the money—and Lansbury Pharmaceuticals."

Jean-Louis took a sip of wine, swallowed, and shook his head. "*Madame*, even if your suppositions are correct, you are talking about events that took place sixty or seventy years ago," he objected. "What possible interest could the company have in it now? And how does that relate to any crime committed in the present?"

"Money," said Julian. He wanted back in. Probably felt that my interrogation techniques left something to be desired. "The government settled with the survivors for a pittance. Everyone knows that. The living orphans were getting older, they didn't have much time left, it was better than nothing, so they took what they could get and the government breathed a sigh of relief. But the orphans have heirs, and Lansbury has deeper pockets than the province and a reputation to uphold—and a lot more to lose if this thing ever came to trial."

"It wouldn't come to trial," said Jean-Louis, marketing expert.

"Exactly," Julian said and nodded. "And a settlement won't make shareholders happy."

Montrachet shook his head and patted his lips with his napkin. "I must be honest with you, *madame, monsieur*," he said. "I think this is a fantasy. We are involved in many projects in many countries. Had this sort of involvement been illegal, even if it did take place—and to be perfectly frank, I cannot speak to that, I know nothing about it—but had it happened, and had it been illegal, we would have heard of it by now. We have a legal department precisely for these reasons: to determine that what we are doing *is* legal. I am sorry if you feel you have wasted your time, but I see nothing here with which I can help you."

At least, I thought, the oysters were good.

"Well, what did you expect?" Julian asked me later, as we walked down the cobbled streets of the Old City. "For him to say, yeah, sorry, *mea culpa*, I've been killing those people to save my company?"

"I thought maybe he'd say, okay, I'll look into it, I'll have you meet someone who can help you," I said miserably, stopping and turning to face him. The afternoon sun was warm and mellow, whispering that it didn't matter, that time had moved on. No, I thought. Not this time. "Julian, we're getting nowhere." I was feeling a little sick. "And if the crown prosecutor goes for this *clochard,* the homeless one your department has in custody, then that will be the end of it all. And they'll all have suffered and died for nothing. Nothing!" I could feel the tears, then, pressing hot against the backs of my eyes. "They were scared and they were tortured and they were killed, and there's nothing we can do about it."

But as it turned out, I couldn't have been more wrong.

CHAPTER TWENTY-THREE

My telephone rang later that afternoon. "Mrs. LeDuc?" An Anglophone voice, brisk and deep. "My name is Robert Carrigan. You may recall we met at the mayor's office. I'm an attorney at Lansbury Pharmaceuticals."

Carrigan: that was the name that had eluded me when I'd had Julian on the phone. Robert Carrigan. The lobbyist, the one who supported the mayor's political campaigns. And I'd been right, he wasn't just in Big Pharma, he was at Lansbury. "Yes?" I said cautiously.

"I understand that you had a conversation earlier today with someone—a Monsieur Jean-Louis Montrachet—from our marketing department."

"Yes?" I said again, trying to keep my voice even. Yes! The bait had been dangled and the fish had snapped it up. Montrachet obviously felt bothered enough by what we said to pass it along to somebody who could, presumably, do something about it. The legal department of which he'd spoken at lunch. And maybe, a small voice in the back of my head was exulting, Robert Carrigan would lead us to whomever had hired the killer, and then to the killer himself. I wasn't interested in the killer himself per se, not if he was just a common or garden variety psycho.

I wanted the one who signed his paycheck.

Oblivious to my thoughts, the voice on the other end of the line continued. "Mrs. LeDuc, I think it would be helpful if *we* could meet."

"Okay," I said as casually as I could. I was remembering what he looked like, the distinguished air about him, the intelligent eyes. I'd thought him attractive, as I recalled. "I can come to your office." In my limited experience with attorneys—though heaven knows the experience is not as limited as I'd prefer—they always want to meet in their offices. More billable hours, no doubt.

"That wouldn't be possible, unfortunately. We're having some construction done." My mind was still remembering our two previous brief encounters. Shining silver hair, excellent taste in clothes, he'd even winked at me. An elegant man, amused and amusing. "You're located in the Old City, right? I can come to you. Say, seven o'clock?"

"Tonight?" I wasn't liking that at all. Too sudden; who knew if I'd be able to confer with the elusive Julian twice in one day? What did one say, anyway? Excuse me, but did your company hire a killer to torture and rape these women who were going to expose its horrific past? How was that for an opener?

"Yes, I think it's best if we discuss this right away," he was saying briskly. "Always important to clear up any misunderstandings before they go further. These things can take on a life of their own, especially when the public gets hold of them—well, you know that better than anybody, I'm preaching to the public relations choir, aren't I?" A pause. "And we wouldn't want to have to bring a lawsuit against the city for anything."

Misunderstandings. Right. That's what's going on here. And the not-so-veiled threat of legal retribution. Then I thought of the mayor and what shade of puce he'd turn if he had any idea this conversation was taking place. Yeah, better get it over with.

I remembered how I'd felt when Dr. MacDougal had me trapped in the office; I didn't need a repeat performance of that particular experience. No empty offices and no echoing corridors, thank you very much. "I'll meet you in front of the basilica on Saint-Sulpice," I said, finally decisive.

A long pause. "I was thinking perhaps some privacy might be best—considering the delicate nature of our topic of conversation," he said.

"Mr. Carrigan—that's your name, right?—I have to say that I don't really care what you were hoping for." I was thinking fast, wondering where Julian was and whether I could get him to meet with us. I wasn't exactly looking forward to a lecture from one of Lansbury's attorneys. He'd already revealed the card he was going to play: he was going to threaten me with litigation around what he no doubt thought of as wild accusations, and having the police present—even in the seemingly innocuous form of Julian Fletcher—might just take the edge off.

"There's an organ recital at the basilica at six," I said; it's useful to be the publicity director and know about all the events in town. "I'll be attending, and can meet you afterward. Or tomorrow, during the day." Let's see just how desperate he is to get together.

He surprised me. "Very well," he replied calmly. "In front of the basilica at seven. Until then, Mrs. LeDuc."

I had a hollow feeling in my stomach that didn't go away even with an orange-chocolate Aero bar, my usual first line of attack against hunger or anxiety. I called Julian and—surprise, surprise—got his voice mail. "*Ici* Martine. We rattled their cage, Julian. I'm meeting that lawyer I told you about from Lansbury right after the concert in the Old City tonight. Robert Carrigan, that's the name I couldn't remember. It would be great if you could come along. Call me back!"

I called Ivan. "Hey, handsome. Want to go to the organ recital at the basilica with me?" I didn't know why I was dreading this meeting so much, but I was, which meant that as far as I was concerned, the more, the merrier.

"At six? I can't, sorry, sweetie. I have some VIPs to coddle here."

"Oh. Okay." I hesitated, then added, "I'm meeting someone from Lansbury right after the concert," I said.

"That's good, babe, isn't it?"

"Yes," I said, trying hard to banish the fear that wasn't going away. "Yes, of course it is." I forced a laugh. "Maybe this will all be over by tonight."

"Maybe," he said. "Are you okay? Really?"

"Yes," I said, unconsciously straightening my back. "Yes, of course I am. I'll see you at home."

"Be careful, babe."

"I will," I promised. "Bye, Ivan. Love you."

It was going to be, I thought, a very long afternoon.

And so that winter was all about the lists. The names—many of them people I didn't know—that I researched dutifully, going through file folders to learn whether there was someone, somewhere, who might actually care if they lived or died.

Just as Bobby had made his choice, I made mine then, too, choosing without conscious choice, doing the only thing that seemed remotely right in the circumstances. I went through list after list, and when I came across the name of someone I knew, I made up a family: a distant cousin, a neighbor, a married brother, and watched, my heart hammering in my chest, as the sister crossed that name off her own list.

Consulted, Jean-Loup agreed that there were bodies. "Not every day, mind," he said. "I don't think they actually want them to die. But they're tryin' things out. The ones that die, they're the mistakes."

"Where do they go?"

He shrugged, indifferent. "Graveyard by the piggery."

"I didn't see a graveyard by the piggery," said Marie-Rose.

"Stones are only there for the nuns," Jean-Loup said. "The rest, they just dig holes and put 'em in. On top of each other, on account of not using too much space. Babies, sometimes."

"Babies!" I was appalled. "What are babies doing here?"

"Gabrielle," he said and shook his head, "what's anybody doing here?"

An unanswerable question, if ever there were one. Some of us were safe, and some of us weren't, and the line between the two was as fragile as the gossamer threads of a spider's web.

CHAPTER TWENTY-FOUR

The concert was interminable.

It shouldn't have been: the guest organist was a well-known musician from Paris and an extremely skilled performer; he knew exactly what to do with the massive pipes and pedals of the basilica's majestic organ, and he did it well. But my mind wasn't on the music.

I had to stop myself from checking the time on my smartphone every five minutes. I fidgeted. I smoothed out nonexistent wrinkles in my skirt. I scratched phantom itches. I slipped my feet in and out of my ballet flats. I even sighed out loud.

It was probably the first time I'd ever been in the basilica and not felt something otherworldly. I told Ivan once that it seemed to me you couldn't go into that place and come out not believing in God, which he of course found both inaccurate and fanciful. It's a cathedral like many other cathedrals, especially European ones, with vaulted ceilings and myriad candles burning at the side chapels flanking the nave; but once you look at the front of the church, your breath is taken away. The reredos—the decorative facing behind the altar— is tremendously large, soaring up almost into the sky, and filled with images, statuary, stained glass, telling intricate stories; and, behind it, the wall and lights are all blue, a brilliant blue, the blue of Our Lady's garments, she to whom the basilica is dedicated. It's exceptionally beautiful, and exceptionally moving.

I was sitting, gazing up at that calm crystal beauty and feeling awash in music, all the while my stomach was tightening in dread. Were things really going to be resolved tonight? Would Julian show up? Was I—and, by extension, the city of Montréal—about to get sued? What was I thinking here?

All in all, I was relieved when it was time to stand and applaud the Frenchman.

I walked briskly down one of the side aisles toward the exit, people around me standing, stretching, reaching for their light autumn jackets and sweaters, holding their programs, talking to each other, easing back from the world of creative soaring music and into the prosaic pedestrian decisions about where to have dinner and whether they should take a walk first and what they all thought of the concert. I passed them quickly, smiling and nodding to people I knew. I always try to make an appearance at as many of these events as I can, for professional reasons, but tonight of all nights I didn't want to get trapped into a lengthy conversation.

The flood of people released from the basilica flowed around me, chattering and laughing, as I stood out on the plaza in front, looking around for Robert Carrigan. When it came down to it,

I wasn't altogether sure I'd recognize him out of context, and I was left with a general sense of his appearance, not anything particularly notable. There were several men hanging about in front of the basilica who actually could have been him.

It didn't really matter, as he would recognize me, no doubt. I'm not famous, but I'm accessible via websites and brochures, many of which include photos; and I had no doubt that any attorney worth his salt would already have a full dossier on me. He'd find me, even if he didn't remember what I looked like.

Or not. Maybe he hadn't made it. Maybe we could do this tomorrow, in my office, with Julian and lots of people around and he'd say no, you're wrong, here's proof that what happened back then had nothing to do with Lansbury Pharmaceuticals . . .

Yeah, that would be the day.

I checked my messages on my smartphone. I checked the time. I called Julian again and again got no answer. I straightened my sweater, smoothed my skirt. I thought about when I'd last brushed my teeth. I wondered when the kids were getting their report cards. I decided I'd go over to l'Aubanerie on Avenue du Mont-Royal sometime this week and buy that dress I'd been looking at for a while.

The crowd around me thinned to a trickle.

I fished out a loonie—our dollar coin—from my pocket and gave it to the street musician gamely trying to make a little money out of the departing concertgoers. He thanked me, as he does every day when I give him something. We each pretend that we don't know each other. He's a janitor in my office when he isn't playing flute for the tourists.

I checked my phone: seven-ten. Okay. He wasn't coming.

I turned away, back toward the church doors, thinking that I'd go in and sit for a few minutes while they were finishing tidying up for the night, and figure out my next move. It's a great place for praying, the basilica, but sometimes an even greater place for thinking.

I was just reaching for the door when his voice stopped me. "Madame LeDuc."

Something jumped in my chest and I turned quickly. Now that I saw him, I did remember: the smooth gray hair, the clear cool eyes. He was dressed tonight in unmemorable clothes; maybe he did that to be unnoticed. But I'd noticed him, down the steps from the front of the basilica, reading a map.

He'd been there the whole time I'd been waiting. I wondered why.

"Mr. Carrigan," I said, hoping that I wasn't squeaking. Somehow squeaking didn't seem to go with the level of gravitas I wanted to project.

He inclined his head. "I didn't mean to startle you."

Of course he'd meant to startle me. "Then why did you?"

"Best," he said, taking my elbow, "if we could wait until there were fewer people about. We're discussing something confidential, after all."

Normally a man's hand on my elbow isn't something I'd even notice, but for all of that, there was something unmistakably creepy about his touch and I pulled my arm away. "A problem that could have been taken care of if we'd met in your office, as I suggested," I snapped. "Or mine." I'd kind of liked the idea that he wasn't going to show, and now I wasn't in the mood for a lecture or a lawsuit threat.

I was thinking, quite honestly and most longingly, of dinner.

Robert Carrigan seemed unaffected by my tone. "It's always best to be as clear as possible, as quickly as possible," he said smoothly. "Shall we walk?"

"Fine."

We walked downhill, toward the waterfront, the cobbled streets slowly emptying as people decided on restaurants for dinner, lights from open doors and windows cascading out onto the uneven cobblestones, the clink of silverware and glasses, the occasional laugh. The sounds of my city.

I glanced at the Lansbury attorney. There was something about him, something that didn't quite fit . . . "May I see your identification?" I asked suddenly. I haven't had much experience with lawyers but it seemed that the ones I had met were forever handing out business cards.

He looked amused, stopped, and pulled a wallet from his pocket. I didn't say anything, just scrutinized his provincial identity card and his driver's license, both of which confirmed he was indeed Robert Carrigan. His employee card for Lansbury Pharmaceuticals sealed the deal. "Thank you," I said.

"My pleasure, of course." We'd reached the Rue de la Commune; and across the street was the waterfront. I half expected him to head that way, as it offered benches, tables and chairs, opportunities for a quiet conversation apart from the bustle of the cafés and restaurants on the Rue Saint-Paul. Instead, his hand again at my elbow, we turned right, passing the souvenir stores, the ice-cream shops, the cafés, all of which spilled onto the sidewalk with tables and postcard stands and guests. "We need to talk about MK-Ultra," he said smoothly.

"Yes," I agreed. "We do."

We looked like any other couple, strolling in the crisp evening air. His tone was pleasant, too, just another fellow remarking on the day. "You realize, of course, that all of Lansbury Pharmaceuticals' participation in the project was completely within the bounds of the law."

"That remains to be seen," I said tartly. Okay, so I was being sarcastic with a lawyer about the law. Just get it over with, I found myself thinking. Just tell me you'll sue, and see how fast I back down.

He didn't go there. He didn't do anything I'd expected him to. "The goals of MK-Ultra," he said, looking down at the sidewalk and not at me, "included investigating a knockout pill that could surreptitiously be administered in drinks, food, cigarettes, or even work as an aerosol. This pill would be safe to use, provide a maximum of amnesia, and be suitable for use by agents on an ad-hoc basis."

He paused, but I didn't say anything; I had no idea how to respond. Why the hell was he telling me this? I was fascinated. I was appalled. I was beginning to get a little scared. "MK-Ultra's brief also included investigating substances that would render the induction of hypnosis easier, or otherwise enhance its usefulness; substances that increase one's ability to withstand privation, torture, and coercion during interrogation and so-called brainwashing, and substances that would produce amnesia for events preceding and during their use."

I had gotten my breathing under control now, and decided that the best defense was a quick offense. "It sounds like a shopping list for Lansbury Pharmaceuticals. Every day is Christmas when you're funded and supported by the CIA, isn't it?"

We crossed at the Place Royal and turned, again at Robert Carrigan's indication, back up the hill on Saint Francis Xavier. "Lansbury Pharmaceuticals was assured in writing that any use of these substances in experimentation was done with the full consent of the subjects involved," he said carefully.

"Oh, really?" I'd forgotten to be afraid. "And where did the orphans at Cité de Saint-Jean-de-Dieu sign their names, Mr. Carrigan? The children, I'm talking *children*, do you have *their* consent forms on file?"

He was staring at me. "What do you know about the children?" His voice was hoarse.

"I know they were put in asylums without being crazy," I said. "I know there was a connection between the Allan and some of the asylums. I know there were people in town this spring and summer looking into what had happened, maybe pulling up evidence."

"You don't know," he said, and his voice had changed. "You don't know anything about the children."

I frowned. What was this about? "They were tortured," I said. It seemed as good an answer as any.

"It was not as bad as people think," he said. "Not for everybody."

He was really losing me now. "I don't think you can forgo all responsibility because some poor souls actually survived!" I exclaimed.

He shook his head, slowly at first then more vigorously, as if he was more than disagreeing, as if he were shaking off memories. We started walking again. "Lansbury Pharmaceuticals had no knowledge that our products were used in conjunction with anyone other than a consenting adult," he said, and his voice was back the way it had been before, the way it was supposed to be: brisk, clipped, professional. As if that other conversation hadn't happened at all.

"Well," I said, going out on a very thin limb, "what if I told you there's been proof uncovered that indicates otherwise?"

We were back on Rue Notre-Dame, coming up again on the basilica from the other side. The area in front of it was now completely deserted except for the pigeons, busily scrabbling about for the infinitesimal bits of ice cream cone or bread or cookies left by tourists.

"I would respond," said Robert Carrigan carefully, "by asking you precisely what proof you're referring to. Claims are easy to make, Mrs. LeDuc. In my experience, they're harder to substantiate."

That's what they had, I thought. It came to me then, suddenly, all in one piece, the way some artists claim that visions come to them, the way some musicians see the whole of a symphony before composing a note. The whole picture, clean and clear and as crisp as the autumn air around me.

That's what they had. One of the dead women, maybe more than one of them, hadn't just put the pieces together the way that Julian and I had. They had found proof, the proof that would nail Lansbury Pharmaceuticals to the wall and cost the company millions of dollars in reparations. They could substantiate the claims. They could prove that Lansbury knew the subjects weren't consenting and still they supplied the drugs. The chlorpromazine. The thioridazine. The LSD. What this horrible man was referring to as the "product."

They could prove it, and so they died.

I'd stopped again, without realizing it, and when Robert Carrigan turned to see why, he saw my face. I'd said I wouldn't be very good at this subterfuge thing, and I was right.

And just as I understood, so did he.

He reached out to grab me and I took off like the favorite in the hundred meters at the Olympics. Across the expanse of gray weathered stone. And into the basilica.

I'd thought that Marie-Rose would be safe. I really had. But that was before she got sick.

She kept coughing in the night and one morning couldn't get out of bed. I pleaded with her to try, but she didn't seem to see me or hear me and the inevitable result was that Sister Marie-Laure, who was infirmarian, caught us. "What are you doing?"

"Sorry, Sister. Marie-Rose isn't feeling well."

"Step away," she ordered me, and bent over the bed, her hand on Marie-Rose's forehead. When she straightened up, her face looked like it was carved out of stone. "Are you taking her to the infirmary, Sister?" The infirmary, I knew, was an antechamber only; the real destination would be the basement.

"It's none of your concern," she snapped. "You have things to do, don't you? What's your name?"

"Gabrielle Roy," I said hesitantly. It wasn't necessarily a good thing, to be brought to the sisters' attention. "But Marie-Rose—"

"Then go, Gabrielle, and tell Dr. Desmarchais that there's a

child taken ill." She saw me hesitate, and slapped my cheek. "Listen to me! Go tell Dr. Desmarchais, and then do whatever he tells you to do."

"Yes, Sister."

I gave one last agonizing look at Marie-Rose, and ran. Down to the doctors' office on the ground floor, where the rooms were brightly lit and everything seemed clean and new. In contrast, of course, to what they were there for. You could almost believe that they wanted to heal people here, that they were really doing something good.

A girl about my own age, someone I didn't know, was sitting in a chair outside a closed door. "What are you waiting for?"

"I don't know," she said, and shrugged. "Sister Béatrice told me to wait, so I'm waiting."

"Is Dr. Desmarchais in there?" I pointed at the closed door. I was wondering if I could claim that I hadn't found him. It wouldn't work, of course; but buying Marie-Rose any time at all seemed the least I could do.

The girl nodded. "Sister said not to disturb him," she said.

I sat down next to her. "My name's Gabrielle. What's yours?"

The eyes flickered at me and back again into the middle distance. She was being cautious, which meant she was smart. "Annie."

We waited an interminable time. I was worried about Marie-Rose, worried about what Sister Marie-Laure was doing to her upstairs, worried what it meant for her to see the doctor; at the asylum, doctors weren't there to protect you. Au contraire.

I stole a glance from time to time at Annie, sitting so still next to me that she might have been one of the statues in the orphanage's chapel.

Finally the door opened and a nun came out carrying a little boy in her arms. He seemed to be asleep. I didn't know either of them, and she left without a word.

Dr. Desmarchais stuck his head out and saw the girl next to me first. "Annie! It's good to see you. Thank you for stopping by. I have something to talk with you about."

He seemed only then to notice me. "Yes? Can I help you?"

"Sister Marie-Laure sent me," I said, sliding to my feet so as to look respectful. "It's Marie-Rose. She's sick."

"I see." He patted Annie on the head. "Just wait here, there's a good girl." He turned to me. "Where are you supposed to be, now?"

"In the file room, monsieur le docteur.*"*

"Very good. Run along there now. I'll take care of your friend."

And he must have done, because I never saw her again.

CHAPTER TWENTY-FIVE

He was behind me.

I knew as soon as I darted into the church that he'd follow me, but I wasn't thinking, not really; like any frightened animal when the hawk circled, I was in a blind panic. Thinking that the shadows would protect me, the scattering of side altars and ranks of flickering candles. No; *not* thinking was more like it. Going on instinct. The hunted will bolt even when it's exactly the wrong thing to do.

And where were the security guards, anyway? They were supposed to lock up, or to keep the odd tourist from wandering in after hours without paying admission. What had happened to *them*?

It didn't matter, not really: they weren't here, and I was.

I wasn't harboring any more illusions about Robert Carrigan. He knew all of Lansbury's secrets, and had been keeping them for years. Who knew when he'd first gotten involved with them, when he'd first decided that the company, above all else, needed to thrive?

There had been something that had come and gone in those eyes when I'd brought up the children at the asylum. I couldn't tell what it was, but it was after that his manner had changed. It was after that he'd decided to do what he had to do to keep me quiet.

Had Robert Carrigan hired a contract killer to take out Lansbury's garbage? Or had Robert Carrigan saved them the trouble and taken care of it himself? Was *he* the killer?

And I had liked him. When we'd first met, I'd *liked* him.

Whoever he was, he was chasing me now. Someone willing to rape and murder, if not by his own hand, then once removed. Someone who was coming after me, ready to add another name to the list of victims. *There might be another woman somewhere*, Ivan had said.

Neither of us had any idea that woman might end up being me.

I'd instinctively swerved to the left when I went in; when I went to the basilica for mass on Sundays it was where I sat, and my feet were moving without any input from my brain. The church was darkened but weirdly alive, the flames from thousands of candles in the numerous side chapels flickering, giving off an odd yellow light that cast more shadows than it relieved and making the very stone seem to come alive. The lights were still on behind the reredos, the blue of the heavenly sky, dotted with gold stars and glowing, I fancied, with the holiness and sanctification of the liturgies that had been enacted there.

There's something about a church, especially a big mysterious one, that makes you want to whisper. Robert Carrigan obviously felt otherwise. "Martine!" His voice echoed around me and off the pillars that spanned my side aisle. "Don't be ridiculous. All I want to do is talk."

Yeah. Like you talked to Danielle and Annie and Isabelle and Caroline. I saved my breath and, like a church mouse in this greatest of all churches, looked desperately for a hiding place.

I'd made my way as far as the confessionals, now, and darted inside the first one. On the penitent's side, of course; even the threat of imminent death didn't seem to relax the shibboleths of my upbringing. As I stood in the narrow space, scarcely breathing, I realized what an infinitely stupid move I'd made. I was trapped inside a box no larger than an upright coffin, just waiting to be discovered.

No: I wouldn't wait here, trembling, for him to hunt me down and find me. You're strong, Martine. You don't have to be a victim.

I wondered how strong they had been, the others. Probably stronger than I was. But I had something they didn't have: I knew who my enemy was, and what he was capable of doing.

I opened the door and slipped out again before I lost my nerve. I was beginning to understand how the rabbit felt, staying stock-still for as long as possible—and then bolting at the very worst possible time, nerves broken, death in sight.

I had no idea where Robert was.

The thought sent me spinning into panic. Beside me, a life-sized wooden statue—of Marguerite Bourgeoys, Montréal's own saint—seemed to move in the flickering candlelight, the lips alive in prayer, the eyes watchful. I crouched beside her, her

painted cloak against my skin. Help me, Saint Marguerite, protect me. She had nothing to say, and I leaned closer to her, feeling
invisible, knowing I was not. Think, Martine, think. You have
the advantage here. You know this place; he doesn't. Use what
you know.

What I knew was that I'd never been so scared in all my life.

"Martine!" I jumped; the voice was close, too close. I stayed
down and scuttled behind a rack of votive candles, probably not
too brilliant a move—their light would blind me to seeing anything else—but the instinct to hide was too overwhelming.
"Martine, where *are* you?" Almost a chant, familiar from childhood games. Childish, that's what he sounded.

He'd changed when I talked about children at the asylum.
His eyes, his voice, he'd become younger though no less terrifying. What was it about Robert Carrigan and these children?

Never mind. Right now what I had to do was survive to tell
the tale.

I felt an atavistic shudder run down my spine and my brain,
finally, clicked into gear. I slipped my hand into my pocket, my
fingers closing around the dreaded smartphone. I pulled it out
and, risking its illumination, navigated to the contacts list, pressed
a button. Ringing. More ringing as I tempered my breath to avoid
making too much noise. "You've reached the voice mail of Julian
Fletcher . . ." That was no good. I whispered into the phone. "It's
Martine, I'm at the basilica, help me, Julian. He's here. Carrigan.
It's him. He's going to kill me." I tried Ivan, got his voice mail too.
I should probably leave Ivan a message, part of my mind was
thinking, in case I wasn't around later to tell him anything.

I couldn't think like that. I had to know where Robert was. I put my head even farther down and focused on the smartphone, clicking on the utilities, then set the alarm for three minutes. I slipped the phone down onto the floor and, cautiously, eased myself out from behind the candles and darted into the shadows of the next chapel over. I couldn't even see who this saint was, somebody male and big and reassuring; he should have been a comfort to me. The small altar was marble, cold under my fingers, and I glanced up into his face, the statue impassive in the flickering candlelight. No help there.

No movement anywhere. What I had to do, I thought, was get up in the organ loft, where only an hour ago the French master musician had been playing. From there, I could see where Robert was.

No, the saner part of me said. You don't have to get into the *loft*, you idiot; you have to get out of here. An adage came floating up out of my subconscious: never climb, eventually you run out of stairs. I had to get out in the open, out where there are people, out where there's safety and no madman chasing me through a medieval maze . . .

I slid around another pillar just as the alarm I'd set went off. Even though I knew it was coming, I jumped.

Robert, however, did nothing. No more calling out. No rushing to see where my phone was. No exclamations of discovery or irritation. It was as if I were alone in the vast dark cathedral. That's probably what he wanted me to think.

For one long moment I considered just staying there. All night. They'd be in, later, to lock up; if not, someone would open the church for morning mass. I could just stay there; in the morning I'd be safe.

In the morning, I thought, I'd be dead. I had to get out of there.

Back behind the reredos was a stairway, down to the restrooms and the exhibit hall. And an exit.

The church seemed brighter now, lit by the thousands of candles burning all over, in front of statues and icons, in all of the side altars, carrying prayers eternally on their flames. I could have used a few of those prayers right now. I felt my way back down toward the front of the church, keeping my back to the wall, in and out of the depressions that held statues, paintings, grottoes. I could do this. I could get out of here.

Still no movement anywhere. I forced myself to breathe. Sure, Martine, everything's safe now. Odd how I'd thought of the murderer as some shadowy figure, larger than life, scary as a nightmare; and then had met him and saw how ordinary he was. Maybe evil looks like that. Maybe evil is so insidious because it's so ordinary.

Maybe someday I'd have the leisure to consider such philosophical questions.

Past the choir stalls, finally, and the staircase, dark and gaping, opened to my left. There was no candlelight back here. It didn't matter: the door at the foot of those stairs was freedom, light, safety. I plunged down them headlong.

And had my wrist grabbed even as I reached for the doorknob. "I don't think," Robert Carrigan said, "that it's time for you to leave quite yet, my dear."

They caught me doing it, of course.

There were four or five doctors at the asylum all the time now, and they all were very busy. There were medications for us to take, injections—some painful, some merely scary—to be endured. Operations to be done. Electroshock, which I hadn't had to undergo but had seen, quite by accident, and never wanted to even think about again. Restraints, chains, straitjackets. Oh, and the prettiest girls—and prettiest boys, too—who spent time with the orderlies behind closed doors, and cried about it later in the night.

And all of it supervised by the doctors. Who always were looking for someone who hadn't been "treated" yet.

Which brought everything back to me and my lists.

I'd been handing them to Sister Béatrice with scribbled notations, and one day she came into the file room and sat across from me. "I'd like to see some of the folders," she said. Her eyes were colder than anything I'd ever seen.

"Yes, Sister," I said. What else was there for me to say?

"Bien," she said. "Let me see . . . Bernard Leveque. Catherine Dulac. François . . . . Hmm, little François has no surname."

"No?" I asked.

"No. No surname. Odd how you were able to locate a sister for him," she said. "You are very talented, Gabrielle."

I hated that she knew my name. "Perhaps I made an error," I said.

"Perhaps you did. Perhaps you've made a great many errors, Gabrielle, and especially the error you made in thinking yourself smarter than we are."

"No, Sister," I protested. "I never said that."

"Or better?" she countered. "Perhaps you think that you're better than we are? Perhaps you think your judgment superior to ours?"

"No, Sister," I said miserably.

"Let's see those folders," she said.

I took them all out. Empty, all of them, as I knew they were, as she'd somehow figured out that they would be: these were the orphans who had nobody to care if they lived or died—or to care if they were tortured in between the two.

Orphans like me.

Sister Béatrice went through them slowly, one by one. When she was finished, she raised her eyes to mine. "You were given our trust," she said. "We took you in when no one else cared about you. We gave you shelter and food and an education. We've given you employment. And this is how you respond. You've lied to us, you've tricked us, you've humiliated us."

What was scariest of all was that she wasn't shouting. She wasn't taking a stick to me, beating the words into me, as they so often did. Her voice was colorless, without inflection, and I found that the most frightening part of all. "Sister—"

"Enough!" The hand blocked any more conversation.

She stood up then, slowly. "You have shown yourself to be willful and disobedient," she said, and I thought no, please, God, no, not back to the restraints again, the cold metal collar around my neck, the immobility; but it seemed she had something else in mind. "Other orphans who are grateful for what they have will take your place here," she said. "Tomorrow I will introduce you to Dr. Cameron."

And then she was gone.

I took a long, deep breath. I knew what that meant.

I pulled some paper from the file cabinet, and began to write:

I suppose that there had been a life sometime before the orphanage, but I could never really remember it—not really, not as a whole. There were only scraps left, a tune that wouldn't leave my brain, a sense of something almost familiar lurking just out of sight that disappeared as soon as I turned my head to look at it . . .

CHAPTER TWENTY-SIX

I floated back to consciousness.

I really mean it: I was floating. It felt like I was in water, but it wasn't water. I wasn't drowning.

Not altogether unpleasant, to tell you the truth.

It became more unpleasant, of course, as my brain cells awoke and synapses fired, albeit irregularly. I knew who I was . . . gradually. I wasn't sure what I was doing floating in the dark, but I remembered my name, which had to be a good thing.

Martine LeDuc. That's who I was. I lived in Montréal. I had a ginger cat . . . no, not anymore; Théo d'Or had died when I was still in college. I started giggling; the cat's name really was clever. A pun in a name. If you spoke French.

Okay. Starting over. Martine LeDuc. That was right, *n'est-ce pas?* And Montréal: I lived in Montréal. That was easy; I've always lived in Montréal. But no more cat . . . there was someone else, though. Someone else close to me? My mother? No: she was sleeping, peacefully or otherwise, up on the mountain for which the city had been named.

Focus, focus: it'll come to you. It has to come to you. Someone else, a man, . . . a tall man, a Russian?

But the sensation of floating was too pleasant to follow the thread of my thoughts, and so for a while I gave in and just floated some more. Couldn't hurt, could it?

Some annoying voice was insisting that it *could* hurt, actually, and that it was time for me to come back. I didn't understand. Irritating little voice. Go away. Leave me alone. I moved my hand to push the thought away, batting at it like a persistent gnat, and found that I couldn't move my arm.

That brought me back in a hurry.

Bon, d'accord. I was Martine LeDuc. I lived with a man, not a cat. A husband, that was it. Ivan the Terrible. No, not terrible: I loved him. It would be good if he were here so he could tell me I'd had too much to drink and take me home to sleep it off. I nodded owlishly, or at least tried to nod, but found then that I couldn't move my head, either.

The floating sensation was receding. Maybe I should open my eyes, I thought, and see exactly what's going on here.

Mistake. Can't see anything. Panic grabbing at my throat and my stomach. I couldn't move, I was blind, I was . . .

And I remembered, then, the basilica in the night and the man, the lawyer, the one who'd killed those women. Robert Carrigan.

Maybe he'd killed me, too. That would make sense. Maybe this was purgatory, and I was going to float here until it was time to see God. But hadn't the Church admitted, finally, that purgatory was a medieval construct with no theological basis? If I wasn't in purgatory I must be dead.

More panic. Breathe, Martine, just breathe. I'd tried to live a good life, I really had. I'd tried to do what I read in the Gospels, I fed the hungry, gave to the poor, turned the other cheek. I hadn't done anything wrong.

More floating. Amazing how you can float and panic at the same time. A rotten feeling, really.

I'd tried to live a good life. I seized on that thought, clutching at it, perhaps even trying to convince myself. I contributed to my church. I volunteered at a women's shelter. And then there were the children . . . I used to think that Lukas and Claudia were a necessary evil that accompanied Ivan whether I liked it or not. To love him meant putting up with them. And that . . . well, that hadn't been fair to any of us. Not to Ivan, who struggled with the long absences when he couldn't see his kids. Not to Lukas or Claudia, who had the right to be people, not just symbols insofar as they related to me as their stepmother.

And not to me, because I hadn't allowed them to inhabit anything but the margins of my life. I hadn't opened myself up to them, not really. Yet despite it all, they had—as the expression goes—grown on me. Now I was wondering: did they know that I loved them? Had I ever told them?

Too late now, anyway.

I tried to move again, which only brought on more panic. Can't breathe, can't move, can't breathe, can't think.

Something touched me and I screamed and flinched, and there was a sense of lightness around my head. And a voice.

"Ah, there you go. We'll take these off, now that you're awake. I'd hate for you to miss anything."

Familiar voice. Male. Self-assured.

Robert Carrigan.

The name clicked, and it was suddenly blindingly clear that I wasn't dead. Not yet, anyway. Who was it that said hell is other people? Sartre?

I still couldn't see anything.

"You're probably wondering where you are," he said, his voice casual, a tour guide, slightly bored. Been there, done that. I didn't respond.

"If you're a very good girl," he continued, "I'll let you see a little something. Hard to tell what's going on around you when you're *deprived of your senses*." He chuckled.

Yeah, I thought, I get it, you don't have to rub it in too hard. My research over the past week flooded back through my synapses. Sensory deprivation: no sound, no light, nothing to touch or feel. And here he was, playing his own little private MK-Ultra games with me. You don't really have to underline the obvious; I do still have the odd brain cell or two.

But maybe he was right to think I was stupid. I'd pretty much done everything he'd wanted, hadn't I?

Hands on my head, again, and suddenly, dazzling light. I blinked, closed my eyes, opened them again. Light sparkling all around me. Blessed, blessed light. Can you drink light, savor it, taste it? Why not?

"Why not?" he asked. Had I spoken those words aloud? I must have done, or he wouldn't have repeated them. "Well, welcome to the sleep room, Martine." I still couldn't really see anything, certainly not him, certainly not the room I was in. It had a familiar ring to it, though, that name: where had I heard it before?

It was too much work to think it through. Too many shadows there. Keep floating in the light.

He was talking again, his voice fuzzy. What was he saying? ". . . effects of soft torture," the calm monotone was going on. "Always interesting to observe how it works on different individuals."

I squinted in the direction of the voice. "Thought you were a lawyer," I said, my words slurring.

"What was that? Speak up, Martine."

"You don't sound like a lawyer," I managed to say. "You sound like one of the doctors. Those doctors experimented on their patients." I licked my lips: I was determined not to sound afraid. Who could be afraid, anyway, floating in the light like this? "But you remind me of someone specific," I added. "That guy . . . One of the CIA's imports from Germany. You sound a lot like Dr. Mengele."

He seemed to find that uproariously funny, and I winced: too much sound is as bad as too little, the volume of his laughter was jangling nerves in my head I didn't know I possessed. I was starting to get a sense of where I was, but there wasn't much to see: there were sheets pinned up all around the bed on which I was lying. A hospital? Above, way high above, a vaulted ceiling. No, not vaulted exactly, not like in the church . . . but curved. A curved concrete ceiling. Where on earth was there a curved concrete ceiling?

Church . . . I'd been in church, I remembered. In the basilica, the biggest church in the city. And that was where he'd hunted me down.

"Funny you should say that, Martine," Robert Carrigan was saying. "Funny that you should mention him. Because once upon a time, I nearly was. A doctor, that is. Perhaps even a pupil of Dr. Mengele. You say his name like it's such a *bad* thing."

"Nazi," I managed to say. "Human experimentation."

He laughed. "You don't think anything *that* important could be done with rats and monkeys, do you?"

"You're no doctor," I said.

"But I might have been. I came close. So close. They were willing to send me to medical school. And apparently I had the aptitude for it, but I decided on the law instead. And, for a long time, I liked it. People respect attorneys. You get to spend all your time playing a chess game, and outsmarting your opponents. I did love the law," he said on a sigh. "But now, lately, I wonder if I chose the right path after all. I wonder if it was a mistake."

I had absolutely no idea what he was talking about. "A mistake?" I repeated, just to keep him talking.

"Well, I'd gotten quite used to the medical side of things, hadn't I?" he said, and his face swam into view in front of me. "Oh. I see. Really. Now, you surprise me. You didn't work that one out?"

"What one?"

He laughed. "My dear girl, you don't really think I'd be willing to carry on as I've been doing as a benefit to my *employer*, do you?" He shook his head, still in apparent merriment, and moved, danced almost, out of my line of sight again. He was enjoying this. "Well, it *does* benefit my employer, of course. And I'm happy to do it, because Lansbury gave me everything. But this goes beyond Lansbury. This is a little more . . . visceral." A pause. "You're so very concerned about the orphans," he said. "Well, I was one of them. One of the poor Duplessis orphans, living out my sad neglected existence at the Cité de Saint-Jean-de-Dieu."

Whoa. *Merde, alors.*

He was right: I hadn't seen that one coming. Okay, so maybe he was the right age, but surely even an experience that horrific wouldn't have driven him to . . . this. This wholesale torture, this sexual assault, this murder.

"I was one of the favorites," Robert Carrigan continued, his voice behind me. "Out of hundreds of children. They recognized that I was special. I was such a good little helper to them, you see. I kept the other kids calm. They liked me. They trusted me. At first I did it to survive. You'd be amazed at what the human psyche will do to survive. What it can take. But after a while . . . it became exciting."

"I have no idea—" I began, but he cut me off.

"Of course you don't," he said. "You're a blundering idiot and hardly worth my time. But we *have* time, don't you know, and it's such a pleasant stroll down memory lane—"

We clearly had different takes on what could be construed as pleasant.

His voice faded for a moment and I thought he moved somewhere else in the room, but then he was back. Not that I could have attempted any kind of escape in his absence. I couldn't even feel my legs.

"At first I did it for survival," Robert Carrigan said again. "Survival and the odd cigarette. We all had jobs, you see. All the orphans, anyone who was *compos mentis* enough to do anything, had to work. No idle hands at the asylum. No, indeed. There was a farm to run, there was food to prepare, and of course there were medical experiments to conduct."

I hadn't been so far off, then, when I called him a *nouveau* Mengele.

He was still talking. "I was assigned to the doctors. There was always a lot to do. Prepare the operating theater. Prepare the instruments. Clean up—ayc, there's the rub, there was always a lot to clean up afterward. And I won't lie to you, it wasn't easy at first. No: you mustn't think I'm a monster. It wasn't always easy. There was a time, yes, there was, a time when it made me sick. A time when I was like everybody else. Even like you, Martine. Some of the children—well, here's the thing: I knew them. That made it more difficult. But the more I helped the doctors, the stronger I got. And the more I liked what I was doing."

I was following, if at a distance. "You worked at the Cité de Saint-Jean-de-Dieu," I said, wishing I could do more than lick my lips. My mouth felt like I'd swallowed ashes. "You helped the doctors."

"You're a little slow tonight, my dear. Try and keep up. Of course I helped the doctors. At first, it was just clean-up detail. Mopping up their mistakes, you might say. I was young and untested. They didn't yet know my full potential. Even I didn't know my full potential."

There was a clatter as he dropped something, and he grunted as he bent down, presumably to pick it up. "Then I started taking an interest. It was extraordinary what I learned. I'll be honest: I'd had no idea I could feel anything anymore. I thought the nuns had beaten that out of me. But down in the basement . . . my whole being, my whole inner self . . . words fail me, they really do. The best way to explain it is to say that I was *uncaged*." His voice grew gentle, reverent. "It wasn't just a coming of age, of having my way with the girls, the sort of thing that every young man goes through. This was different. It was more than that, deeper than that. It was spiritual." Another pause. "There's something remarkable that happens when someone's about to die and they look into your eyes. Something deep and holy passes between you. It's an *incredible* intimacy."

You are *incredibly* off your rocker, I was thinking. "How did you get from being an orphan in an asylum to Lansbury Pharmaceuticals?" I asked. I had to ask something; I really didn't want to hear any more about how magical it was to kill somebody.

"They weren't monsters," Robert Carrigan said. "Everyone has the wrong idea about them. They were trying to advance science. They wanted to learn the limits of the human brain, the human body, the human spirit. They were willing to keep at it, to try again and again and again to learn. They were the bravest of the brave. No one understood; no one ever understands. The world wants medical breakthroughs but the world doesn't want to pay the price for them."

"So the orphans did," I said.

"Come on, Martine! Oh . . . I *can* call you Martine, can't I? It's a custom with me, a ritual, you might say. I always knew their names: I always said their names at that last moment. It was the least I could do for them, really. And my darling Martine, we're going to get very, very intimate, you and I, very, very soon." He paused, and then, as though bestowing a great privilege, he added, "And you may call me Bobby."

I didn't say anything. I wasn't liking the way he was using the word *intimate*. I wondered how much of this he had shared with Isabelle, Caroline, Annie, Danielle.

"They were of no importance, the orphans," Robert said. "Persons of no importance. Hadn't their families made that clear? Hadn't society made that clear? You can't require us to lock people up, tuck them away so you don't have to think about them—and *then* have issues with how they're treated. It's absurd. People can't have it both ways."

"Lansbury," I reminded him. I didn't want to start gagging.

"Lansbury was part of it from the start," he replied. "Even when I was a boy in the asylum, when I was first getting involved, Lansbury Pharmaceuticals was underwriting the experiments. You think it was the *hospital* that paid the doctors? You think Ewen Cameron made money from the *asylum*? Not for a second. It was all Lansbury, from the beginning." His voice got dreamy again. "From *my* beginning, too. My first awakening."

He stopped and I heard the screech of a metal drawer opening. I didn't want to think about what he was doing, what horrible instruments he was taking out of that drawer. Panic was rising and I was finding it hard to breathe. There was a voice inside me that was starting a mantra: I don't want to die, I don't want to die . . .

Robert found whatever he was looking for and shut the drawer. "Lansbury's rep was almost always around. Everyone thought he was one of the doctors, but he wasn't, he was the pharmaceutical rep. The salesman. And he's the one who got to know me best. The doctors appreciated my help, but it was the rep who really saw my value. He was the one who offered to send me to medical school. I was in seventh heaven!"

I had to shut him up. My inner voice with its stupid mantra wasn't getting me anywhere. And it was scaring me. "So how did you end up an attorney, Counselor?" I asked instead. "Second choice? Medical school didn't want you?"

A louder clatter this time, and Robert swore viciously from behind me. I must have hit a nerve. Too bad I couldn't hit any of my own. "They said"—and his voice was filled with rage—"they said that I didn't qualify on psychological grounds."

I laughed. Well, I *tried* to laugh, but it came out sounding like something between a squeak and a rumble. I moistened my lips before I tried to talk again. "You wanted to go into medicine so you could continue torturing people, and the medical establishment didn't feel that was okay? You surprise me."

"Lansbury Pharmaceuticals sent me to law school instead," he said, and I was sobered to realize how quickly he'd gotten control of his anger back. That didn't bode well for me. "They've taken care of me, every step of the way. I owe them everything."

"So much that you have to repay it with murder?"

He laughed. "Actually, I probably owe *that* to them, too," he said. "When I found out that that little *pute* was getting too close and I realized I had to do something about her . . . well, in the process, I rediscovered a part of myself that had been buried too long. Inadvertent but strangely logical, isn't it, to come full circle like this? Poetic, almost."

"Isabelle Hubert," I said, nodding again like I'd discovered something significant. *Pute* was a rude colloquialism for prostitute.

"Isabelle Hubert," he agreed. "Stupid cow thought she owed it to her mother—her *mother*, of all people—to expose the asylum. Asking all her clients questions about it. Trying to find out what no one was supposed to find out. I had to close her down. It doesn't work like that."

Light dawned. "She asked the wrong person," I said slowly. "One of her clients was a bigwig at Lansbury."

"Senior vice president of research," Robert agreed, and I could almost feel him nodding behind me at the terrible gaffe that had cost Isabelle her life.

"And he told you that something had to be done?"

"Exactly. Though I don't imagine he thought I'd take such a *personal interest* in it all. I expect that he meant me to do something to stop her legally, rather than permanently. But my solution was much neater."

"They don't know it's you who's been doing this?"

"Of course not. This wasn't anyone's idea but my own. Give me credit for *some* creativity here." There was the sound of liquid being poured behind me; it was unnerving. I was so parched I wished it were being poured down my throat. "No one at Lansbury told me to kill anybody. That was all my own doing. Oh, someone there may have had suspicions. But I doubt it. I've been very, very careful. No one could prove anything, even if they thought they knew what I was doing. I was on my own with the killing." A pause. "But what a discovery it was. All these years since I left the asylum," he said reverently. "All these years had passed, and I'd thought that part of me had been cut off. That I'd never feel those feelings again. But it was only dormant. When I got her alone, I knew right away what I had to do. I didn't even have to think about it. It brought back such memories! I felt alive again, alive for the first time in years."

"Torturing her, you mean."

"For heaven's sake, Martine. You have no idea what you're talking about. You're misinformed by the popular press, by stupid TV shows. It's nothing like that. I'm telling you, by the end, the torturer and the victim are bonded forever as one. There's no greater intimacy than being there for the last breath, for being responsible for that last breath. Being with her, it was like the first time I ever did it, back at the asylum. And she screamed beautifully. It was touching, really, amazing. I could *almost* feel her pain, we were that close. We were *so* close."

"But—"

"You see, words just can't explain it," he interrupted. "The wonder of it. The magic of it all. You'll understand, Martine, you'll see, and you'll agree, there's nothing else like it. Being locked together, gazing into each other's eyes while you take your last breath. There's nothing in the world more exciting."

I tried to fight down the panic. Lansbury had no idea what they'd unleashed. They must've asked their attorney to make the problem go away, expecting it to be done through paperwork and settlements and nondisclosure agreements. But Robert found his own way to make the problem go away, and he wasn't going to stop. Not once he'd rediscovered his darkest demons.

"It wasn't just Isabelle, though," I said, trying to steer him away from that particular memory. "You killed Annie. She was there, too, at Saint-Jean-de-Dieu. Didn't you remember her? Hadn't you known her? Didn't that make you feel something?"

"Of course it did!" he exclaimed. "You see, you do understand! Believe me when I tell you, Annie was the best! We shared so much before she died . . . so many memories. Her father was one of my heroes, one of my role models. It was a great honor, believe me."

I was starting to gag now. I couldn't move my arms. If I threw up, chances were good I'd choke on my own vomit. On second thought, maybe that would be a good idea. I really wasn't anxious to experience Robert's idea of intimacy. "And the Allan?" I asked, swallowing hard. "What about the Allan? Did you work there, too?"

"I've always taken an interest in the work of the Allan," he said. "It's amazing, really, what you can make people do, with the proper—"

"Incentive?"

"—stimuli," he finished.

"So there is a connection." Between the Allan and the Cité de St.-Jean-de-Dieu.

"Of course there is. You really think Montréal is that large, that we wouldn't have pooled resources? You're as naïve as the police, as the public. No one understands what I've accomplished here. No one understands what a coup it was, taking care of these women."

"You made their deaths look like the work of a serial sex killer," I said. It was difficult to get the words out, my mouth was so dry and so parched; and it was a stupid statement. Of *course* it looked like the work of a serial sex killer: he *was* a serial sex killer.

"The rapes?" he asked. "The park benches? Tell me something, Martine, was that part too over the top? Really? I wondered, you know. Maybe too showy. Maybe too dramatic. And putting them all out there, it was the hardest part, of course. Timing it right to prop them up on the benches without being seen, tough, but oh, what a gesture! And when it hit the papers! It was like reliving everything again. *Very* exciting, Martine."

There was a pause. Then, "I've even picked out your bench. You should feel flattered, considering all the thought I've put into you. You know, it's absolutely true what they say, that anticipating something is almost as exciting as doing it. The Christmas Eve syndrome, I like to call it. I've been thinking about which bench would be yours for a long time now."

A far-too-loud scraping sound and his face swam back into my field of vision. He'd pulled up a chair next to the bed. "But enough of that. There's still time to talk about the bench. Here's something: I'll bet you can't guess where we are."

"Ask me if I care," I managed to say.

"Well, Martine, you really *should* care. I'd think you'd be curious. After all, you've been a busy little girl, running all over town, calling up Ottawa, figuring it all out. The police couldn't solve it. The mayor couldn't solve it. Of all people! The publicity director! *Very* good, Martine, very exciting indeed. So I thought you'd appreciate seeing one of the places you've been so obsessed with."

My eyes went to the strange high rounded ceiling again.

"Not that you can see much," he added. "We had to camp out here, since they're using the rooms upstairs as a proper hospital. They renamed it, but you know, the patients there, they say they keep hearing little children crying in the night. It's funny. Ghosts, they say. I wonder what kind of hallucination that is? Do you think—my goodness, could it be that they're doing too many *drugs*?"

I tried to say something and couldn't. I passed my tongue over my lips. "We're at the Cité de Saint-Jean-de-Dieu," I mumbled.

"Oh, I just love your accent when you say that, Martine," he said. "So Francophone. Not like my accent at all, despite all my years of speaking French: I've worked hard to retain my Anglophone identity. And, of course, you got it in one. That's exactly where we are." He was fiddling with something, and as he moved, it caught the light: a hypodermic.

I guessed I'd be doing the floating thing again.

"Such a clever girl," Robert was saying. "Yes, that's where we are. We're downstairs. All the way downstairs." He shook his head. "Disappointing, I have to admit. I'd have liked to use one of the basement rooms. That would have made everything just perfect, you know? Maybe even the one where I worked all those years ago, where they used to try performing lobotomies— wouldn't that have been fun, such great memories—but it's all locked down now, closed up, and there's a guard and security checks. I wonder if they were able to clean up all the blood. We couldn't get it all, not every bit, it permeates everything, and it has such a distinctive smell, blood, sweet and metallic at the same time . . ."

He sighed, presumably with reminiscence. "No, my dear, we're in one of the steam tunnels that connect the buildings. As close as I could get to my beloved basement. They used to use the steam pressure to run the electric generator, and to heat the buildings. All very practical. I explored them when I was a boy, I even got burned once or twice for my efforts."

He laughed, and there was an echo. "But you shouldn't be disappointed, my dear. I suspect your little orphans spent time here, too. Maybe there are even bodies. Maybe there were ones who tried to escape. Sometimes a child would disappear, and none of us had anything to do with it . . . and now some of the smaller tunnels have collapsed. Naked limestone does that when it's not maintained. Who knows what—or who—we might find in the rubble?"

Steam tunnels. I tried to focus on what that meant. Tunnels that carried steam pipes to heat big buildings. I blinked and looked around me: this was a big one, the top of it ten feet up with pipes running along the curved ceiling. Something out of some steampunk nightmare, all industrial and cold. Concrete and metal. A great escape route, maybe, if I could only move something more than my eyes.

I focused back on Robert. "You're enjoying this."

"Well, of course I am! It's like Christmas and birthdays rolled into one, all the Christmases and all the birthdays they never let us celebrate at the asylum. Well, I'm celebrating now, Martine. I'm celebrating now! Annie was my favorite, of course, but we had history, you can't compete with a shared history. Still, you'll do nicely. Maybe you'll make second place. You'd like that, wouldn't you, Martine? To be my second favorite?"

That did it. Gag reflex, and my system didn't like it one bit. Lights flashing, and no breath, no breathing at all . . . "Whoa, there!" A clatter as the syringe was set down and then a sharp sudden pain in my arm and suddenly my airway cleared.

I'd never felt so grateful to breathe.

"You gave me a little scare just then, Martine," Robert said. He, too, sounded a little breathless. "Can't have you nodding off just yet, especially not permanently. We have so many games to play before you leave. So much fun and so many games. Like I had with the others. Are you hearing me, Martine? Give me a nod if you do. This is supposed to be a conversation. One just between the two of us. And I so hate talking to myself. It makes me look a little—you know—*crazy*." He laughed. "Not that these walls haven't seen their share of crazy, mind you. But I'm supposed to be one of the sane ones."

I managed to nod.

"Good girl. So where was I? Oh, right. Talking about the steam tunnels. I brought them all here, just like you: Isabelle, and Caroline, Annie, and Danielle. All my lovely ladies. And you, of course."

I steadied myself. "And who's after me?"

"What makes you think there's anybody else?"

I would have shrugged if I could. "You need this too much. This isn't just about Lansbury anymore, it's about you."

"My dear, dear Martine. You're cleverer than you look. I like that about you. We're going to have such a lovely time together, Martine."

Martine, Martine, Martine . . . He'd said my name more times in the last five minutes than Ivan had said it in the past

month. Good thing it wouldn't wear out from so much repeti-
tion. For some reason, I found that thought uproariously funny.
I would have laughed out loud, only I seemed to be unable to
move my vocal cords.

Robert noticed. "Yeah, it takes you that way, doesn't it? Pretty
much paralyzes your nervous system. Don't worry, it'll wear off.
I don't want you to *not* feel anything. I want you to feel it *all*."
A long sigh. "You're thinking that only a deranged individual
could do something like this, aren't you? That's what they all
think. The bad apple. The evil seed. The monster that comes
around a few times a generation, who gets arrested, sentenced,
taken out of circulation, and leaves everybody safe and everything beautiful once again."

Something like that, anyway.

"But corporations are far deadlier than any person, no matter how psychopathic he or she happens to be," Robert continued. "You hear about things, you know, these public shootings,
sixteen dead, twenty shot, oh, the horror. Well, corporations
kill that many people before breakfast, girlie. And where's the
indignation over that? Where's the outrage? Take my advice:
you're better off with a psychopath than you are with any corporation, Lansbury included."

Whatever he'd injected me with had taken away the floating
feeling and replaced it with numbness, a feeling of cold, like I
was bathing in ice water. Ice water . . . They'd done *that* here, too,
if I remembered correctly. Hydropathy, another of the mid–
twentieth century's torture treatments. They hammered their
heels on the bottoms of the tubs. They passed out, their bodies
racked by shock. Maybe he'd found some drug to simulate

hydropathy. Like swimming near an iceberg...icebergs... must have been like this, for the survivors of the *Titanic*, the dark Atlantic Ocean surrounding them, the dark Atlantic night...

Whoa. I *was* drifting again.

Focus, Martine. Focus. On what? On his voice, still droning on, didn't he ever shut up? I just wanted him to be quiet. I just wanted to be left in peace.

"We were doing a lot of work back then with neuroleptics," he was saying. "Dreadful side effects, of course, but really, who cares when you see what we learned from it all. All in the aid of humanity, right? And, besides, what drug doesn't have them?"

I closed my eyes. A thought started to make sense and then drifted away—I tried to catch the tail end of it, but off it went, taking a string of unrelated words with it as it went.

Maybe I'd catch the next one.

"They block the flow of neurotransmitters," he said. "Chlorpromazine, phenobarbital, Thioridazine. All of them *interesting*, mind you, though not all of them interesting to the government, who were the ones paying us the big bucks for our experiments. And we needed the money. But I'm not going to give you the good stuff," he added, his tone changing, as though remembering he was speaking to me. "The LSD-twenty-five that Cameron liked so much. That was definitely good stuff. He came here, not everybody knows that, but they couldn't be transporting children over to the Allan, now, could they? So Cameron came here." His voice got a little dreamy. "There was a whole protocol," he said. "Administer the drug, wait fifteen minutes, then electroshocks. Sometimes I'd write it down for him, record the patient's responses. I liked that, I liked being near him. He was a brilliant man, simply brilliant. And there were some very interesting responses." He looked at me. "I'm not set up for it now, of course."

Thank God for small favors, I thought.

His voice grew cheerful. "Well, time to get this show on the road," he said. He came over and pulled my eyelids back, inspecting whatever he saw there. "Hmm. Coming out of it slowly, aren't we?" He stepped back, did something out of my field of vision, and I realized that he was answering a smartphone. God knew how he got a signal down here. "Robert Carrigan."

A length of time while he listened to somebody. "That's not convenient. I'm taking care of it, but you have to give me some time." Another, longer space of time. Fine with me: when he was on the phone, he wasn't doing anything to my body. *Keep talking*, I urged the unknown person at the other end of the line. Just keep talking.

There was a decisive click, and immediately he was back with me. "A minor interruption, my dear Martine. It seems that my presence is required elsewhere. Lansbury calls, and I must obey. It's only a mere postponement, I promise. But remember what I said before about anticipation: we'll have to wait a bit before we begin the rest of our time together. You can stay here and think about it. Imagine it. Come to grips with it. When I come back, we'll share. You can tell me what you imagined, and I'll show you what I imagined. I wonder if our fantasies will have anything in common."

"You could change your mind," I told him. Perfectly silly thing to say.

He smiled, and leaned over me, tucking some of my hair

behind my ear, gently, the gesture way too intimate, way too close. "My dear Martine," his voice was thick, "there's nothing in the world that will keep us apart. We have things to share, places to go together that you've never dreamed of."

He must be planning to enter that phrase into the Bulwer-Lytton contest, I thought irrelevantly and a little hysterically. Do people even talk like that? "I can wait," I managed to say.

"Oh, I won't leave you alone," he responded. "That would be rude of me, and I've always been a gentleman. Well, almost always. Here's a little something to keep you company. Just sit back and enjoy. It's very fast-acting, this batch. Into your system, out of your system. I won't be too long."

Another pinprick in my arm, and a rush of heat coursing through me, I could almost see it running through my veins, along my nerves. There had been drugs in the autopsy reports. I'd dismissed them; everyone had dismissed them. Bad mistake.

He was there, and then he was gone. Just like that. Who knew time was so slippery?

I became vaguely aware that there were hands touching me, tugging at my shoulders. "Come on, come on," someone said.

I'm not going anywhere with you, buddy, I thought. You're going to kill me. Not in the mood right now.

"I'm not going to kill you. But you have to come with me."

I frowned. Had I said it out loud? And who'd answered? It was a different voice. Was he changing his voice to confuse me? I didn't need that: I was plenty confused already. "I can't possibly carry you," said the voice. "You have to help me."

Someone speaking French.

Oops, that wasn't right. Robert Carrigan spoke English.

I squinted in the direction of the voice. "Violette!"

"Yes," Violette Sobel said grimly.

"Violette Sobel!" I was still amazed that I'd recognized her. Or amazed that she was here in the steam tunnel. Or just pretty much amazed by anything that didn't have to do with my impending torture and death.

"Yes," she said again.

"I'd like to sleep," I confessed.

"No time for that," said Violette. "Come on, Martine. He will return soon when he realizes it is us who made the telephone call."

"Us?"

"Come on," she said again, and there was an undercurrent of fear in her voice. "We have to go."

I swung my legs over the side of the table, and the tunnel tilted dramatically around me. I clutched at her and then realized that I was grabbing for balance at a woman who was nearly seventy. Yikes.

That didn't seem to occur to Violette. "Come on, Martine, come on." She pulled me off the table altogether and I stumbled and would have gone down if she hadn't been holding me up. "It's the yoga, isn't it?" I asked.

"What are you talking about?"

"You're so strong. Julian said you do yoga."

"For heaven's sake," she said impatiently. "Come *on*, Martine."

Her arm was around my waist, and she seemed to know where she was going. "This way, this way." Standing up had cleared my head considerably, and after the first few stumbling steps I found that I could take on some of my own weight, which must have been a relief for her. "Where are we going?"

"Out of here," Violette said grimly.

"How did you find me?"

"Later," she said. "There'll be time for that later."

"Or not," said Robert Carrigan.

He was standing over by the table I'd just vacated. There were bright lights trained on it and they were casting a tremendous shadow up on the tunnel wall. Was that Robert's shadow? *Someone* looked very big and very scary.

And it had a syringe in its hand. My knees buckled at the sight.

Violette's arm came around my shoulders again, and it felt warm and strong. "Stand," she hissed.

"Yes, stand up," agreed Robert. "Well, well. Annie's adopted sister! What a pleasant surprise this is."

Violette didn't answer him; presumably she wasn't finding the encounter as pleasant as he seemed to be. She kept looking the other way, down the tunnel, in the direction she'd been dragging me.

A door slammed somewhere behind us, off in the other direction, and a shout. "What was that?"

Julian's voice—I thought it was Julian's voice—came echoing up toward us. "Robert Carrigan! SPVM!"

Carrigan had turned to face the sounds, peering into the darkness, and Violette wasn't wasting any time. "Now," she hissed again, and this time we managed a pace that might have put a two-year-old to shame. "This way."

Behind us, suddenly, a loud bang, echoing, and a sharp exclamation of pain. "What was that?" I asked again.

We could hear voices, swearing, and then the sound of footsteps echoing behind us—a whole barrage of them, it seemed to me. The echoes in the steam tunnel seemed to pass us and then doubled back until they surrounded us with whispers of sound, fading and returning again. Auditory hallucinations, no doubt, but the footsteps sounded real. Violette gasped and pulled me off to the side, as far aside as she could, and we fell together against the brick wall of the steam tunnel and Violette began pulling me underneath a giant steam pipe.

I looked back toward Carrigan's little operating theater.

The bright lights behind the men down the tunnel showed them in silhouette, dark and flickering and very scary. Robert Carrigan saw what was waiting for him, presumably, and decided to get out. There was a moment of hesitation and then he was running, running down the tunnel, seemingly straight at us.

Just as Robert came up even with us in the tunnel, his vision fixed on his escape and not on anyone cowering underneath the steam pipes, I stuck out my leg. It caught him right on the shin, and he went down, loudly, swearing as he did. It sounded like a herd of—something. My brain was still struggling with what was and wasn't real.

Now we had him and I had no idea what to do next.

It was moot: he wasn't moving. Later I learned that the syringe he'd been carrying had stuck into his shoulder; he must have flung his arms forward to break his fall, and fell right onto the needle instead. He wasn't getting up without help, and neither Violette nor I felt inclined to offer any. Imagine that.

I looked at Violette. "Did you see that? I did that!"

"You did," she assured me.

"I'm a hero," I said.

"Come on, hero," Violette said crisply. She'd clearly had enough of me. Together we stumbled along a widening section of the steam tunnel, Julian's voice echoing behind us, others joining in.

We went through a door and up a short flight of stairs. The stairs were challenging, and my legs felt like rubber. I was having a hard time with the perambulation and it felt like Violette was dragging me, which I didn't understand. Why the rush? The last I'd seen Robert Carrigan, the police were taking quite good care of him. It would have been nice to just sit down for a while. Besides, this whole dragging thing seemed incredibly silly when you considered our disparate ages.

A door opened ahead of us and we were suddenly bathed in more light, flashing blue and red. "You've got her?" A different man's voice.

"Just barely," said Violette. "Here, she's all yours. I've never managed anyone so difficult."

"Well done!" Stronger arms now. "Madame LeDuc, come on, we're going to the hospital."

I blinked. "This *is* the hospital."

"Not for you, it isn't." Another man, another syringe, and after that, nothing but black.

This isn't my story, but I want to add why it is I have these papers, and it seems appropriate, somehow, to append it to this journal.

I was sitting in the foyer waiting for Dr. Desmarchais to take me home—and what a word that was, home!—when one of the older girls, someone I may have met before but really couldn't remember, came through.

There was something about her. I don't know what it was. Something furtive. Something scared. And something surprised, too. She asked me what I was doing, and I told her, my voice holding the wonder of it all, told her that I was going away, that Dr. Desmarchais was adopting me as his own daughter. I was to call him Papa now.

"Annie," she said then, as if just remembering my name. "Annie, you have to help me."

I don't know what I said. I am so ashamed now, but all I could think of then was getting away. Of going home. Someplace where it was warm and there was enough food and there was no basement.

She looked around to make sure we were really alone, and then she thrust a collection of papers at me. I just stared at them, and she pushed them down deep in the pocket of my new warm coat. "Keep these," she said.

"What should I do with them?"

"Keep these," said the older girl. "Don't show them to Dr. Desmarchais, please? Don't show them to your new family, not to anybody."

I knew what she was thinking then. She didn't want them changing their minds, bringing me back: she couldn't put me in that kind of danger. "Hide them and take them out again when you're older and then you should share them with everyone. Will you do that for me?"

I remember that I nodded. I still hadn't said much at all.

I thought she was going to cry. "And, Annie, remember my name, yes? Gabrielle Roy. Please remember it."

"Annie!" The voice was behind us: Mother Dauphinée, who rarely put in an appearance, was there next to Dr. Desmarchais. "It's time for you to go home, dear!"

I looked at Gabrielle, and she was already moving, already at the door. "Gabrielle Roy," I said, as loudly as I could, and then Papa took my hand and led me out into the fitful morning sunshine and into my new life.

CHAPTER TWENTY-SEVEN

They kept me in the hospital—the Royal Victoria, and not the psych ward, thank you very much—for three days for observation. "You got yourself quite a cocktail in your system there," Julian said. "They're still trying to sort it all out."

"But you arrested him, right?"

"Of course we arrested him. Didn't you see? Right there in the steam tunnel. You did a great job, by the way, tripping him. He knew those tunnels better than anyone; he might have gotten away." He smiled. "We wouldn't have found either of you, though, if it weren't for Violette Sobel. The old girl was amazing."

I put my hand to my forehead: I was dealing with the absolute mother of all headaches. "How did she know?"

"Seems Annie Desmarchais left behind a lot of breadcrumbs," Julian said. "And Violette felt guilty after you talked to her about Annie's death, guilty she'd been so cold, so unhelpful. Violette was starting to twig on to a lot of things on her own, just because she knew her sister. Annie was smart, and she was closing in on Lansbury, figuring out what we'd figured out, about who made the money, who was behind it all."

He turned and walked over to the window, looking out. "And Annie had this—diary, I guess you'd call it, just a bunch of papers written by this girl, Gabrielle, an orphan who was buried in the graveyard across the road from the asylum. Which apparently still *is* a graveyard—despite what the Sisters of Providence would like us to believe—under the liquor board's warehouse. We'll be looking into *that*. We'll be looking into a lot of things that I'm sure my boss, *monsieur le directeur,* would just as soon not look into, but there you are; life's simply unfair sometimes. I brought you a copy, by the way. Thought it might make for interesting hospital reading." He tossed a large manila envelope on my bed.

I didn't pick it up at first. "And Violette?"

He shrugged. "We guilted her into it, I guess. Or you did by way of accusing her of not caring. Anyway, Violette was remembering everything that Annie had ever told her about the asylum, trying to make sense of it. About the basement. About the experiments. She knew more than she wanted to know, and you made it all resurface."

"I didn't realize I'd been that rude," I said, grimacing.

He grinned. "Seems to have done the trick, though. Once she started, nothing was going to get in her way. She retraced her sister's research, connected the dots, whatever. And she got action. Desmarchais is almost as big a name in this town as Fletcher." He smiled again happily. "She'd got hold of all her sister's research, and part of that was the architect's plans. Before, and after, as you might say. Including the warren of steam tunnels, vertical and horizontal, under the hospital. And notes that Annie had left about the basement being part of the hospital now, but the steam tunnels being abandoned and disused. Anyway, the old girl—and she's a lot braver than she'd have you believe—did a little recon of her own, she wanted to see where the awful experiments had taken place, and stumbled onto Robert's little setup in one of those steam tunnels."

"When Carrigan wasn't there," I said, nodding.

"Obviously." He frowned. "You're a little slow. Must be the drugs. Anyway, anyone with half a brain could see that they were practicing some pretty bad medicine down there. She may not have recognized it as the killing space where her sister died, but she knew it wasn't exactly Romper Room, either. And so she called me."

"When was this?"

"Yesterday afternoon."

"And it took you this long—" I stopped. "You didn't answer the phone," I said flatly.

"I didn't call her back until evening," Julian said. "Last night it was. And then I saw *you'd* called, and I listened to your voice mails."

I remembered that second frantic call. Hiding in the confessional, every shadow in the church a threat, and the real threat at the end of it all. I swallowed and didn't say anything. I had a feeling it would be a long time before I could think about last night without feeling sick. I wondered how long it would be before I could go back to the basilica.

"So we thought, he's not going to keep her in the church, no way, that's too public. And Violette had this feeling she couldn't explain, that somehow she was being led to the steam tunnel, and was on and on about that's where you'd be."

"Maybe she *was* led." I wasn't beyond believing anything.

"Maybe." Julian was more prosaic. "I think the impromptu science lab more than tipped her off. By the time Violette got out to the old asylum, Dr. Strangelove there had arrived with you in tow. But don't believe for a moment that you were in real danger," he added stoutly. "We were there, waiting in the wings. I'd have taken him, syringe and all."

"Uh-huh."

"In the meantime, in case you were wondering how I've been spending *my* time, I'd been persuading both my boss and yours that Lansbury Pharma needed looking into. We got the Sureté in on the act and apparently they had a productive conversation with the powers-that-be over there. Persuaded them it would be a good idea to call their boy in for a little meeting. They were the ones who fingered Carrigan, actually."

"The phone call that saved me," I said, remembering Robert's disappointment when he'd answered.

"Well, them and us. My boss was standing next to them when they called. That was Violette's idea, actually, too."

"She was amazingly brave," I said in wonderment. So many brave women in this story. Isabelle, Caroline, Annie, Danielle, Violette . . . Juliette Hubert, who'd gone over the wall . . . and a lost little girl named Gabrielle, whose journal I would read as soon as Julian left.

"Seems to have run in the family, bravery," Julian said. "Oh, and you'll be happy to know, Carrigan had picked out your bench. Wrote it all down, along with sketches of you, deceased, sitting on it. He was going to put you over at Parc Lafontaine."

"Now that's something I didn't need to know."

Ivan spent the three days I was at the hospital by my side. Being Ivan, he didn't give me any lectures on my irresponsibility or ultimatums about never putting myself in harm's way again. Being Ivan, he was just there. With his computer tablet and his English-language news sites.

I had a lot to be thankful for.

Two weeks after I left the hospital and was back to the more or less usual insanity of my job, Violette Sobel came to my office. She was perfectly dressed, perfectly coiffed, and seemed vaguely embarrassed by her role in having saved my life. "I'm pleased that you're well, Madame LeDuc," she said formally.

"Thanks to you, Madame Sobel." I didn't really know what to say. How do you thank someone for *that*?

She made a brushing-away gesture with her hands. "I came by to tell you something we thought you'd want to know. I'm going up into Montrégie on the weekend," she said. "It seems that *détective-lieutenant* Fletcher has located the half sister of Gabrielle Roy." She glanced at my face and smiled. "Her name is Annette Latour. She only learned of Gabrielle's existence when their mother died five years ago, and knows nothing of her life. She is eager to learn more. I thought she should have the journal." She hesitated. "And I thought you might wish to come with me."

"Yes," I said, stifling thoughts of too little, too late. But I'd read Gabrielle's journal, and anything to honor her, to keep her name alive . . . "Yes," I said with more conviction. "I'd like that very much."

AUTHOR'S NOTE

Much of what my fictional protagonist Martine LeDuc learned about Montréal's past is, unfortunately, true.

The Allan Memorial Institute—sometimes colloquially referred to as the Allan—now houses the psychiatry department of the Royal Victoria Hospital, part of the McGill University Health Centre. Although currently a respected psychiatric hospital, the institute is also known for its past role in the CIA's MK-Ultra project. The agency's initiative to develop drug-induced mind-control techniques was implemented in the institute by its then director, Donald Ewen Cameron, from 1957 to 1964.

The institute occupies the mansion formerly known as Ravenscrag, which is, as Martine has noted, a *seriously* creepy-looking building. Look it up online if you don't believe me: just search the terms *Ravenscrag Allan Institute Montréal*. One can believe that all manner of things went on there, and in fact there are quite a few theories drifting around, many of which verge on the conspiratorial. It doesn't matter: what is verifiable is quite bad enough.

Project MK-Ultra was the code name for a CIA mind-control research program lasting from the 1950s through the 1970s. It was first brought to wide public attention by the U.S. Congress (the Church Committee) and a presidential commission (the Rockefeller Commission) and also the U.S. Senate. The project attempted to produce a perfect truth drug for use in interrogating suspected Soviet spies during the Cold War, and generally to explore any other useful possibilities of mind control.

Those "other possibilities" are the stuff of which nightmares are made.

Lansbury Pharmaceuticals is the product of my imagination, but the experiments—at both the Allan and the asylums—with substances that included LSD, chlorpromazine, phenobarbital, and Thioridazine, had to have been carried out with the collusion and cooperation of more than one pharmaceutical company. To this date, none has been identified or investigated. Their roles in this affair have never been explored.

Meanwhile, elsewhere in Montréal . . .

Beginning in the 1940s, under Québec Premier Maurice Duplessis (along with the Roman Catholic Church, which was in charge of running orphanages), and continuing into the 1960s, a scheme was developed to obtain additional federal funding for thousands of children, most of whom had been "orphaned" through forced separation from their unwed mothers.

The federal government offered more monetary support for asylums than it did for orphanages, so this move was primarily financial, although the possibilities for medical experimentation soon overrode the mere fiduciary rewards.

In some cases, children were shipped from orphanages to existing insane asylums. In others, orphanages were merely rechristened as mental healthcare facilities. One writer[1] said that you could go to bed one night in an orphanage and wake up the next morning in an asylum: I found that particularly moving.

Many years later, long after these institutions were closed, the children who survived them and became adults began to speak out about the harsh treatment, medical experimentation, and sexual abuse they'd endured at the hands of the psychiatrists, Roman Catholic priests, nuns, and administrators.

Was there a connection between the work being done at the Allan Institute and the psychiatric experimentation undergone by the Duplessis orphans at the Cité de St.-Jean-de-Dieu asylum? If not proven, it's certainly plausible. Some authors contend that it happened:

> Some of the Orphans interned at St.-Jean-de-Dieu Hospital remember being treated by Ewen Cameron, the psychiatrist who conducted appalling and inhuman experiments on human subjects at Allan Memorial Institute of McGill University as part of the notorious "mind-control" programs of the U.S. Central Intelligence Agency from the late 1940s through the early- to mid-1960s.
>
> Bruno Roy, president of the Duplessis Orphans Committee, examined records of hundreds of Orphans, and

---

[1] *Collusion: The Dark History of the Duplessis Orphans*

said that Cameron's name, indeed, showed up in children's records.

Cameron was known to use chlorpromazine in his experiments, combining drugs, electric shock, lobotomies and other savage incursions on patients.

His associate Heinz Lehmann, who did undergraduate and postgraduate teaching at McGill and became clinical director at Allan Memorial in 1958, is regarded as the psychiatrist who discovered the use of chlorpromazine on psychiatric patients in 1953.

Yet today, evidence reveals the Duplessis Orphans, railroaded into psychiatric hospitals as retarded and mentally ill, were being administered the powerful drug as early as 1947 with debilitating effects.[2]

The sense of many has been that the reparations awarded the remaining orphans is not consistent with those offered to others who have been abused by the system (notably the government reparations offered to indigenous First Nations children forcibly sent to Canadian boarding schools during roughly the same time period); as of this writing, a legal case is being brought[3] to discover why these reparations were so low.

There still remains controversy over the old cemetery at the Cité de St.-Jean-de-Dieu asylum. The asylum buildings them-

[2] www.freedommag.org/english/press/page07.htm
[3] www.montrealgazette.com/health/Quebec+government+asked+disclose+Duplessis+orphan/6619543/story.html

selves now comprise Louis-Hippolyte Lafontaine Hospital (and the giraffe and sign about watching out for "our children" are indeed actually on its grounds: you can't make this stuff up); but the Québec liquor board now owns the site of the asylum's cemetery.

The paperwork for the purchase from the Sisters of Providence included an unusual provision about the order not being responsible for the "condition of the soil." Before the liquor board purchase went through, the graves were supposedly exhumed, though very few remains were in fact actually transported. Since then, the site has thrown up some bone fragments that are consistent with human remains. There's a better than decent chance that there are still nameless forgotten children buried beneath the liquor board's warehouse.

In any case, the cemetery did not shelter *all* the children who died at the asylum; they're only the ones whose bodies were not sold to medical schools and who were not identified when the cemetery was relocated.

A partial list of those identified includes the following names. Please take a moment to read them all.

IN MEMORIAM[4]

List of minors (under age 21) buried in St.-Jean-de-Dieu Asylum Cemetery, 1933–1958

---

[4] Extract from Saint-Jean-de-Dieu Hospital burial registry, Québec Superior Court, 1966–19.

Date/First Name/Surname/Age

04/26/33 —Anonymous child — (a few hours)

02/17/35 — Anonymous child —

03/29/35 — Marie May Saint-Laurent — 17 years

05/07/35 — Marie-Jeanne Bisson — 14 years

11/23/35 — Pugliesse — 1 day

02/04/36 — Joseph Paul Adélard — 2 days

11/07/36 —Marie Cronier — (while being born)

11/18/36 — Anonymous child — 2 days

01/21/37 — Joseph Monette — 1 day

05/09/37 — Maria Kaziniera Tayer — 1 day

05/26/37 — Marie Germaine Thérèse Isabelle —1 year and
8 months

08/22/37 — Martin Dufour — 8 years

12/05/38 — René Sauriol — 17 years

12/18/38 — André Piché — 7 years

01/06/39 — Gaétan Lapointe — 9 years

02/25/39 — Child of unknown parents — 0 years

04/15/39 — Marie Roséline Léonard — 3 years

07/27/39 — Florence Smith — 19 years

12/26/39 — Joseph Richard Caddington — 1 year and
9 months

08/14/40 — Jean Paul Godmaire — 3 years

12/14/40 — Anonymous male child — 0 years

08/17/41 — Jean-Louis Francoeur — 13 years

10/17/41 — Stillborn child —

12/20/41 — Lucien Couture — 3 years

01/20/42—Dieudonné Parent—15 years

03/07/42 — Stillborn child —

05/30/42 — Thérèse Caron — 15 years

05/31/44 — Anonymous child —

06/01/46 — Pricille Vallières — 20 years

08/11/46 — Thérèse Rancourt — 17 years

05/27/47 — Huguette Latour — 7 years

10/24/47 — Child of Eva Brière and Daniel Forgues — 5 days

11/12/47 — Simone Racette — 18 years

03/28/49 — Jacques Millette — 16 years

04/18/49 — Georgette Fontaine — 6 years

06/03/49 — Yvon Mader — 9 years

07/17/50 — Yvon Aubé — 10 years

02/07/51 — Jean Noël LaLonde — 7 years

07/05/51 — Stillborn male child Bilodeau —

07/09/51 — Antoine LaMarche — 9 years

06/04/52 — Wilfrid Bélair — 13 years

07/07/52 — Female infant Allard — 0 years

03/11/53 — Lise Fitzgerald — 11 years

12/17/53 — Serge Potvin — 9 years

07/15/54 — Léon Jean Fugère —

11/26/54 — Marie Barbeau — 8 hours

04/30/57 — Stillborn male child —

04/24/58 — Royal Fournier —19 years

10/04/58 — Anonymous male child — 4 days

They deserve to not be forgotten.